Bronwyn Scott is a commun... at Pierce College and the pro... three wonderful children—one boy and two girls. When she's not teaching or writing she enjoys playing the piano, travelling—especially to Florence, Italy—and studying history and foreign languages. Readers can stay in touch via Facebook at Facebook.com/bronwyn.scott.399 or on her blog, bronwynswriting.blogspot.com. She loves to hear from readers.

HOW TO COURT
A RAKE

Bronwyn Scott

MILLS & BOON

First published in Great Britain 2025
by Mills & Boon, an imprint of HarperCollins*Publishers* Ltd,
1 London Bridge Street, London, SE1 9GF

www.harpercollins.co.uk

HarperCollins*Publishers*, Macken House, 39/40 Mayor Street Upper,
Dublin 1, D01 C9W8, Ireland

How to Court a Rake © 2025 Nikki Poppen

ISBN: 978-0-263-34509-4

03/25

This book contains FSC™ certified paper
and other controlled sources to ensure responsible forest management.

For more information visit www.harpercollins.co.uk/green.

Printed and Bound in the UK using 100% Renewable Electricity
at CPI Group (UK) Ltd, Croydon, CR0 4YY

For B and all the good girls
who play by the rules (mostly).

Adventure is out there
and so is your very own Caine Parkhurst.

Chapter One

London—late June 1826

Caine Parkhurst had the instincts of a bloodhound. He could scent trouble a mile away although he was seldom that far from it. A single man in a ballroom at the height of the Season didn't have the luxury of distance. He was smelling some of that trouble now as he and his brother kept company with a pack of Parkhurst male cousins in the sweltering June crush of Lady Barnstable's ballroom.

'Here they come,' Caine growled in low warning tones, nudging Kieran into alertness with a slight nod indicating the approach of a gaggle of giggling girls who were much too young to be circling a ballroom unchaperoned and just much too young, period. He made a grimace. Was that what youthful womanhood looked like these days? From the vantage point of his rather august thirty-eight years, eighteen seemed extraordinarily young and extraordinarily uninteresting. What did such a girl know of the world? She'd know even less of the particular world he inhabited—a much darker world than this chandelier-lit, sparkling sphere where safety was assumed. The world of the Four Horsemen offered no such assumptions. Death was always a knife tip away. Not that London understood that. They saw the Four Horsemen only as rakes.

'Maybe they won't stop,' Kieran laughed, unconcerned. But then, Kieran was more tolerant of social foibles than he was. 'I certainly wouldn't, not with that grimace you're wearing.'

'No, they'll stop. Five pounds says I'm right. Trouble always smells the same: lilacs, lavender, and lilies.' Sweet smells, innocent smells, sometimes cloying smells worn by idealists and fools who knew nothing beyond the fairy-tale walls of their castles, never even suspecting that tonight his world crossed paths with theirs. Word had it, a saboteur might be in their midst, intent on obstructing a private shipment of funds and arms bound for the Greek independence cause.

Kieran gave a shrug of acceptance, his keen gaze homing in on the group now that there was money in play. He picked out a few. 'There's Townsend's niece, Blackhurst's cousin, and the one in pink is

Darefield's girl, first Season, significant dowry to back her. She'll go fast.'

'If she can keep that insipid laugh of hers under control.' Caine scowled. He'd met Darefield's daughter at Somerset House when the art show had opened back in May. She'd made an impression and not for the best. It would be the last time he'd let his sister rope him into attending such an event, whether she was a pregnant duchess these days or not. His gaze lit on the last girl in the group, elegant, willowy, serious. A young woman who'd seen a fair share of Seasons. A clear outlier for this coterie.

'Lady Mary Kimber's a rather odd member of such a group,' Caine remarked. Odd because she was at least two years older than these girls. Was this her third Season? Perhaps her fourth? Yet even Lady Mary, who was generally regarded as an example of perfect English womanhood, looked shockingly young to him—one of many consequences, perhaps, of his participation in his grandfather's diplomatic world, shadowy edges and all. If patriotic intrigue didn't kill a man, it had no qualms about stripping away his innocence.

'They'll pass us by. They just want a peek at a questionable gentleman or two.' Kieran was all nonchalant confidence. Caine hoped his brother was right. His cousins might be here for the debutantes and dancing, but he and Kieran weren't. They were putting in an appearance tonight to satisfy their grandfather, the Earl, who had specifically requested they keep their ears to the ground in case the saboteur gave himself or his plans away.

He and Kieran were here at Lady Barnstable's, while Lucien was at Lord Morestad's birthday rout. Given his own amorous history with Lady Morestad, Caine had felt it in poor taste to attend her husband's birthday party. Meanwhile, Stepan had taken up his post at a deserted inn near Wapping to prepare the horses and await the call to action if it came, which it very well might. Intelligence, via his grandfather's trusted informant, Falcon, had brought to light earlier today that an Ottoman sympathiser was moving among society's higher echelons. Thus, the Four Horsemen's appearances tonight at various events across town in case there was further word about how and when the attempt to interfere with the shipment would come.

So far, nothing more had materialised and now it seemed that nothing might. That was the hope. If an attack was to happen at all, it would have to happen within the hour, which meant it would occur at the docks. By now, the arms would be loaded and the money would be en route under guard. The ship would sail at midnight with the tide.

The money in question was no trivial sum. It was a substantial amount of privately raised funds to support the Greek independence movement. The last thing the Greek cause needed, or England for that matter, was to have six hundred thousand pounds and a significant arsenal of weaponry fall into Ottoman hands. England was keen to support the independence movement, but less keen to publicly acknowledge that support as an act of official policy. If this shipment came to light, the government would have to answer for this lavish display of 'private' support and arms, which would displease certain European allies.

'Besides,' Kieran was still talking about the silly girls who continued to advance, 'their mothers would murder them if they talked to the likes of us. The Four Horsemen are off limits to debutantes. We're far too dangerous to their reputations.' That reputation was indeed their best protection from becoming outright prey: four gentlemen brothers, grandsons of an earl, sons of a third son, none of them with significant prospects of their own, all of whom rode like hell, raked like hell and had reputations to rival Lucifer himself.

Caine had taken great care to make sure everyone knew just how wildly they lived, shamelessly promoting the idea that the drawing room of Parkhurst

House was akin to a St James's gambling hell and that they were not strangers to the Covent Garden opera singers. Matchmaking mamas approached the Four Horsemen with extreme caution if they approached at all. However, their naive daughters were less concerned with such considerations and perhaps more concerned with the mystery of what lay behind those reputations.

He and his brothers were the wild Parkhursts. Their cousins were the desirable Parkhursts and therein lay Kieran's miscalculation. The giggling girls might not stop for the Four Horsemen, but they'd definitely stop for Alexander Parkhurst, one of the Season's most eligible bachelors as the scion to the heir of the Earl of Sandmore. Unfortunately, he and Kieran had the dubious privilege of standing next to that eligible *parti*. Attention by association as it were. It was Caine's estimation that they would pay for that proximity, collateral damage in the making.

'Ladies.' Alex bowed politely to the group of girls in acknowledgment of their attentions. Caine made no such conventional overture. Beside him, Kieran swore under his breath, his wager lost.

The 'ladies' in question curtsied, eyelash-fluttering gazes moving with adolescent excitement between the gentlemen in the group. Townsend's niece offered Alex her hand. 'I believe we were introduced at my aunt's Venetian breakfast last week.' Ah, that explained the chit's boldness, then. She was presuming on a prior introduction. If it had been up to him, Caine would have said something like, 'Forgive me, I do not recall'—probably without the 'forgive me' part—but Alex was cut from a much better cloth of manners. Then again, his cousin had prospects to preserve. Alex didn't have the luxury of speaking his mind.

'Yes, I believe we discussed your aunt's rose garden.' Alex smiled—whatever suffering he felt over doing the pretty was neatly hidden away behind grey eyes that reflected polite, neutral interest. That might have been the end of it if the orchestra hadn't chosen that moment to start back up, the sounds of instruments tuning inviting guests to return to the dance floor. The Townsend girl's gaze took on an expectant quality and Alex, damn him, felt obliged. 'Would you do me the honour of this dance?'

Townsend's niece—Caine had no idea what her name was and didn't care to learn it—blushed prettily and made a polite show of concern for leaving behind the party of girls with her. How would it be, she protested, to dance if her friends were left on the sidelines? Caine's cousins, the *decent* Parkhursts, leapt into the breach, making offers to the other girls until only he and Kieran were left with Lady Mary Kimber. She'd hung back during the bold interaction. Perhaps she'd been rightly mortified by the behaviour of her companions. 'I'll get us some punch,' Kieran offered, effecting his escape.

'You'd better get me my five pounds. It looks like I won this wager,' Caine growled as Kieran slipped off to the refreshment room. In this crush, it would take him a good twenty minutes to make the journey. Until then, Caine was stuck with Lady Mary Kimber, daughter of the Earl of Carys, one of the most impeccably mannered, well-dowered girls on the marriage mart, the personification of dutiful and beautiful, and the least likely to seek out the company of the Four Horsemen.

Her father had made no secret in the clubs that Lady Mary was meant for a duke. She had, in fact, spent a week at the end of May at the Duke of Harlow's house party expressly for that purpose. But Harlow had come back with his intentions firmly and rebelliously fixed on a pretty nobody from Dorset despite Lady Mary's beauty, bloodlines and bank account. Her father had thrown a fit over it at White's a few weeks back.

'It seems our friends have deserted us,' she said to cover the awkwardness of the growing silence. It was skilfully done. The line offered him a choice to take it up as commiseration or as an invitation to ask her to dance. A gentleman would do the latter. He was not that man. He was on a mission from his grandfather.

'I am not dancing tonight, Lady Mary,' he explained bluntly. Even if he was dancing, it would not be with her. Lady Mary Kimber was no more his type of woman than he was her type of man. He liked a lick of fire, an edge of steel, a certain sensual confidence in his women. He had an opera singer he consorted with in Piccadilly on occasion who ticked all those boxes quite nicely and expected nothing in return that he wasn't willing to give. He did not see the dutiful Lady Mary checking those boxes and she was most definitely the sort of woman who would have expectations.

'A ball seems an odd choice of entertainment for someone who doesn't wish to dance.' Her grey eyes gave him a challenging stare, one slim brow arching in an attempt to call his bluff. *Did* she think he was bluffing? Her boldness surprised him. Maybe she did tick one of his boxes after all.

'I am here supporting my cousin,' he offered in explanation.

'Ah, the *decent* Parkhurst,' she said with a cool detachment that translated into the smallest of smiles on those soft pink lips of hers as if she hadn't just rendered him an insult, or at least tried to.

He laughed, rather enjoying this unexpected show of sharp wit. 'You'll have to do better than that if you want to offend me.' Such wit rather begged the question as to why she hadn't bagged the Duke of Harlow. Had Harlow not liked the sharp honesty? She'd certainly not lost him on account of her looks. Lady Mary was objectively pretty, albeit in a non-standard sense. No blonde hair and blue eyes here. Instead, her beauty lay claim to quicksilver eyes, glossy nut-brown hair and a willowy figure with enough height to give her a sense of poise the other girls lacked. There were other attributes, too: the slim, elegant column of her neck that begged a man to run his hand down its length and those sensual lips that invited kisses without trying. His eyes were riveted by them and his thoughts followed.

'Offending you was hardly my intention, Mr Parkhurst. I was merely stating a fact.' There was more of that delicious coolness she seemed to culti-vate so well in a heated ballroom. With a little prac-tice she could freeze a man at twenty paces. What a duchess she would be with a look like that. Harlow was definitely missing out.

'Neither was insult *my* intention, Lady Mary. I simply find it expedient to make my position known from the start. It saves people from disappointment later on.' By people, he meant naive debutantes who had a fancy to take to the floor with a notorious rake.

She gave a dry laugh. 'I assure you, forgoing a dance with you will *not* disappoint me.'

'What does disappoint you, Lady Mary?' He couldn't resist the words any more than his gaze could resist moving over her mouth. What he could do with those lips… He'd not meant to instigate flirting with her. He knew better. She was off limits by his own self-imposed rules. And his curiosity was piqued. What *did* lay beneath all that collected coolness? Something did—the sharpness of her wit was proof that not all of her was calm and smooth.

Her grey eyes met his, a little flame rising to the challenge, licking in their depths. 'Starving children in the London streets, oppression of native peoples in Britain's colonies, the suppression of women here at home who are denied the right to lead their own lives. That is real disappointment, Mr Parkhurst.' She was testing him with her response.

Really, it was an impressive answer. His grandfather would approve of such an agenda, as did he. 'And the Duke of Harlow, is he on that list as well?' Caine ventured boldly.

'The concept of disappointment assumes that I've failed to claim something I wanted. Harlow was my

parents' dream, not mine.' Despite the casualness
with which she dismissed society's latest specula-
tions, the shadow in her grey eyes said she could not
entirely dismiss the sting of Harlow's choice, however much she'd like to.

No one liked being overlooked. She had his empathy there. He knew a little something about that
himself. In his own way, because of a lack of a title
or real prospects, he and his brothers were often
overlooked after a fashion because they were sons
of a third son.

She gave him a cool glance. 'Make no mistake, I
did not want Harlow. If he has found happiness elsewhere, I wish him well.'

A woman who did not want a duke was rare in
his experience. Something stirred inside Caine. Intrigue? His innate need to protect? Maybe even a
little anger at Harlow on her behalf. Lady Mary
Kimber was showing herself to be made of sterner
fibre than he'd given her credit for. Beneath the rose
silk and lilies-of-the-valley perfume, she possessed
the steel of conviction, the strength of self-knowl-
edge. She understood who she was—to herself and
to others. 'What *do* you want, then?'

With another sort of woman, this would be the
opening move in a seduction because that's how all
his flirtations began and ended: seduction intended,

seduction accomplished. He didn't flirt without a particular end goal in mind. He wasn't certain why he was bothering now when such an end was out of the question. Lady Mary Kimber was not for seducing, ergo, not his type.

'Not a duke, no matter what my parents are determined to say.' The sharp point of her chin jutted up defiantly.

Not just her parents but society. Caine paid enough attention to the gossips to know that, in the span of two Seasons, she'd lost two dukes—one of them to Caine's own sister. Her father was furious. Society made it out to be her fault she couldn't captivate a man. Perhaps she just hadn't met the right man? Which raised the competitive edge in him to prove that Harlow was somehow a lesser man because he'd not appreciated her. But she wasn't looking for Caine's type of appreciation.

'Yet, you are the one who will pay the price,' Caine probed. By all accounts, her Season was going poorly. She'd lost the Duke of Harlow—she, who had everything to offer such a man. She, who had been bred for such a man. Worse, she'd lost that man to a nobody and quite publicly. All of society had been watching that house party. Just as they were likely watching her now, noting how her group had been asked to dance while she'd been left on the sidelines.

An unusual pin of guilt pricked at Caine. Any censure directed at her now was his fault. But no doubt she'd be the one to pay for that, too. Men could get away with almost anything, but not women. He could imagine what the social columns might make of it in tomorrow's papers. Beyond them on the dance floor, sets were forming for another dance. His conscience stirred to wakefulness.

'Lady Mary, I find I've changed my mind.' He offered his arm in a surge of unusual gallantry. 'Would you care to dance?'

The sharp point of her chin went up and her quicksilver eyes flashed. 'No, Mr Parkhurst.' Not 'no thank you', or any other gracious refusal. Simply and bluntly: no. Those eyes flashed again and he expected to hear thunder follow. 'I do not require your pity.'

Caine felt his own temper rise in answer. He didn't like having his gesture thrown back in his face. 'Perhaps I'm the one who needs *your* pity,' he cajoled. The competitor in him was wide awake. Now that he'd made the offer, he wasn't going to tolerate being turned down. Perhaps she didn't understand the necessity of accepting? They could not stand here much longer. The room was starting to watch. Eyes always followed the Horsemen. And eyes followed Lady Mary Kimber. Put the two together and there was no chance of escaping notice: the *ton*'s most competent young lady with society's most reckless rake.

He laid a light hand on her glove-covered arm and lowered his voice to a private tone. 'Please, Lady Mary. People are starting to stare. It does neither of our reputations any good. We are inviting comment.' Particularly her, although to explicitly remind her of that would likely earn him another lightning bolt from her eyes. He could care less what anyone thought of him outside of his family. She did not have that luxury. After losing Harlow, her reputation was in danger of becoming frayed, her pristine image tarnished.

'Well, when you put it in such practical terms, I can hardly refuse, can I?' she quipped drily and reluctantly took his arm, the scent of lilies undercut with vanilla wafting past his nose—the smell of trouble. But how much trouble could one dance with Lady Mary Kimber, the *ton*'s most dutiful daughter, actually be?

Chapter Two

How much trouble could one dance be? Mary argued with herself, especially when that dance was designed to mend her reputation, not rend it. Yet, when she took Caine Parkhurst's arm and felt the firmness of the muscles beneath her gloved hand, she had the unmistakable impression that this was very much a case of a wolf in sheep's clothing and she was most certainly a red riding hood led astray by her own curiosity and a pair of dark eyes with mysterious depths.

Worst of all, she knew these things and she'd not put a stop to it. Instead, she'd followed this particular wolf on to the dance floor just to see where it led, although her conscience did make one last bid for retraction as they drew closer to his cousin's set. The logic that had propelled her on to the dance floor had been flawed. What had she been thinking to accept? In what world did dancing with Caine

Parkhurst, rake extraordinaire, a man who'd turned his town house drawing room into a gambling hell, a man who seduced women for entertainment, make anything right?

She wasn't mitigating trouble; she was courting an obscene amount of it. She ought to have stood her ground and refused him. In fact, she shouldn't have *stood* anywhere near him. She would have been better off walking away once it was apparent everyone else in her group was dancing. Decent, unmarried women didn't stand on the sidelines conversing with one of the Four Horsemen and they definitely didn't take to the dance floor with one of them. In a matter of minutes she'd managed to do both. She had no excuse. She was not newly come to town, a gullible young miss in the throes of her first Season. She *knew* better.

And she did not want to *do* better. It had been her choice from the start. She'd convinced herself there was no harm in idle small talk. After all, she made small talk with viscounts and dukes all the time. But that had been her mistake. Caine Parkhurst was nothing like the Duke of Harlow. The Duke was a gentleman to the bone. Harlow dressed like one, he looked like one. He acted like one.

Caine was something else entirely. He was something wild and untamed, from the messy, ebony waves of his hair to the unorthodox all-black evening clothes relieved only by a single diamond stickpin winking in the folds of a black silk cravat. He looked like the devil incarnate—wicked, sensual, a walking invitation to sin and, to her surprise, it was an invitation something in her was tempted to accept.

Curiosity spurred her hard. Like Eve in the garden, she wanted a taste of what the devil offered, perhaps because he was the antithesis of all she'd come to know since entering society's lists. Tonight, on the sidelines, they'd not made small talk. They'd *jousted* with words for spears, cool glances and arched brows for shields. And it had been far more invigorating than discussing the weather in Hampshire with a viscount. Then again, she was coming to believe that everything about Caine Parkhurst was designed to be invigorating to the feminine mind.

And she was definitely invigorated. At two inches over six feet and sporting the shoulders of Atlas, he was larger than life. She could go toe to toe with him, but not nose to nose. She was used to looking many men in the eye. Even at her stature of five foot seven inches, rather tall for a woman, she was aware that Caine Parkhurst towered over her, the breadth of him an obvious contrast to the slenderness of her own frame. Beside him, she did not feel too tall, too overpowering. She did not need to cultivate a stoop to accommodate a shorter man. She did not need to worry about daunting a gentleman with her mere presence simply by standing next to him and making him feel less the man.

Caine Parkhurst was breathtakingly impressive, intimidating, intoxicating even and, from the unexpected rush of her pulse as they took to the dance floor, it was absolutely clear why mothers steered their daughters in the opposite direction when he was in the room. Just as it was clear why women of all ages were drawn to him against their better judgement. He smelled deliciously, like the call to adventure all sharp citrus, exotic sandalwood, and rugged masculinity—two things in short supply for a well-bred English woman, which only added to the intrigue of him.

She did not think she was the only woman who wanted to solve that riddle. The complex scent complemented what rumour spoke of him: that here was a man who cared not a fig for rules and propriety, a man who did as he pleased and took what he wanted. A man who had nothing to lose. In that moment, she understood the pull he had over her. He was all she was not. She must always give a care for propriety and it was wearying. Such care eroded one's soul and she was on the brink of losing hers. The small part of her that society had not yet claimed wanted him for herself and all that he represented: freedom. If only for the length of a dance, these moments would be for her.

Then it would be back to reality. Unlike him, she had something to lose—a reputation that had taken a battering recently. She was acutely aware of the consequences of being overlooked by two dukes in two years; first Creighton and now Harlow. It had raised the question: if she was indeed the impeccable example of propriety, why had two dukes passed on her? This evening, if she'd continue to stand there, that question would have extended to asking why a man not as grand as a duke had not taken to the floor with her? People would begin to ask, 'What is wrong with her?' She was in danger of being demoted from a diamond of the first water to wallflower.

Truly, she'd really not had a choice. Refusing Parkhurst's invitation to dance would simply draw more attention than what they were already receiving. Accepting was the lesser of two evils. It wouldn't stop all the talk, though. There would just be different talk. Talk she hoped her mother wouldn't hear about. But it was too late to change her mind now.

They joined Alex Parkhurst's set and Caine made a bow to her as the music began. The dance was a lively scotch reel, which required switching partners, and she was spared the intensity and perhaps the scrutiny that came with dancing solely with him— something that brought a bit of irrational disappointment. Part of her was aware it would have welcomed the scrutiny of those dark eyes. On a positive note, the reel did offer the opportunity to study him in contrast to his more urbane cousin. Both were tall and dark-haired; both had the strong Parkhurst jaw and aristocratic nose. But Alex had none of his cousin's muscular breadth. His was a more elegant, town-fed build whereas Caine was barely leashed virility, wildness caged in a tailored evening coat.

Caine flashed her a smile as he danced past on to his next partner and her knees went unexpectedly weak at the dazzle of that smile, wide, open, honest, his tousled curls flying. Two surprises hit her at once as she moved on to dance with Alex. First, despite his claims to not dancing tonight, Caine was having fun. He *liked* to dance. It was there in his smile, in the posture of his body, which suddenly seemed less guarded. Second, he was actually good at it, something unusual for a big man, especially one better known for his athletic pursuits. Everyone knew Caine Parkhurst rode like the devil, shot like the devil and boxed like the devil among other skills that were best unnamed in the presence of ladies.

The rotation finished, she returned to him and

they danced facing each other, doing an energetic little kick step. The joy of the dance had her laughing out loud and smiling back at him, the wicked thought coming to her that she could dance all night with this man, that she *wanted* to dance all night with him, to claim this freedom, this surge of joy.

She'd no more thought it then Kieran appeared at his shoulder, inserting himself into the set and rapidly whispering something at his ear. Caine's smile disappeared, his features stern. She caught the words, 'We ride for Wapping.' Caine reached for her wrist and pulled her out of the reel, the warm intimacy of his touch jolting up her arm even as he said the words that would take him away. 'I must go.'

'What? Now? In the middle of a dance?' It took a moment to comprehend that he was leaving her— nay, *deserting* her in the middle of the dance floor where everyone would notice. 'You *begged* me to dance with you, you can't leave me now,' she sputtered a stunned protest. Her temper rose. How dare he! He knew how this would look. He had no idea how this felt. Something inside her wilted, her moment of freedom was slipping away even as her considerable pride surged to the fore, ready to protect her as it always did. She would need it to get through the aftermath.

His hand lingered at her wrist, his gaze steady

on hers. 'I am sorry.' Then he was gone, winding his way through the dancers on his brother's heels, leaving her to calmly depart the floor on her own with her head held high against the stares and whispers that would reach her mother's ears by breakfast: Lady Mary Kimber had been left on the dance floor by none other than Caine Parkhurst, a man she should not have been dancing with in the first place. She was always being left. First the Duke of Creighton, then the Duke of Harlow and now the rogue, Caine Parkhurst, whom one would think couldn't afford to leave an heiress in the lurch. How would she live it all down? Would society ever let her? There was going to be hell to pay and this time it would not be easily dismissed.

Caine dismissed the ball and Lady Mary along with it, although the latter had been dismissed with more regret than the former. He *had* felt badly about the timing of Kieran's interference, which had required his immediate departure. Lady Mary hadn't deserved that, but when England summoned, one answered the call immediately. He exchanged his dancing shoes for boots in the coach and, by the time he and Kieran arrived at the address near the London Docks at Wapping, all his thoughts were firmly centred on catching the traitor set to sabotage tonight's critical shipment.

The cause of Greek independence might very well rise or fall on the midnight tide and, with it, the balance of power in the Mediterranean. Democracy was at stake, as was the long arm of the English empire. There was no room or time for thoughts of a dark-haired miss who challenged him with her wit and for a brief while made him forget why he disliked ballrooms so much. It was also a reminder as to why he eschewed entanglements. They made for distraction when he could least afford it.

Caine was on the ground, Kieran behind him, before the coach came to a complete stop. He barked orders, taking stock with a swift perusal of the deserted stable yard. 'Stepan, the horses!' he called for his brother. Time was of the essence and the traitor had the advantage of it at present. The clatter of horses' hooves answered. Stepan emerged from the stable, two dark horses in hand.

'Argonaut is ready. Your pistol is in the halter, your sabre in its sheath.' Stepan handed over the reins and Caine clapped him on the shoulder in appreciation.

'Good man, I knew you'd have everything prepared.' He nodded an acknowledgment to Luce over Stepan's shoulder as the youngest Parkhurst came out with the other two horses, all of them brothers bred from the same sire. Four dark horses for four dark brothers.

They were all assembled now, the Earl of Sandmore's Four Horsemen in a deserted obscure innyard, Britain's very own apocalypse on horseback, swift and decisive in their judgement, a reminder to foreign powers that a nation tangled with Britain at its own peril. They mounted up and Caine looked to Stepan. 'What's the news?'

'Their plan is to put an explosives expert on board and wait until the ship is out to sea before blowing it up. Falcon sent word the expert was being rowed out tonight just before sailing.'

'And the explosives?' Luce enquired. 'Are they already on board?'

'Doesn't matter,' Caine interrupted, eager to be off. There was a mile to cover between them and the docks. 'Not at the moment at least. Explosives are irrelevant if the expert isn't on board to detonate them.' For all they knew the expert was going to ignite the ammunition already on board. Doing it at sea would make it look like an accident and very likely there'd be no witnesses after the fact, Caine thought grimly. 'Is that all we know?' It was deuced little to go on. 'How are they getting him on board?'

'Perhaps he'll claim he's a last-minute crew member, or that he comes with an important message for the Captain,' Kieran posited. 'He'll use the chaos of departure to his advantage. Everyone will be too busy getting ready to sail to maintain the usual protocols.'

Caine nodded his agreement. He could see it play out now in his mind: the expert, disguised in sailor's garb, paying an unsuspecting oarsman in want of coin to row him out to where the ship waited for the tide, then pressuring the unlucky crewman who spied him to haul him up so that he could deliver his message. The crewman would be torn between outright dismissing the unknown sailor or risking his Captain's displeasure over missing the message.

Once onboard, the traitor would be left to wait in the Captain's quarters until the Captain was available, during which time the explosive expert could either take on the role of a stowaway and hide himself or make his role compelling and join the crew as a late-come member, perhaps even have a false message to deliver. The latter seemed most likely to Caine. But the point was to not let it get that far. 'Our goal is to ensure that man does not reach the ship. We must stop him at the docks.'

A simple task in theory. Harder to execute in practice. They'd have to split up. The docks boasted two and a half miles of jetties and quays. Coupled with the bustle of dockside activity and the darkness, their traitor would have cover and distractions galore. It would be no mean task to pick out one man from hundreds hurrying about their jobs.

Caine glanced about the circle of his brothers on their horses. It was his job to see that they all came back from each mission, every time. He didn't like them pairing off. There was safety and power in numbers, but time was against them. 'To Wapping then, as fast as we can.' They wheeled their horses around and set off. In the distance, the bells of St Peter's tolled the hour as Caine led the Horsemen through the dark streets. The thrill of the hunt fired through his veins. This was his hour; the midnight hour, the witching hour, the riding hour, when the Four Horsemen rode for the honour of England in the black of night.

At the docks, Caine gave the silent gesture to split up, Kieran with Luce and Stepan with him. This was a pairing from childhood. With two years' age difference between each of the four brothers, Caine and Kieran had each taken one of the younger brothers under their supervision and tutelage. Perhaps for that reason, Caine felt more responsible for Stepan. Stepan was his. His to protect.

They slowed the horses to a walk, carefully

winding through the crowds on the dock, using the horses' height for better visibility of the wharves. Stepan leaned over and touched his arm. 'There, do you see that man?' He gave a nod to a man in the act of haggling with a boatman. Gold flashed, exchanging hands.

'Did you see *that*?' Caine growled, his sharp eyes picking out another flash of a different sort of metal. 'There's a pistol beneath his jacket. A rather fancy and impractical weapon for a sailor.' He jerked his head towards a nearby tavern. 'We'll go from here on foot. We'll be less noticeable. Let the boy look after the horses.' He dismounted and roused the scrap of a boy serving as an ostler.

Stepan put his knife in a sheath at his hip, Caine tucked his pistol beneath his greatcoat, hidden but quickly accessible, and stepped into the midnight melee of ever-busy docks. 'When we reach him, let me do the talking,' Caine urged. 'Stay back a bit.' In case there was trouble, in case Stepan had to run.

Stepan made a disapproving frown as they neared their target. 'If it comes to swimming, you let me go in. I am by far the better swimmer.'

Like hell Caine would allow that. But there was no sense in arguing. The man they'd spied was preparing to step into the boat. Caine called out, stopping the man with his voice. 'Papers, Sir.'

It was enough to make the man halt. He turned, beady eyes narrowing and assessing. Hesitating. Proof enough that this indeed was their man. A man with nothing to hide would not hesitate to comply. 'I've already cleared it with the harbourmaster,' the man said in tones too authoritative for a sailor used to taking orders.

'It's not the harbourmaster who is asking.' Caine pulled back his coat, revealing his pistol. 'I am a special emissary for the Crown. We've received word there may be nefarious activity tonight. We're checking everyone. I'm sure you understand.' All of it true. Kieran and Luce were no doubt doing the same at their end of the docks a mile away. Caine tensed. This was the critical moment. If this was their man, he'd have to try something now—jump into the water and attempt to swim out to the ship, or run here on land, which would require getting past him and Stepan.

The man gave a cold grin. 'Special emissary? I don't know about that. But I know what you're after, eh? When money talks, it's always a good conversation.' He reached into his pocket and held up a wad of pound notes. 'Perhaps this is the paper you're looking for.' He stepped closer as if to put the notes in Caine's hand.

Stepan called a warning, 'He's got a blade!'

Caine saw the covert steel the man must have withdrawn with the pound notes too late. How the hell had he missed the motion? He jumped back to avoid the jab that would have taken him in the abdomen, the tearing sound of fabric ripping in proof of how close it had been. Then Stepan was there, grappling with the man. Stepan shook the knife free of the man's hand. The blade and pound notes fell to the wharf as they wrestled. Stepan took the man to the ground, but they were evenly matched in size and weight. Stepan no sooner had him pinned than the man used his legs to flip Stepan over.

'Get away from him!' Caine drew his pistol. Even in the dark at this range, he'd get a good shot at the traitor, one that would disable him, but not kill him, if only Stepan could disengage. Caine wanted the man alive. He had information Grandfather needed: who had hired him? Who was the mastermind behind the sabotage? But there was no chance. The risk of hitting Stepan was too great.

'Surrender!' Caine barked. 'And you will live.' When all else failed, one could always try reason. Continue to fight and Stepan would knock him senseless given the chance. Stepan had the advantage at the moment, the fight nearing the edge of the wharf. Stepan was overpowering him and the man had nowhere to go.

The man gave a grunt as he scrambled away from Stepan, reaching the end of the wharf. Stepan made a grab for his ankle and missed. 'Let him go,' Caine instructed, levelling his pistol. This was the distance he needed for the shot. Just a second more… Damn! The man jumped into the water. Coat, boots and all. Stepan was on his feet, shedding his own coat and tugging at his boots.

'You're not going after him.' Caine raced forward, rapidly scanning the water, looking for a shot. He could shoot from here if only he could see. But the water was dark. 'I'll find a boat; we can row after him.' He gave a mad glance around, but the boatman was gone and for a busy dock there wasn't a skiff in sight.

'There's no time. You said so yourself. We cannot let the man reach the ship.' Stepan's pronouncement was followed by a splash.

Caine turned, the space beside him empty. Damn it! 'Stepan!' he called, desperately searching the dark water for a sign of his brother. What the hell was Stepan thinking? The water was cold even if it was June. Thirty feet from the dock, he saw Stepan surface and he knew his brother's thoughts: that he'd outswim a man in a greatcoat and boots, that it wouldn't be hard to find and overtake him because the man's destination was obvious—the ship that sat out in the basin, waiting its turn to make its way to the Thames and the open ocean.

'Stepan!' Caine called again at the sight of his head, but Stepan didn't turn. He dived beneath the surface and disappeared.

Damn and double damn, he should have fired sooner. Now Stepan was in the water, searching for a killer in the dark. If anything happened to his brother, he'd never forgive himself. He raised a plea to the sky.

Stay safe, Stepan, until I can reach you. Hold on, I am coming. Followed by, *Please don't find the man.*

At the moment, he did not care if the man reached the ship. They would track the ship down somehow and warn the Captain. He cared only that his brother was safe.

Caine raised his pistol to the sky and fired a shot, hoping Kieran was close enough to hear it above the noise of drays and ships. Then he raced along the shoreline, boots pounding, looking for a boat that would row him out to the last place he'd seen his brother, praying that they would find him.

Chapter Three

They found the traitor's body at dawn, aided by the first light of morning. 'That's him,' Caine confirmed, toeing the bloated and bloodied body with his boot where it lay on a stretcher. Kieran and Luce were with him, all of them wet and cold, furious and worried, after a night in rowboats trolling the docks. They had the traitor, but they had no idea where Stepan was.

Caine turned from the body, his anger evident as someone came to cover it up and bear it away. 'He was the last person to see Stepan and he's dead, so there's no help there.'

'How do you reason that? He was in boots and a coat. He could have simply drowned,' Kieran asked as the three brothers moved away from the crowd of assorted constabulary.

'There was a knife wound on his arm. It wasn't from their scuffle on the dock.' The bruises, the black eye, they were all from the fight. But not the knife wound. 'Stepan had his blade with him.' He rubbed at the space between his brows, pushing back against the frustration welling within him, the helplessness, maybe even at the very real memory he had of his brother taking the knife from the saddle sheath at the tavern just hours earlier. 'I saw him strap it on.'

'Which meant,' Kieran said slowly, 'that Stepan found the man and they fought.' Caine gave a grim nod. It was the last that was worrisome. The fight had ended in at least one dead man. He hoped not two. When he'd offered up his prayer that they find Stepan, he should have been more specific. That they find his brother *alive.*

'Perhaps he swam out to the ship,' Luce suggested. 'If he was tired, or hurt, or even directionally confused in the dark, unsure of where shore was, he would have headed for the ship.' It was a good idea, a hopeful idea. Caine managed a small nod at his youngest brother. Luce had been impressive tonight in organising a small fleet of boats to comb the harbour.

'I will check again with the ship's Captain.' Luce stepped away with purpose in his step. Caine understood Luce's need to do something, to feel useful. It kept hope alive. Thinking there was something yet to do or to try was the manifestation of optimism in the face of crisis. To simply walk away, to give up, was to admit the search was over. And if the search was over, it meant the unthinkable had happened. That Stepan was dead.

'He has to be out there.' Caine looked across the water to where the ship still sat at anchor. The sailing had been postponed in light of the growing situation. It would sail tonight though, the delivery couldn't be delayed any longer, and it would sail safely. In that regard, the mission had been a success. 'What do you think, Kieran?'

Kieran shook his head and scuffed his boot on the dock. 'I don't know what *to* think. Stepan would have sent word by now, he knows that's protocol.' Kieran sighed before stating the obvious. 'He's not sent word, which means he can't send word. Best case, he's unconscious somewhere. Knowing him, he's washed up in some pretty girl's bed and is recovering on feather pillows and linen sheets.' Kieran forced a chuckle.

'Or worst case—' Caine caught Kieran's gaze '—he's dead, sunk to the bottom of the pool, or washed down the Thames. I can't imagine it though. He's a strong swimmer.'

'Skill doesn't matter if one is unconscious,' Kieran

argued gently, putting a hand on Caine's shoulder in commiseration. 'I can't imagine it either, though.'

They stood in silence, waiting for Luce to return. Caine knew he had to make a decision. They could not justify lingering here much longer with no new developments to support waiting. Luce approached with a shake of his head and Caine felt as if the last spark of hope had been snuffed out. 'No word.'

'Then it's time to go.' Caine looked each of his brothers in the eye, offering them his strength. They all knew the implicit message behind this choice. 'Grandfather will be waiting.' England would be waiting. Democracy was safe for now; England's private support of Greek independence was safe. If it came to it, would it be worth the price of a good man's life? His *brother's* life?

Caine watched the reality of the situation hit Luce. For a moment, his brother's features threatened to crumble, disbelief became a shadow in his eyes. Caine willed himself not to look away, to let his own sternness lend Luce the fortitude to conquer the despair.

Not here, not now, he coached Luce silently. *Show nothing of your feelings to these people around us. We don't know who is watching. Give away no weakness.*

He glanced at Kieran. 'We won't give up. This is

not over.' It wouldn't be over, he vowed, unless there was a body and he knew definitively that Stepan was gone from this world. Until that time, he would bring to bear all his resources to find his brother and bring the men responsible to justice.

Mary's mother was meting out justice along with the sausage at breakfast. Usually, Mary met each day eager with plans. She kept her days full and herself busy. This morning, though, she approached the breakfast table with dread and she was not disappointed. She'd not even sat down before her mother began.

'It's all over every society column in the all the papers.' Her mother waved one newssheet to emphasise the point. 'You were dancing with the *disreputable* Mr Parkhurst *and* he left you on the dance floor like the cad he is. One can hardly be surprised by his behaviour, but one *can* be surprised by yours, Mary. You should have known better.'

Mary calmly finished fixing her plate. This barrage of critique was not unexpected, unpleasant as it was. She wasn't going to let it spoil her appetite. Breakfast was her favourite meal of the day. Nor was she going to let it ruin her memories of a few moments of enjoyment. That had been the decision she'd arrived at in the carriage on the way home.

The ending of her evening had been unfortunate. The consequences would also be unfortunate. But her enjoyment was not. She would protect it as her pride had protected her last night, as she'd departed the dance floor.

That enjoyment had been an awakening of sorts, a claiming of something that had fluttered around inside her for a while now, something that was tired of being caged and limited, tired of being her parents' pawn in a game she didn't want to play. Last night something had got out and she'd liked it.

'Well? Why don't you say something?' her mother scolded as Mary took her seat.

Mary looked at her mother and it was like looking in a mirror of the future. If she wasn't careful, if she did not put a stop to the nonsense, this would be her in twenty years: disappointed perfection, the elegantly coiffed dark hair with the beginnings of grey at the temples, the faint whispers of lines at her eyes, the drawn tightness of a mouth that had spent too many years pursed in disappointment, in her daughter, in her life, even though she had everything a woman might want, everything that she'd been raised to aspire to and to which she was raising her own daughter to aspire to despite her own firsthand knowledge of the disappointment that waited.

'What would you have me say? That it didn't happen? Would you like me to say that I sent him from the floor and that's why he left me? That would also be a lie.' She paused, enjoying the little surge of rebellion. 'Do you want me to say I didn't enjoy dancing with him? That it was a chore to lower myself to dance with a well-known rake? I can't say any of that. It would *all* be lies. Even the last. I enjoyed dancing with him very much and I *would* dance with him again.' Should she ever get the chance. She thought it would be unlikely, though. While the dance had been something of an epiphany for her, she doubted it had the same impact on him. He'd probably forgotten her the moment he'd left the floor.

Her father set down his paper and spoke from his end of the table. 'You should not speak to your mother like that. She has tried her best for you, as have I, and we deserve your gratitude, not your scorn. We most certainly deserve your apology. I suggest, Miss, that you take the day and think about what happens to young girls who are in their fourth Season and cannot capture a husband even with all the required assets at their disposal.'

Boldness took her and she met her father's hard stare evenly. 'I had offers, Father. My first Season there were two viscounts and my second Season there was an earl and the wealthy Baron's heir. *You* were the one who insisted on a duke, who insisted we turn away perfectly decent offers.' She'd not minded losing them. While the men had been acceptable to her, they would have married as strangers. There'd been no spark of attraction, but she'd thought it would have been possible to build a future with them, a friendship over time. But nothing more, so she'd let her father send them on.

Her father frowned, anger roiling in his eyes. 'You have become impertinent beyond toleration. You are ungrateful and spoilt. We've arranged two dukes for you and you have lost them both.'

'I cannot control where another's heart leads,' Mary shot back, even though she was courting her father's wrath. She should not push him like this, he was not a gentleman when angered.

'Hearts? Do you think this is about *hearts*? About love? What folderol! This is about alliances, about power,' he raged. At the moment, she was a convenient target for her father's spleen over his still-open wound regarding Harlow. He had threatened to financially ruin Harlow in order to leverage the Duke for her and that had failed spectacularly. There'd been economic repercussions. He'd been dismissed from the lucrative investment group, the Prometheus Club—it's chair, the Duke of Cowden, siding with Harlow over the matter.

Her father smacked an open palm on the table,

sending the teacups rattling. 'That's it. It all ends this Season. I am fed up with dressmakers' bills that accomplish naught but depleting my account.' He pointed a finger at Mary. '*You* will wed before Parliament rises. There are still offers out there. Someone will want what you bring to the table. You've fine bloodlines.'

'Or else?' Mary goaded, hiding her nerves over that pronouncement with a show of contrariness. Her father was a stubborn, determined man who usually accomplished what he set his mind to. Marrying her off was his one unusual failure.

'There is no "or else".' He narrowed his gaze. 'You would like that, wouldn't you? To remain unmarried and be on your own without a care to what you owe this family.'

Mary sat up taller, meeting her father's gaze. 'What I would like is to be wanted for myself, not for my money or my bloodlines or my father's connections.' Was that too much to ask? She wanted what Harlow had found with Cora Graylin and had been brave enough to claim.

'Bah! What nonsense. You've not been bred for such plebian tripe. Even so, you've not the luxury to pursue it.' Her father made a wide sweeping gesture to the breakfast room. 'Do you see a son lurking behind the curtains?' He was being cruel now. 'You cannot afford freedom, Mary. When I die all this goes. Where will you live? How will you live? What becomes of your mother without your good marriage? If you won't think of me or yourself, at least think of her after all she's done for you.' This was one of his favourite strategies—using her mother as guilty leverage.

'You've made provision for us both. We can live in reduced cirumstances,' Mary retorted. This was not the first time he'd trotted out that argument. He'd started using it when she'd made her debut. But it was the first time she'd openly countered it.

Her father's eyes flared at the rebellion. 'How dare you make that decision on your mother's behalf. It is too presumptuous by far. You used to be more biddable, Mary. Is this what dancing with a rake turns one's daughter into? A contentious shrew who does not respect her elders?' He rose, not waiting for her answer. 'Spend the rest of the summer looking to your trousseau, Mary. I will start entertaining offers today and I will be looking for the wealthiest titled man I can get, age notwithstanding.'

That man would not care what her passions were, what her dreams were, what she thought about… anything. Caine Parkhurst had, though. In her mind she could hear his seductive tones asking, *'What do you want?'* She could still feel the heat of his gaze on her as she answered as if he were genuinely intrigued.

She stayed silent until her father left the room, her hands clenched in the crips folds of her napkin, an anchor against her rising fear. She did not want marriage to an old doddering man with clammy hands and rotting breath. Neither would she let her father see her distress, but she was well aware that he could contract her marriage to whomever he wished. She hoped his own pride would be some protection against that. He would want a son-in-law in truth, a grandchild perhaps to make up for the son he felt he'd been denied. An old man could not be a guarantee of either.

She drew a steadying breath and turned to her mother. 'Will you talk sense to him? Make him see reason? That marriage is nothing to be trifled with?' Make him see that her *life* was not to be trifled with, bartered away like a bauble in the marketplace.

But her mother merely set aside her napkin and shook her head. 'You've gone too far this time, Mary. There is nothing left I can do and, in truth, I must think about my own interests since I have no son to protect me.' Only a daughter who had failed her despite Mary's best efforts over the years to be everything to them: the perfect daughter who excelled at all things, who turned her hand to all the arts, even the ones she didn't enjoy, without complaint. There was sadness in her mother's grey eyes, regret for what might have been. For a moment, Mary felt it, too.

Guilt pricked at her. Mary did not want anyone affected by her decisions, but she knew her father had spoken truly. Upon his death, which hopefully would not be for several years yet, the estates and titles would pass to a cousin who had his own wife, his own family to instal at the family seat, his own daughters to bring out and fête at the town house. There would be no room for a widow and her unmarried daughter among them.

'Perhaps you are right, Mother. It is time we think of ourselves,' Mary said quietly, the dangerous truth of her situation settling about her. For her, ballrooms had suddenly become battlefields. If she didn't fight for her freedom, it was clear no one else would.

Chapter Four

Caine threw the letters patent down on his grand-father's polished desk with an angry flourish, disgust vibrating through his body, his words. 'This is a prison sentence, to say nothing of an attempt at blood money to recompense us for the loss of Stepan.' The King's audacity knew no borders. The man sought to reward their efforts and sacrifice at Wapping with titles which would only be made hereditary *if* the three brothers married within the year. If not, the titles would revert to the Crown upon their deaths.

It was a rather neat deal for the King. He was able to give something with the hopes of getting something in return. Either he'd get the titles returned to him eventually or he'd see the remaining Horsemen tamed by matrimony. But it was clear to Caine that this generous offer did not truly reward the recipients.

'Caine, please see reason.' His father spoke from the sofa where he sat with their mother. 'These are advantages that I cannot give you.' Father was always apologising, in his own way, for being a third son, when Caine had never felt there was anything to apologise for. They'd been raised well and with love and they'd had more opportunity than most. Unlike his wild sons, their father was a quiet, country gentleman who liked his history, his horses and his books and left the wildness to his wife. Aside from his dark hair and Parkhurst brown eyes, his sons had taken after his vibrant, blonde wife, proving that opposites did attract on occasion. And when they did, they created rather extraordinary progeny.

Caine's gaze slid towards his mother, pale and exhausted by the tragedy of having lost her third son, but her eyes remained sharp and alert, meeting her eldest's gaze with covert encouragement. Mother had always understood him a little bit better than his father had. Mother understood this was a bribe.

'I cannot sit here, even if the rest of you can—' Caine gestured to his father and grandfather '—and pretend this is an incredible gift when the raw truth is that we are being prettily coerced to give up our freedom and toe the line of aristocratic decency.'

'Are you finished?' Grandfather Parkhurst, the Earl of Sandmore, spoke for the first time since introducing the subject, his tone one of regal patience. Even in his late eighties, the Parkhurst patriarch exuded shrewdness and authority. One crossed him at their own peril.

That was not to say the man was cold. The Earl of Sandmore loved his three sons and his grandchildren with a passion. He'd taken an interest in their lives from the day each of them had been born and that interest had continued into adulthood. In return, the family served the patriarch, each playing their parts and doing their duty according to their birth. Alex was in the heir line. He would eventually inherit. Sandmore's second son had no children, but his third son, Caine's father, had four sons and a daughter. The continuity of Sandmore's spy network would carry on through Caine and his brothers.

Caine took his seat, trying not to feel as if he were ten again and Grandfather had caught him stealing cheroots during a summer visit. To be fair, Grandfather had followed the scolding up with, 'Now, if you ever want to pick a lock *properly*, you need to know a few tricks so that you're not caught.'

Perhaps that had been the day Grandfather had seen his true potential. Criminals weren't the only ones who needed lock-picking skills. Gentlemen operating on the dark side of diplomacy did, too. Alex would always be the heir behind his father, but Caine had always felt that *if* Grandfather *had* a favourite grandson, it was probably him, which made any set down smart all the worse. Alex might be in the official heir line, but Caine was unofficially inheriting something far greater. Even at thirty-eight, the scolds could still sting.

Luce turned from the window, the summer light pouring in behind him, giving him the appearance of a dark angel with a halo. 'Caine is right. No one in this room thinks the offer from the King is anything other than the opportunity of a gilded cage. The *ton* is tired of us raking through their ballrooms and their daughters. Now the King can look magnanimous by entitling three men who have no official prospects while addressing the need to bring us into line. Meanwhile, those who served and sacrificed for England are sacrificing once more.' Luce gave a brittle laugh, his words infused with a sharp wryness. 'This time on the altar of *holiest* matrimony. Make no mistake, *we* are not the winners in this scenario.'

The sharp sarcasm and harsh laughter were new, Caine noted, a sound most unlike his brother. The events at Wapping had hit all of them hard. It had been Luce's first personal brush with loss and the aftermath had turned the smooth edges of Luce's usual easy elan jagged. Caine nodded his appreciation to Luce for the support.

As for himself, Wapping had simply turned him angry. He was riddled with it—anger at those who'd perpetrated the crime and at himself. Why hadn't he shot sooner? He played those moments over in his head tirelessly, looking for a solution or, more honestly, a way to turn back time, to stop those choices, those moments from happening at all. He was angry at the King, too. While he sat here in his grandfather's home trying to go back in time, the King was pushing him forward into a future he didn't want, a future he didn't have time for.

'The point is…' Caine levelled a stare his grandfather's direction '…there's no time for courtship and all the social niceties that goes with it. The people behind the attack on…the cargo…' it was easier to say that than to say the attack on his brother 'are still at large. Their trail will only get colder the longer it takes us to search for them.' And exact justice, Caine added silently.

There was a scold in his words for his grandfather. He'd wanted to start hunting immediately, but Grandfather had called their parents, insisting it was time to draw together as a family and required that the three brothers remain with him at the Sandmore seat while he sent out the elusive and anonymous Falcon instead.

While there had been comfort in having his father and mother near, it had been a difficult week for Caine having nothing to do but cool his heels and grieve the whereabouts of Stepan. He would not let himself think of Stepan as dead. Not yet. As long as there was no body, there was still a chance.

That phrase had become a mantra for him. What had *not* been foremost in his mind was returning to London in order to spend his evenings dancing with debutantes. Unless it was with one debutante particularly: Lady Mary Kimber with her wide smile and her hair starting to fall free from its pins as they danced. Not that she'd have anything to do with him now. He'd left her on the dance floor, her face briefly stricken as she recognised the damage done to her though none of it was of her own making.

And there *had* been damage. He *might* have looked at a scandal sheet or two during the past week—out of sheer boredom, of course—and noted her name had appeared in less than congenial references. If he returned to London, he owed her reparation. But that was hardly any more reason to go back to town than the King's whim that he start bride hunting. Marriage was out of the question for a Horseman.

It was the height of selfishness to ask a woman to share the life he led—a life full of darkness and danger. He would not drag a woman and children into that lifestyle, to have them used as leverage against him. It would put them in peril and it would make him vulnerable, incapable of doing the job he did so well.

Grandfather gave each of them a strong look, his gaze lingering on Caine the longest as if reading his mind. 'Perhaps you are looking at the King's offer of titles in the wrong way. Let me remind you of what we know about the events in Wapping.'

He ticked each item off on long, elegant fingers. 'First, we know that the mission was a success. The cargo was secured as was our commitment to Greece under terms amenable to our government.' Which meant, unofficial aid had been rendered without exposure. 'Second, we know that the explosives expert whose body was dragged from the harbour is merely a pawn. The mastermind is at large. Third, we know from Falcon's reports that the mastermind is someone who moves within society's higher echelons. He will be hard to catch and even harder to prosecute if he is indeed a peer.'

Grandfather paused for effect, spearing them with the Parkhurst dark gaze. 'The man you want to find is lurking in plain sight in the very ballrooms you want to eschew. What better way to hunt than to hunt under the cover of being ambitious bridegrooms? Can you imagine it?'

Caine could indeed imagine it. Once word got out he and his brothers had received titles for patriotic services rendered, they would be seen as men with prospects. Their usual rakish shield would be stripped away. Every hostess in London would target them and now they wouldn't be able to refuse. The King had all but commanded they seek out brides. Caine had not considered being able to use that command as subterfuge.

Grandfather nodded, validating his point. 'Perhaps the King is not so single-minded in his reward after all. He wants the culprits caught as much as you.' Grandfather gathered up the letters patent from where Caine had tossed them. 'Now that's settled. Let's settle this.'

He handed one to Luce. 'You should be Viscount Waring. It comes with a nice estate in Surrey not far from your father's and the library has an excellent collection of the classics. You and your father will have a good time with that, it needs some work.' Grandfather smiled and clasped Luce on the shoulder.

He moved on to Kieran. 'You should be the Earl of Wrexham. The estate is on the border of Wales and Cheshire and it needs a sense of itself. It has coal and other untapped resources, the key being untapped. It's lain fallow too long. It will be a good exercise for your mind and your body and I know how much you like a challenge, for all your easy ways, my boy.'

'Well, isn't this rich?' Caine scoffed when Grandfather reached him. 'What do you have for me? Another run-down estate in need of an heiress? These estates *compel* us to marry. We can't possibly sustain them without endless coffers. Surely you see how the King has connived this to his benefit.'

Grandfather coolly tolerated the rebuttal and carried on. 'You shall fashion yourself the Marquess of Barrow.' He handed Caine the letter. 'There's a horsing estate that goes with it and you're not far from Newmarket. I thought that would please you. Sometimes, I think you like horses more than you like people, present company excluded.' Grandfather cleared his throat and gestured for Luce to pour them and their parents a drink from the decanter on the sideboard.

'No one can make you marry. You may choose to not keep the titles beyond your lifetimes. You may even choose to not interest yourself in your estates. You will still have the use of the Parkhurst town house in London unless it suits you to live elsewhere. But these are all decisions that are up to you.'

He waited until Luce had put a drink into each of their hands before raising his glass. 'All I ask is that you use this opportunity to find the traitors who have done harm to your missing brother and who would have done harm to the image of England abroad and bring them to justice. I wish my grandsons happy hunting wherever their endeavours take them. The clock is running, gentlemen.'

'To the clock.' Caine raised his own glass. 'Horsemen, saddle up and be ready to ride within the hour. London calls.' And with it, the next adventure. His blood was already humming now that he had purpose once more. The traitor would not elude him again and time was of the essence.

The next time Mary saw Caine Parkhurst, rake, rogue and rascal extraordinaire, he was a marquess, surrounded by young women at the Carfords' ball. The inequity of the universe could not be clearer. *He'd* left *her* on the dance floor and her reputation suffered the snub while he'd been elevated to one of the elite titles of the peerage. Now, he outranked even her father—a fact that just maybe she took a little perverse private pleasure in.

She might also have taken a bit of pleasure in

knowing that Caine Parkhurst would resent being put in the position of eligible *parti*. Perhaps the universe had a sense of humour, after all, although she wished it was a little more discriminate in where that sense of humour was aimed. She could use a good turn these days.

Since her father's ultimatum, she'd taken a more proactive hand in the offerings on her dance card, paying careful attention to the young men on it: who could she cultivate with tolerable results? Who had the potential to be a life partner without causing her grief and regret? Because if there was one thing her father was not, it was flexible. Once he decreed something, it was the law. He never backed down from his position once it was staked.

She knew other men admired this about him, called him steadfast and reliable for it. She rather thought it stemmed from a fear of being wrong. She often felt that minds should be free to change if new information came to light that impacted a previously held opinion. Not that her belief mattered. If he was determined she would wed by Season's end, she was determined to at least have a hand in the matter.

She sipped her lemonade and watched Caine from across the room. His shoulders seemed broader, his near-black hair more tousled, his profile more darkly handsome. There was something different about him. Or was that simply because he'd become re-spectable in the *ton*'s eye? Now that the Duke of Harlow was all but off the market, matchmaking mamas were scrambling to refocus their attentions. For them, the timing of the Parkhurst elevations could not have been better. The one eligible Duke had been replaced with *three* suddenly eligible gen-tlemen—a viscount, an earl and a marquess.

How lovely, Mary thought acerbically, that a man could have his future arranged so neatly. With one flick of the royal wand the three dastardly Parkhursts had joined the ranks of the decent Parkhursts. But at a price, she reminded herself. The papers had been rather tight-lipped about what had happened in Wapping and why the brothers had been there in the first place, but everyone knew Stepan Parkhurst had been lost. Just as everyone surmised without saying it aloud that the titles were a recompense for whatever had happened. It had been two weeks since their dance, since Wapping. Still, it was something of a surprise to see him out at a ball with the loss of his brother so raw. But perhaps the titles had some-thing to do with that as well.

Caine's dark head with its thick tousled waves swivelled in her direction, his eyes resting on her. She nearly choked on her lemonade. Perhaps she'd been staring too long and he'd somehow *felt* her gaze. She'd heard that some people could do that—feel when others were looking at them. Or perhaps she was being fanciful and this was nothing more than chance.

She took another sip of her lemonade and this time she did choke when it was plain that it wasn't chance at all that kept his gaze on her—on her lips. He was looking at her lips. A delicious frisson took her as she watched a slow, stalking smile take his mouth. He was coming for her, seeking her out, and every eye was trained in his direction, especially the eyes of the women he'd left behind. Drat the man. He was bringing her to attention in a ballroom once again.

'Lady Mary.' He bent over her hand, kissing her knuckles while his dark eyes remained fixed on her face, lingering on her lips. A warm wave of awareness moved up her arm at his touch. How was it that *his* touch was so *noticeable*? There were other noticeable changes, too. His eyes were darkly serious—more serious than they had been the last time—a silent reminder that he'd lost a brother not long after leaving her on the dance floor. Against her better judgement, her heart went out to him. She wanted to acknowledge that loss, wanted to offer words of comfort, but she didn't know him well and a ballroom was not the place to do it. Here, all she could do was flirt.

'Lord Barrow.' She made a small curtsy, remembering his new title. 'To what do I owe the *honour* of your presence?'

His mouth quirked at her emphasis on honour and the implication that the honour was indeed a dubious one. 'My lady, I believe I *owe* you a dance.' Ah, he was here to make reparations.

'You think a dance will repair my reputation after last time?' she replied coolly, playing the ballroom game. Her heart wanted a different conversation altogether—what happened in Wapping? Her pride wanted to send him packing. She didn't need a pity partner. Her dance card was full enough. But the thrill of pleasure his touch sent through her argued otherwise. No one on her dance card tonight moved her like this.

'I'm decent now,' he bantered, his words light, although his gaze remained dark. His actions belied those words. He had not relinquished her hand as a decent gentleman would have done and the low rumble of his voice was too intimate and entirely more appropriate for a bedchamber than a ballroom. All of which suggested he was mocking those that thought so.

She laughed, too, a low throaty, conspiratorial chuckle. 'Are you now? I'm not sure a title can change a man. A wolf in sheep's clothing will always be just that.' That was too much, she reprimanded herself the moment the words were out of her mouth. He had a way of making her say things, do things, she'd otherwise keep to herself.

The response seemed to please him. He tucked her hand through his arm. 'Dance with me and find out.' The dare glittered in his eyes—the first light she'd seen in them—and hovered unspoken on his lips. Mary knew she'd never really had a choice in the matter now any more than she'd had a choice the first time. From the moment he'd taken that first step towards her, the matter had been decided. When one was Caine Parkhurst, asking was a mere formality.

Chapter Five

She'd agreed to a dance. What she got was a waltz—
proof that the universe was still toying with her.
Proof, too, that her mind had not exaggerated the
memory of him: the magnetic pull of his dark gaze,
the warm command of his touch where his hand fit-
ted to the small of her back as if it had been designed
to do explicitly that, the hard muscled breadth of his
shoulder where her own hand lay on him taking in
the hard form beneath the fabric. Every inch of his
body vibrated with masculinity and power. It was
enough to make even a level-headed woman giddy.

He smiled down at her, teeth white and straight,
eyes intent with a gaze that drew a woman in, that
made her a part of whatever mischief lurked behind
that gaze. 'Shall we give them all something to talk
about, Mary?'

Mary. The low, husky gravel of his voice elevated
her plain name to the realms of the sensual, sending

a frisson of erotic awareness through her, as if she were Mary of the Magdalene sort and not the Virgin. This was how lovers might speak to one another. Never had her ordinary name sounded so delicious. Or so wicked, given that he had no leave to use it.

She ought not be surprised. Permission was not something Caine Parkhurst asked or waited for. It was part of his roguish charm—a man who did not stand on niceties, a man perhaps better suited for an era less dependent on manners for the definition of a gentleman. His recklessness inspired reckless-ness in turn and she was overcome with the desire to be equal to it, to him.

'We might as well.' She laughed up at him, try-ing out her own boldness. In answer, his hand tight-ened at her waist and drew her close until her skirts flirted with scandal. It occurred to her in those mo-ments that this might be the closest she'd ever been to a man. 'They're bound to talk, regardless.'

'My thoughts exactly,' he murmured, and moved them into the dance.

It was a quick waltz and Caine wasted no time get-ting them up to pace, taking her through turns with a rapidity that left Mary breathless, her cheeks flushed from the exertion and the sheer thrill of waltzing at top speed. 'I've never dared to dance so fast,' she said with a laugh as he guided them through a sharp turn, expertly avoiding another couple.

'You're a good dancer.' She managed to catch her breath long enough to make conversation. Caine had a keen sense of navigation on a crowded floor and an innate confidence in his own skill. She was struck once more by the agility and enjoyment on display when he danced.

'You seem surprised by that.' Caine took them through a corner using a reverse turn as if on cue to illustrate the point.

'Big men aren't usually so gifted with such grace,' she managed to say, still somewhat in awe of the reverse he'd just executed. It was one of the most difficult parts of the dance and he'd managed it effortlessly.

'Aren't we?' He raised a dark brow, his gaze fixed on her, the hint of a sinful smile teasing his lips. 'Are you an expert on big men, Mary?' A low purl of naughtiness rippled through his words and her breath caught for entirely different reasons than the speed of their dance. She didn't understand his reference entirely—no decent girl would—but she understood enough to know his innuendo was wicked. While she wasn't an expert on big men, she suddenly wished she was, especially if that big man was him.

'It's only that you don't dance much. I assumed it

was because you didn't enjoy it or lacked skill,' she confessed openly, smartly letting his innuendo go untended. That was a battle of words she hadn't the experience to win. She cocked her head and took in the dark gaze, the smiling lips. 'Surely you see the contradiction. If you love to dance so much, why do you do it so seldom?'

His gaze lingered on her, meltingly warm. 'Perhaps because there are so few partners worthy of my efforts.'

She felt the heat rise in her cheeks yet again at the implied compliment—that *she* was worthy. His flattery irrationally pleased her perhaps because it was true. She was a good dancer. What hadn't come naturally had been drilled into her by countless dance instructors. Heaven forbid the Earl of the Carys's daughter not be an asset to any ballroom she graced. One could not catch a duke without dancing. 'I'm glad I do not disappoint.'

His gaze had gone from melting to smouldering and, despite the heat of it, she felt a shiver, a portent of excitement at his words. 'You definitely do not. In fact, one might say you exceed expectations.'

He'd gone too far there. Regret flickered low in her belly. 'Are you flirting with me, Lord Barrow?' She didn't want flirting from him. He flirted with everyone.

Her disappointment must have shown in her eyes. 'Do you really want me to answer that?'

No. She didn't. She'd not wanted to be *everyone* in this moment. She'd wanted to be unique to him, not just another partner, not like all the other women he flirted with.

Silly ninny, her logic berated her. *Your hopes are too high for an apology dance—how quickly you've forgotten why he's dancing with you at all.*

And her logic was right.

Caine leaned close, his mouth grazing her ear, the adventurous citrusy sandalwood scent of him brushing her nostrils, reigniting the thrill of awareness that rippled through her when he was near like this. 'In my experience, it is best not to call out flirting. It ruins the mystique.'

Heaven forfend she ruin the mystique and embrace the reminder that he was flirting to be nice, although one did not usually associate such a milquetoast word as 'nice' with Caine Parkhurst. He was worthy of strong words like dashing, reckless, fearless, shocking, scandalous. But he was not merely 'nice'.

The Viscount who'd courted her during her first Season was 'nice'. Harlow was 'nice'. Caine Parkhurst, who said wicked things about big men and used her first name without permission, was not nice. Which begged the question, why was he being nice now?

'What do you get out of this? No one asked you to make it up to me.' She did not believe for an instant that Caine Parkhurst was doing this out of entirely altruistic purpose, not when he had a brother to mourn.

'I should think it obvious,' he replied with a wicked smile. 'I get to dance with an accomplished partner, a chance to make reparations and I get a break from the suddenly adoring crowds of insipid debutantes while satisfying my hostess's desire to see me on the dance floor doing my duty to the ladies present.'

'I see. One stone, three birds, as it were.' This time Mary was careful to cover her disappointment. Caine would call her out on it if she didn't. She *had* learned that lesson, at least, even if she hadn't learned there were consequences for asking Caine Parkhurst bold questions.

Caine chuckled. 'Don't ask questions of an honest man if you don't want honest answers, Mary.'

She tilted her head. '*Are* you an honest man, Lord Barrow?'

'I am. Honest enough to admit I am sorry our dance is ending. Honest enough to prefer you call me Caine.'

She shook her head, feeling prim and prudish, the very epitome of what society had made her into, as she uttered the words, 'You know I cannot. It is far too improper based on the newness of our acquaintance.' But how delicious such a privilege would be, to be able to claim that kind of intimacy with this man who had the devil's own reputation, but the decency enough to make reparations.

Perhaps it was yet another contradiction in the character of Caine Parkhurst, or perhaps someone who knew him well would understand how the pieces all fit seamlessly together. Perhaps they would understand, too, that he was more than what London rumour made him to be? What would it be like to be that person—the person who was privy to the heart and soul of rakish Caine Parkhurst? Did he, like her, hunger to be truly seen? Was there even such a person who saw him?

That person would not be her. Soon, their dance would be over, he would bow over her hand, thank her for the dance and be gone, her questions unanswered, her comfort unoffered. The music stopped and a little wave of sadness swept her. She would not see him again, not close up at least. They would cross paths at various entertainments now that his new title was of interest to so many, but his duty to her was discharged. She would not dance a breathless waltz with him again.

She prepared to curtsy to him and depart, but he reached for her arm. 'Would you care to walk in the garden with me?' His voice was low, his eyes intent as if he very much wanted her to accept.

There was no flirtation now, no obligation to satisfy, and the lack of a structure in which to understand the request startled her. There was no reason for this invitation except genuine preference for her company and that was perhaps more intoxicating than anything else he'd done. Here was the real danger.

She had no guidebook for this, for going into a garden with a known rake where the protections of the ballroom did not exist. She would be on her own. She ought to say no. Two weeks ago she might have refused. But that was before she'd become a woman living on borrowed time—the sands in the hourglass of her freedom were running swiftly now. If she was to be led to the altar like a sacrificial lamb, she would not go quietly. If her father did his worst, she would have at least a few memories to take with her.

'Yes, a walk in the garden would be lovely.' She offered him a conspirator's smile, inwardly celebrating her boldness and the thrill of satisfaction that came from it. 'If anyone should ask, I find the ball-room has grown…heated.'

'As have I.' He offered a private laugh that did funny things to her stomach and made her glad she'd chosen boldness.

Heated. Crowded. Overpopulated with too many people he didn't want to spend time with. Under-populated with people that he did. Caine had not intended to do more than dance with Lady Mary Kimber and discharge his self-imposed duty of recti-fying things with her. Normally, he wouldn't bother. His usual sort of woman understood the rules and risks of being with him. In fact, they thrived on it. But Lady Mary had been unsuspecting.

Despite her surprisingly sharp wit, she had not been prepared for what dancing with him might mean that night at the Barnstables' ball. He'd in-tended to dance with her tonight, but he'd not in-tended to like it quite so much, or to be loath to leave her company when it ended. Perhaps the reason was nothing more than the logic of comparison. She was far better company than the mamas and daughters who stood waiting for his return.

Outside, he steered them towards less travelled paths in the hopes of privacy. The fewer people en-countered, the better. The ballroom was work—a chance to seek information about the saboteur under the auspices of bride-searching. Out here, the garden represented a moment's escape. He didn't *want* to stop to talk to anyone. There would be time for that later when he returned inside.

'This is much better.' Mary played with the gold locket at her throat, the gesture belying her nerves.

'Is it? Are you uncomfortable being out here with me?' That would be a first. Most women went to great lengths to be in the dark with him.

'No, of course not.' She let go of the locket. 'It's just that I want to discuss something and I am not sure how to go about it. I do not want to pry and I am cognisant that we are mere acquaintances.' Her grey eyes were genuine, sincere. He gave her a nod of permission. 'What happened in Wapping?' she asked softly.

With anyone else, he would indeed have found the question intrusive, a blatant bid for gossip. With Mary the question seemed genuine. But it didn't change his answer. He covered her hand with his where it lay on his arm, wanting to convey his own sincerity in his response, yet one more way in which he found himself taking pains to sheathe his jagged edges when he was with her. 'I regret, Lady Mary, that is something I cannot divulge.'

'I am sorry about your brother.' The words came

out on a careful sigh as if she was not sure she should offer them. The words were intimate and, personal. Perhaps she was thinking they were too personal.They did not know one another well. Out of habit, Caine waited a heartbeat, for her to ruin it with the enquiry that always followed—'Do you think he's truly dead?' He'd had to field that impertinent probe more times than he could count in the last two weeks. But the words did not come.

Something softened within him at her innate sensitivity and he offered her what he'd offered no one else—an answer to that question although she'd not asked. 'I have not given up hope. My brother is infinitely resourceful. If anyone is a survivor, it is he. Even now, he might be making his way to us.'

She gave him a gentle smile. 'You are very brave to live with such hope. You do him a credit, even though such hope must be as exhausting as it is a source of strength.'

Caine paused to study her in the lantern light, struck by her words, by what she saw. 'Exhausting is exactly the right word for it.' He laced his fingers through her gloved ones, absently studying the size differential between them. Her fingers were long, elegant and slim, capable of great delicacy like the woman herself. His were strong, capable of great power, to protect, to pummel as needed.

'I rise in the morning with hope renewed that perhaps today will be the day there will be word of him. I go to bed each night with those hopes dashed.' He shook his head. He'd talked of this with no one, not wanting to burden his brothers. They had their own grief. They didn't need his. What they needed was his strength, his unrelenting confidence that it would all be all right.

'Each day that passes that flame of hope wanes a bit more. I wonder how long I should keep it up? When weeks become months? When months become a year? When does hope become ridiculous?'

'Why don't you ask the Church? They're going on nearly two thousand years of hope, aren't they? And as long as there's no body, they can continue on, can't they? Just like you.'

Caine stared at her for a long moment before he threw back his head and laughed at the stars, a great rippling chuckle taking him. He was seldom wrong about people, but he'd been wrong about her. Never had he thought such words would come out of her well-bred mouth. 'Lady Mary speaks heresy.' He smiled, feeling lighter than he had in weeks.

'Oh, hush! Someone will hear you,' she scolded, casting a worried glance about her. They were deep in the garden now, past the ornamental bushes and decorative fountains where other couples lingered in decency.

'No, they won't,' he countered in measured tones, letting each of his words make their point. It wasn't being heard that should bother her. It was the prospect of not. She was in the dark, alone with a notorious rake who'd already managed to bring scandal to her once. He should offer to take her back into the light, back on to well-trod garden paths or into the ballroom. He should put himself back to work searching for saboteurs and fending off eager mamas with daughters in tow.

They should return to being the Marquess and the lady, or the rogue and the rose. What they should *not* do was stay out here as Caine and Mary. The longer they talked, the more the mutual intrigue between them grew and that was dangerous. He recognised a woman's interest when he saw it and he'd unmistakably roused Lady Mary's. It was there in her gaze, in her wit, in her questions, her sensitivity. It was not what a woman's 'interest' in him usually looked like, but it *was* interest none the less. He intrigued her. And, damn it all, if she didn't intrigue him as well.

To stay out here was to court all nature of temptation. Already his mind was wondering what it would be like to capture her mouth, to taste the sweetness of her on his tongue, to feel the softness of her body as he held it against him, his hands at her hips, tutoring her with his touch. There was something intoxicating about the idea of offering her such tutelage, to put that sharp tongue of hers to good use, to bring her, however briefly, into this world of his, to satisfy her intrigue, to show her what it was like to tempt a rake. But to do so would be to ruin her. She didn't deserve that.

He offered her what she *did* deserve—his protection. 'Would you like me to take you in?'

'Back there?' She gave the distant ballroom a disparaging shake of her head. 'No.'

Gravel crunched, followed by the flutter of feminine laughter, the jovial slur of a man's voice who'd had too much to drink. Her eyes went wide with the implication of discovery. She froze. He was already in motion, gripping her hand and pulling her through the garden towards the edge, hoping the light colour of her gown didn't give them away. At the edge, he found what he was looking for—a door into the back of the house, into a dark room not in use for the evening. He rushed her inside and shut the door behind them. 'We'll be safe in here.' But he thought it was rather a case of out of the frying pan and into the fire.

'Will we though?' Mary said drily. 'Forgive me

if I respectfully disagree. I think you and I understand "safe" a little differently.'

'Do we indeed?' Caine laughed. For the second time that night she'd managed to surprise him.

Chapter Six

Safe was a relative concept these days, demonstrated most aptly by the idea that she was safer in a dark room with a rake than she was at the breakfast table of her own home. Mary would go as far as to argue that the person most at risk in this room right now was he. A marquess caught alone with a gently bred young woman would have no choice but to marry her. That was certainly not an outcome either of them was looking for out here.

She studied him as he toured the room, turning up a lamp so that they could see, taking care to draw the curtains against the lamp's light so as not to attract notice from the garden with its glow. He was careful, attentive to detail. She'd never stopped to think about such characteristics before. They seemed to be the antithesis of what a rake was: a man who was care*less*, reck*less*. Perhaps this was how he'd survived so long without being caught. He took precautions to ensure his freedom.

He stopped at a sideboard displaying a row of decanters. 'Port or brandy?' He held a decanter up in each hand, giving each a swirl. 'No sherry, I'm afraid.' She liked his assumption that she was entitled to the option of drink as much as he was.

'Port, please. I've always wanted to try it.' The rebel in her was alive and well tonight: dancing with rogues, walking in dark gardens, sipping port—a man's drink—alone in a room with a marquess of dubious reputation. It felt *good*.

Caine brought her a glass, his fingertips brushing hers, a gesture that set the butterflies of awareness fluttering in her stomach. Tonight, her body was sharply cognisant of his every nuance, every touch. Perhaps this keenness was akin to that special vividness felt by the dying. A star never burned as brightly as it did right before it was snuffed out, its energies spent, its presence swallowed by the universe. One last brilliant gasp. She was that star. Ever since her father had delivered his decree. This was her last gasp. At the end of the Season, she'd be snuffed out, carted off in marriage to become a matron, someone's wife. No longer belonging to herself.

'Sip it slowly. It's meant for relaxing, for long conversations by the fire.' Caine's dark eyes were watching her as she took a swallow, his gaze following the liquid down the column of her throat. 'Do you like it?' He took the space beside her on the sofa, his leg brushing hers. For him it was no doubt a gesture without thought. Not so for her. She was aware of every inch of him.

She let the taste of the port linger on her tongue before giving a slow smile. 'I *do* like it. You may have corrupted me. I could easily get used to a glass of this after supper.' What she liked more was the man who'd poured it and the promise of a long conversation. With him. The very thought of exchanging such intimacies turned this foreign room into a private space rife with fantasy—what would it be like to sit on a sofa every night beside this man who ignited her with a simple touch? To sip port with him, this rogue who'd seen to her safety, who'd been cognisant of her reputation, who'd given her a waltz to remember and who was also a man wild and untamed, who followed no rules but his own.

Therein lay the fantasy—thinking such a man would be content with firesides and fortified wine, that a woman like she could domesticate a man like him, that such a woman could hold him.

She took another swallow to cover the sudden bitterness that came with the realisation that she could not aspire to such a man. She was too calm, her existence to staid. She was a *good* girl. And look what that had got her so far…angry parents and lost proposals. All it would get her in the future would be an enforced march down the aisle to a husband of her father's choosing.

'You look like a woman debating her choices.' Caine nudged her knee with his leg in a gesture meant to convey casual enquiry. 'Care to talk about it?'

'You assume there *are* choices.' She gave a dry laugh before sipping her port.

'You are a woman with a dowry, connections and status. I would think there are choices aplenty. Creighton and Harlow are merely two men in a pool of several who would be appropriate for you.'

'And any one of them will do? Does that standard apply to you? With your title there are also several women who are now available to you. Why not get married next week, then, if anyone will do?' She scowled. 'I expected a little broader thinking from you of all people. It would be nice if the breadth of a man's thoughts matched the breadth of his shoulders on occasion.'

Caine chuckled and hung his head in a good-natured admittance of defeat. 'Apologies. Of course, you want the same choices as a man, not only in drink but in larger considerations.'

'Port is a start, but, yes, I suppose I do. My life should be worth no less, my happiness no less important, my choices no more limited. And yet those are the items regulated by others, by *their* wants, *their* words, while *you* can do as you like.'

'You're talking about the consequences of me leaving you on the dance floor.' He gave her an apologetic look, dark and warm. How could a woman not forgive that look? 'Was it terrible?'

She'd not meant to confess anything to him. Perhaps it was the port, the intimacy of sitting side by side on the sofa in a dimly lit room, maybe it was just the simple invitation of his eyes or the soft murmur of his voice that suggested her secrets were safe with him, that her honesty was welcome, both of which were not welcome in her own home.

Fleetingly, she wondered how many other women had confided their secrets to those eyes? The answer didn't seem to matter, didn't change the words that came from her mouth. 'My parents were furious over the ballroom incident. As a result, my father is determined to have me married by Season's end.'

She paused, realising it might sound as if she were blaming him. 'I think my father's been looking for a reason to marry me off since Harlow went in the other direction. If it hadn't been the ballroom, it would have been something else. He can always find reasons. He never wanted a daughter. I've never been enough for him.' It felt good to confess it out loud to someone even if that someone was a rake and a stranger. Here in the quiet though, Caine Parkhurst didn't *feel* like a stranger.

His hand curled over hers, his touch warm and easy—yet another way in which men had choices that women did not. He might touch someone at whim. A proper young lady, though, must never dare to take a man's hand. His hand, his arm, must all be offered first. 'What will you do?'

'There is little I can do other than try to beat him to the choice. I cannot alter his decision, but I can perhaps influence who the man is. I think my best hope is to find a man I prefer, a man he cannot object to, before he finds one *he* prefers that *I* cannot object to, albeit for different reasons.' She let out a sigh that held all her exasperation.

'They're all the same and I fear that when they look at me, they think I am interchangeable, too, that they don't see *me*, but a placeholder for whatever comes with me.' Her plan had not got off to a good start. The start had, in fact, been quite dismal. The field of candidates had not significantly changed since the year she'd come out, except perhaps to get smaller.

'You are not alone in that thought. You look at

the men and they all seem the same to you. I look at the girls and I think that, too. There is no life to them, no individuality.' Caine offered her a melting smile. 'I don't think that when I look at you, though. You're not like the other girls, Mary. Don't worry on that account.'

'But *you* can make your own choice. You can decide who it will be and you can decide when.' That was all she wanted, too, but those simple variables were being denied her, had always been denied her. The Dukes had never been her choice either. She'd not known either of them. Creighton had been raised in India and Harlow had never been anything but resigned. Resignation wasn't exactly what a woman wanted to see on her husband's face.

'Is that what you think? That I'm entirely in charge?' He gave a dry laugh. 'Well, maybe I am when it comes right down to it.' He leaned close and she breathed in the scent of him like calming salts from a vial. 'Shall I tell you a secret?'

A delicious shiver took her. Secrets in the dark with a rake? Did he really think she could say no to that? The lure of possessing a secret held by Caine Parkhurst was irresistible even though the rules said she ought to. But why resist? What was the point? The whole rotten lesson of playing it safe, of being good, was that there was *no* grand reward for it.

Good behaviour had changed nothing for her. But breaking the rules had opened up experiences she'd not dreamed of.

Tonight, she'd veered from the staid goodness of her life. She'd danced with a notorious gentleman, walked in the garden with him, drank port with him, confessed her own secrets to him. Why not be his confessor now? She smiled and slid him a glance, whispering the word that would take her one step further down a decadent path. 'Yes.'

'You have to mean it.' Caine was only half teasing. It was a real secret. 'I've not told anyone. Only the King, my grandfather and my family know.' With the exception of the King, everyone else was entirely trustworthy.

He watched her nod solemnly, the light of the single lamp limning the delicate, classical lines of her profile. The semi-darkness enhanced her beauty, called attention to the elegant length of her neck, but it could not erase the edge of desperation that edged her voice. She *knew* she couldn't escape her fate. She was doing the best she could with what tools she had.

To Caine, that was real bravery: to fight on knowing the odds were supremely stacked against you. Something in him had answered to that, awakened.

Empathy for young, privileged girls was not his usual suit. But Mary Kimber was proving to not be the usual.

'This is serious, Mary.' He had his mouth at her ear, breathing in the spring scent of her soft lilies and vanilla. She smelled fresh, clean, pure, all the things his world wasn't. He should not drag her in, should not lure her with an irresistible temptation, yet, he wanted to offer her misery his company, to let her know that she wasn't alone.

'I must marry within the year if I want my title to survive me.' He leaned back from her ear, watching her face take in the revelation. 'You're not the only one who doesn't get to decide when.' It wasn't quite the same. He had more time than she did, but one might also argue the opposite. She'd been expected to marry from the time she was eighteen, more time to accustom herself to the idea of it, whereas he'd had no pressure to marry and had not truly expected to.

He lived a dangerous life, chasing down saboteurs at midnight. A family, a wife, would become complicit in that life, collateral to be held against him, used against him. Such ties would make him vulnerable, fallible. Weak. No matter how much he might want those things in theory, he could not force his life on others.

He felt the press of her hand overlaying his. 'I am sorry,' she whispered. 'Truly.' She was uniquely poised to mean it, to understand.

'So you see, we have something in common. The rogue and the rose, both facing enforced marital obligations.' He chuckled to make light of it.

'I am no rose,' she demurred.

'Yes you are, Mary. You've got more thorns than I anticipated and I'm usually a good judge of character.'

She laughed, a light, natural sound void of the usual debutante affectations. 'Are you suggesting I'm thorny? I would think a rake with your reputation would be more adept with compliments. Usually a rose is known for its blooms, its delicate scent.'

'Don't settle for the usual, Mary.' He laughed, but the reply was offered in all seriousness. Her company was surprisingly delightful. What had started out being an attempt to do her a favour had left him thinking the roles had been reversed and she was the one doing him a favour. An idea came to Caine. 'Do you have any candidates in mind?'

'No. Do you?' Mary took a sip of her port and he let his gaze linger once more on her throat as she swallowed. He wanted to stroke that neck, wanted to trace the lines of it with the tip of his finger from jaw to the edge of the lace on her rose silk gown, to feel her skin grow warm beneath his touch, to see the pulse at the base of that elegant throat speed with excitement caused by him. He knew how to rouse a woman and she would rouse quickly. The curiosity, the interest was already there even if she tried to fight it, tried to reason it away. He would enjoy the tutoring. There was much he could show her, so much she ought to have the right to experience.

Caine shifted on the sofa, crossing a leg over one knee, aware that his body was already rousing as a product of the conversation. 'No. I've not found any prospects either.' He gave a shrug. 'Maybe I won't find anyone.' This was the real secret. 'If I don't find someone suitable, perhaps I will let the title lapse with me, rather than settle for someone unsatisfactory.' It appealed to him to show the Crown that he could not be brought to heel with a title. He gave Mary a slow smile. 'You're the first to know.' This was not something he'd voiced yet with anyone, not even Grandfather.

'Some would call that a very brave rebellion, indeed. Many would also call it foolish,' Mary challenged softly. 'I am happy for you that you have the choice. We are different then, not quite as alike as you originally posited. *You* still get to choose. No one, not even the King, can truly force you if you are willing to pay the price, which is not so very great.

You get to keep your title for your lifetime. It's still more than you started with.'

Whereas for her it was all still captivity. He saw the unspoken juxtaposition of her argument. She was just trading jailers. Not for the first time that night, Caine thought this woman beside him, who followed the rules so diligently yet thrilled to the sipping of port, who dared to dance with him on not one occasion but two, deserved something better than the fate that awaited her. Perhaps there was something he could do for her, something he could give her.

He reached a hand to cup the fine curve of her jaw, his touch slow and sure so as not to startle her with the intimacy of it, but there was no mistake—this was not how a gentleman touched a lady. Her eyes followed his hand, he felt her skin warm against his palm. 'You are all petals and pearls. I've never seen skin so fine.' His thumb stroked the high, elegant arch of her cheekbone, her quicksilver eyes going dark at his words. He moved his thumb to the rosy bow of her lips, drawing them apart, tracing the lower one in a slow, lingering caress.

Her hand gripped his wrist, her fingers too slender, her grip too small to encircle its girth entirely. 'What are you doing?' The question came out on a breathy sigh. She was teetering—wanting to know as much as she felt she ought to put a halt to it.

'Say my name,' came the whispered growl. '"What are you doing, Caine?" and then maybe I'll tell you.' His mouth was at her ear again, feathering a gentle breath against it, his hand moving to rest at the base of her neck, feeling her pulse accelerate.

'What are you doing, *Caine*?' She breathed the words and he smiled against her skin.

'Can you not guess? Surely you have imagination enough,' he teased softly, his teeth nipping at her ear, eliciting a gasp of pleasure. He trailed kisses along her jaw, slow and deliberate, making his destination clear, giving her time to object. He did not kiss unwilling women. But there was no objection, only a sigh that ended with a little sob of want and the shift of her head as she turned into his kiss, her mouth meeting his.

He led her into it with the gentle instruction of his mouth, coaching hers to open, coaxing her to taste, to tangle in mimicry of his own.

Copy me, follow me, it said. *Come with me a little further on this path we've walked tonight and I will show you a garden of delights.*

And she did. He felt the moment when she gave herself over to him, to this brief adventure. There was the press of her body against his, the realisation that kissing was not for mouths only. She tasted deliciously of the port, smelled of English springtime, sweetness and seduction rolled into one. Did she realise what she was offering with the crush of her breasts against his evening jacket? He dared not take it, not when she was caught up in the first throes of passion newly discovered. The moan that purled up her throat was his sign that they'd reached the end of that path. He should not take them beyond this point.

He withdrew from the kiss gradually, cupping her jaw once more as he released her mouth, letting his eyes hold hers so that she could see his want, his regret that the kiss must end. He did not want her to doubt, or to think he withdrew from disappointment when just the opposite was true. He'd enjoyed kissing her, more than he would have thought a few weeks ago. Hell, a few weeks ago he'd not even conceived of kissing Lady Mary Kimber.

But a lot had changed in two weeks. Stepan was missing, a traitor was at large, he'd been made a marquess and given an ultimatum to wed. The Four Horsemen had gone from hellions to husband material, a sure sign of end times.

Her grey eyes were wide in posthumous realisation of what they'd done, of what she'd experienced. Her elegant fingers went to her lips as if she could touch the memory of him, a gesture that he found provocatively erotic. Her voice was a sensual husk when she spoke. 'Why did you do that?' There was no scold in it.

'Because you deserve to know passion, at least once,' he said in quiet tones. Because now she would have something to hold on to against all the kisses to come. He could not change her fate, but he could gift her with a memory.

She blushed, her gaze downcast, a soft smile on her lips. 'Thank you, Caine.' Then she rose. He did not stop her. It was beyond time to return to the ball.

He stood with her. 'I will go back by way of the garden.' She would go back to the ballroom through the hallway to ensure they arrived separately. He held her gaze, forcing her to look at him. 'Will you be all right?' He felt protective of her. She gave a small nod of assurance and turned for the door.

'Mary,' he called at the last. 'If you ever have need, send word.'

She glanced over her shoulder, her features already schooled into politeness, her mask firmly, admirably already in place. 'Of course, thank you,' she said as if he'd offered her a glass of punch, as if they'd not, moments before, had their tongues in one another's mouths. The door shut behind her and Caine raised an appreciative toast to the empty room. Lady Mary Kimber was a cool customer indeed. Who would have thought?

Chapter Seven

Caine focused his thoughts on the half-composed list that lay beside his breakfast plate. It was no easy task considering his thoughts felt they had better places to be—back in the dimly lit library kissing Mary Kimber, worrying about Lucien holed up in his new estate with his grief and refusing to engage in the Season, worrying about Kieran who was perhaps engaging in the Season a bit too much—and always there was that insistent faction of thoughts that remained committed to being on the dock in Wapping searching for Stepan, steadfastly convinced his brother was out there...somewhere.

Where his thoughts *needed* to be, though, was on creating a list of likely suspects behind the sabotage. Caine reached for his coffee cup, hoping a hot swallow would centre him, burn his distractions to oblivion or at least drive them to the back of his mind. The arms sabotage had to come first, nothing else could follow until that was resolved, not just for England but for Stepan. If he couldn't have his brother, he would have his revenge.

The sound of boots on hardwood announced Kieran's presence. Caine checked his watch as his brother entered, fully shaved, and dressed. 'This is awfully early for you.' Since the titles had been bestowed, Kieran hadn't been home before four or up before noon. Caine missed his morning riding partner. 'To what do we owe the honour?' He snapped his pocket watch shut.

'I have calls to pay,' Kieran replied cheerily, filling a plate with a hefty scoop of eggs.

Caine raised a brow. 'So, you're taking the marriage challenge seriously?'

'I'm serious about promoting the illusion that I am.' Kieran winked as he took his seat.

'As am I,' Caine retorted, feeling there was a scold wrapped somewhere in Kieran's words.

'You're not doing a very good job. You dance, but you have to pay calls, you have to follow up on your intentions or else you're still a rake.' Kieran shot his cuffs for emphasis and gave a devilish grin. 'A gentleman pays calls, Brother.' He flicked a finger at a folded newspaper at his place. 'How does Lady Mary Kimber feel about your attentions?'

He took a sip of his coffee and Caine didn't like

the slow smile on his brother's face as if Kieran knew something he didn't. 'You haven't seen the pages this morning, have you? Your dance and subsequent departure to the gardens was noted. Page five. My valet delivers a copy to my room before I come down.'

Caine scowled. Mary wouldn't thank him for the attention.

Kieran chuckled. 'Finally, I get one over on you. Let me enjoy my victory.'

'While you're gloating, perhaps we could talk about Wapping.' He tapped the list beside him. 'I've been trying to construct a list of potential suspects based on what we know and what we can reason.'

Kieran nodded and his smile became grim. 'Let's hear it.'

'I'll start with what we know. On the night of the arms and cash transfer, those who did not want to see England offer support to Greece attempted to sabotage the shipment. This poses two questions. First, who *knew* about the transfer? It was, after all, a transaction arranged by *private* parties. That means a very specific and very limited number of people knew the details. Second, even if someone knew, *why* would they want to stop a shipment they had supported?'

Kieran drummed his fingers on the table and

Caine watched the implication dawn on him. 'That would mean the Ottoman sympathiser was an insider?' He frowned. 'A traitor at the very heart of the transaction.'

Caine nodded. That had been his conclusion as well, *if* his hypothesis was correct.

'Fair enough.' Kieran leaned forward. 'Who's on the list? I am thinking I don't want to know.'

'For starters, anyone who is a member of the Prometheus Club. That would be the inner circle.' The Prometheus Club was a newly founded investment group headed by the Duke of Cowden and the Duke of Creighton—their sister's husband. It was designed primarily for titled gentlemen to grow generational wealth and break the mystique that a gentleman didn't work with money. It was a brilliant project in Caine's estimation and a much-needed one. Too many gentlemen lived in a cycle of debt. 'The six hundred thousand pounds was raised primarily by the club and their personal contacts.' He read the list, 'Cowden, Creighton, Carys, Colby, ten names in all and Harlow has applied for membership.' This was the hard part. These were names of families they knew. It was difficult to see any of them as Ottoman supporters.

'Harlow will be a good addition. Sounds like they could do with some variety, all those names start-

ing with a C,' Kieran joked to add some levity to
a situation that was growing more personal by the
moment. 'You might want to check that list, though.
I thought I'd heard through very quiet channels that
Cowden had suspended Carys and Colby in favour
of supporting Harlow after the scandal at the Duchess of Cowden's ball.'

'What was the scandal?' Caine had apparently
overlooked it and it obviously had not lasted very
long, but had left an impact.

'Harlow was planning to announce his engagement at Cowden's ball, but that night Colby's daughter told everyone Miss Cora Graylin had stolen her
ballgown in an attempt to woo the Duke of Harlow
for herself. In essence, Lady Elizabeth told everyone that Miss Graylin was a fraud. Miss Graylin
left in disgrace and the engagement was not announced. It put quite the damper on the festivities
and Cowden wouldn't tolerate anyone ruining one
of his wife's entertainments or maligning a friend.
He and Creighton put Colby and Carys out immediately, not that its common knowledge.'

Caine's eyes narrowed as he thought. 'When was
this?'

'When you were in Newmarket with Stepan looking over the colts.'

Caine did the calendar maths. 'A week before

Wapping. Well, that adds an interesting element to the game, doesn't it. What if the sabotage wasn't political but personal?' He floated the idea, watching Kieran's brow furrow in thought while his own stomach churned at what he proposed: that Carys and Colby had tipped off the saboteur out of revenge against Cowden and Harlow.

Kieran frowned, apparently finding the supposition as outrageous as he did. 'That's expensive revenge all because Harlow didn't marry one of their daughters. They'd be blowing up their own money.'

'The loan and armaments were insured. I heard that straight from Cowden. And insurance would have paid out much sooner than the Greek repayment on a war loan. It makes me interested in taking a look at Colby and Carys's ledgers. Perhaps they are in financial straits,' Caine posited.

Kieran shook his head, still in disbelief. 'Fine, so perhaps insurance covers the money, but it's not *just* the money, it's the people affected. Losing that shipment would affect thousands of lives and the very survival of the independence movement. We're talking far-reaching consequences that could reshape Mediterranean shipping lanes and trade routes, to say nothing of Christian–Muslim relations in Europe. To use the shipment for personal revenge is the height of selfishness.'

It was that last part Caine couldn't get past, the one sticking point in his theory. Would someone really sell out a country, a people and their own country's best interests all for matrimonial revenge? It was hard to believe. Too hard. It was even more difficult to believe that Stepan had possibly died because of such selfishness. A Horseman's death was something they all risked every time they rode. But that death was meant to be a noble sacrifice in England's service. Not this. Not a meaningless death over a petty squabble.

'What sort of person would go to such lengths for so little personal gain?' Kieran ask the next logical question if they were to test the idea to its fullest.

'A desperate man. It increases my curiosity regarding the state of Carys and Colby's finances.' Still, a man would have to need a lot of money to be willing to tip off an act of sabotage against one's own country's interests.

'Or a man with no scruples,' Kieran offered. 'Someone who doesn't feel responsible for the unseen lives affected.'

Caine sighed, not liking where this was definitely leading, but he couldn't ignore the facts despite his desire to protect Mary. 'We'll start with them. Of all the Prometheus Club members, they're the ones with any sort of motive to act in this manner. It's not so much the marriage revenge that appeals to me, it's knowing they've been put out of the group and now, perhaps, are bent on ruining the group as the group has ruined them financially speaking.'

'And hope you're wrong?' Kieran took forkful of cold eggs and spat them out. He wiped his mouth with a napkin. 'You've been spending time with Lady Mary. I thought there might be some feelings developing there.'

'Not those kinds of feelings,' Caine said shortly. 'I have found her interesting to talk to.' And to kiss and to share thoughts with that he shared no-where else. She'd been a revelation in their short acquaintance.

'Well, I suppose that's all to the good since investigating her father for sabotage is bound to put a crimp in any friendly feelings, especially if you're right.' It would, indeed, and he regretted that because if it came down to choosing between justice for Stepan or protecting Mary, he did not envy himself the choice.

Kieran raised a dark brow in question. 'What is it?'

'Nothing.' Caine shook his head, dismissing such morbid thoughts. They were not at that point yet. 'It's good to talk with you like this. I've missed you by my side riding in the park and I've missed breakfast brainstorms with you. It's been lonely without you here.'

The sentiment caught Kieran by surprise. He cleared his throat. 'It's been lonely without you, too. There's been a lot to sort through. Perhaps it's been a mistake to sort through it alone.'

Caine reached across the table to grip his brother's forearm. 'Not any more. The Horsemen stick together. Always.'

Kieran's gaze brightened. 'In that case, go upstairs and get ready to go out.'

'Where are we going?' Caine asked warily. He'd thought to stay in and work on the list, see if he could come up with who the personal contacts of the members might have been.

Kieran stood. 'To the florist. You and I have calls to pay.' He nodded to the newspaper. 'Thanks to society gossip, you have the perfect reason to call on Lady Mary Kimber. I'll be calling on Lady Elizabeth Cleeves, Colby's daughter. And we don't dare show up empty handed.'

Caine rose and clapped a hand on Kieran's shoulder with a laugh. 'I like it, simple but elegant. We have the cover of courting the daughters and we can use it to gain access to checking their ledgers. We can confirm if money was involved or even if we're barking up the wrong tree.' His bloodhound instincts told him they weren't, though. What a man didn't do for money, he often did for love and Colby and Carys had both motives working against them.

At the florist, Caine produced a large cut-glass vase of Bohemian crystal. He and Kieran had made a stop beforehand. 'I'll take the red roses from the front window.' Women had been crowded around the window, staring at the blooms from the sidewalk, so lovely were they. 'All of them. They should be sufficient to fill this vase.'

'*All* of them? There are four dozen, my lord.' The florist's eyes widened in barely disguised protest.

'Yes, *all* of them.' No one else would have the roses, at least not today.

'Yes, my lord. Shall we strip off the thorns?'

'No, leave them.' Mary might appreciate that the most. She alone would see the deeper meaning.

The florist nodded, choosing not to argue the point, although his expression indicated he found the decision odd. 'Will you send a card, my lord?'

'No, she'll know who they're from.' Caine grinned at the man's discomfiture. In the span of a minute, he'd broken two sacrosanct rules of flower sending and marked himself as not a gentleman in truth. But his money spent the same and so the florist merely nodded again.

'It will be a pleasure, my lord. They will go at once.'

Outside, Kieran laughed. 'I thought you were going to give the poor fellow an apoplexy. Yes, to thorns, but no to a card. And four dozen roses when everyone else sends a dozen.' Kieran let out a low whistle. 'Perhaps with a message like that, you don't need a card after all.'

Caine grinned. 'My thoughts exactly.' The order would make Mary smile. At least that was what he hoped. Part of him wished he could be there to see her face when they arrived.

'Still, isn't that a bit extravagant?' Kieran nudged him in the ribs as they continued down the street in the bright July sunshine.

'Hardly for what I am about to do to her.' He hoped Carys was clear of any participation. He hoped that Mary would never have need to connect his continuing friendship with her to anything other than his personal preference for her company.

'*You're* not doing anything. If anything is amiss, it is her father's fault. He's made these choices,' Kieran reminded him. 'It all assumes our hypothesis is right. We don't know that yet.'

Right or wrong, at some level it didn't matter.

The choices weren't Mary's choices. That was the point. If her father had sabotaged that transport, she would suffer once more for choices made on her behalf without her consent. Even as it was, she'd been reduced to playing the pawn and she didn't even know it. If Caine had his way, she'd never know it. He did not want her thinking last night's kiss had been connected to anything other than his own desire. She deserved truth and honesty and light. An association with him could give her none of those, only roses with thorns.

The roses came shortly after luncheon—forty-eight red roses in glorious full bloom and scent, thorns intact, in a cut glass vase that caught the sunlight, sending rays of light throughout the drawing room as if the vase was made of diamonds. A huge red silk bow was tied about it, tails flowing over the mantel, a display that put to shame every other bouquet in the room.

'Who is it from?' her mother gasped in delight at the sight of it. The footman had been so impressed by it, he'd interrupted lunch to announce its arrival. 'The Viscount has already sent a bouquet.' Some unexceptional carnations in pale pink. Mary could hardly pick them out in the room amid the splendour of this new arrangement.

Mary walked over to the vase while her mother continued to run through the list of suitors. Mary didn't need to guess. She knew who'd sent these. Roses with thorns could only come from one man.

'Is there no card?' Her mother frowned. 'How odd. Who sends a bouquet of this magnitude and doesn't claim credit for it?'

'A man who doesn't need an introduction,' Mary said softly. A man who kissed like sin in the dark, who dared even to defy a king's command in order to pursue his own desires. She fingered the length of red silk ribbon. After the roses faded, she would keep the ribbon as a talisman, as a reminder of having known a man who was brave enough to live free and when she'd been in his company, she'd been brave, too.

She gave a surreptitious touch of fingertips to her lips, the memory of their kiss as vivid now in the bright light of afternoon as it had been in her dreams last night. Her body still thrummed with the echo of it as she took her seat beside her mother and smoothed her lilac skirts, prepared to receive callers for their at-home.

Normally, the prospect of an at-home would have bored her. It was a duty to be tolerated. The Viscount would call, the others who'd sent bouquets would call and she would give them their requisite fifteen minutes of polite conversation. But today, there was a new ripple of anticipation. Caine Parkhurst was coming for her and her body was alive with the thrill of that knowledge.

At half-past two, she looked up from conversation with an earl's young heir to hear the footman say the words she'd been waiting for all afternoon. 'The Marquess of Barrow for Lady Mary Kimber.'

Elation shot through her, obliterating all else. She instantly forgot the last words the young heir had spoken. All that registered was Caine. She could have looked at him all day, framed as he was in the doorway of the drawing room, his dark waves tousled as if he'd just come from a ride, his blue frock coat taut across his shoulders, breeches tight-fitted and boots polished. Hers was not the only breath that caught or the only gaze that lingered on this blatant display of roguish English manhood, but hers was the only one mattered, the only gaze he returned.

He strode directly to her and bent over her hand. 'Lady Mary, I see you have received my roses.' Around them, the whispers began, fans fluttered.

She gave a coy smile and lowered her gaze, playing the game with him. 'Yes, I did. Thorns and all, my lord.' At the covert press of his fingers against her hand, something private and warm passed between them. She raised her gaze to look up into those mysterious dark eyes, home to a thousand wicked promises, a thrill of excitement rippling through her. The devil was loose in the garden—and not just any garden—*hers*. Should she fear it or embrace it?

Chapter Eight

Curiosity lit her quicksilver gaze, but there was a tentativeness to it, too. For a moment, Caine wondered if he'd presumed too much on last night's kiss. After all, it had been done in private. No one knew it had happened. But today's roses, his appearance here at her mother's at-home, was very public by contrast. Everyone would know it had happened. Gentle, unmarried ladies were admittedly not the usual targets of his skills. 'Have I gone too far?' he asked in low tones. If so, he would make a tactful retreat and approach more slowly from another direction, not unlike the tack he'd take with a skittish filly.

She gave a delightful, throaty laugh, matching his low tones. 'Does such a place exist for Caine Parkhurst? Or perhaps it does for the Marquess of Barrow?'

'They are one and the same, Lady Mary. Neither of them knows limits. I was thinking of your-self. Perhaps I had gone too far for you?' He was aware that the noise level of the room had decreased from the buzz that had stirred upon his arrival. People were straining to hear what they were saying to one another. 'Would you care to come out with me to the Park? I have the phaeton and the bays,' he tempted. Everyone knew Lady Mary Kimber excelled at many things but enjoyed only three: horses, archery and botany.

She slid him a half-smile. 'We can hardly be more conspicuous atop a phaeton at the high hours in the park than we are in my mother's drawing room at the moment. I'll get my hat and let my maid know.'

'I say, Parkhurst, that's not fair, stealing Lady Mary away,' the young man who'd sat with her previously complained when she left the room.

Caine laughed and slapped his driving gloves against his thigh. 'It's Barrow, now.' He outranked every man in this room these days. He'd damn well get some use out of the nuisance of the title, even if it just was to see the chagrined look on the face of that popinjay of an earl's heir. 'I'm hardly stealing her. There's only fifteen minutes left of the at-home. Perhaps *you* should have come earlier.'

The meaning was clear: Caine had done all the men in the room a great favour by coming late.

They'd had their chances. 'No one is forcing Lady Mary out for a drive, gentlemen.' Caine made his way to the hall, letting the final implication settle in the room behind him—that Lady Mary *could* have chosen to stay with all of them, but she'd chosen to go out with him instead. It was no longer his actions that ought to be called into question, or Mary's, but theirs.

What did it say about the quality of their company? At best, it said they didn't measure up to a marquess. At worst, it indicated she preferred even the company of a rogue to their lukewarm conversation. Either way, no one in that room was coming out of the comparison favourably.

Mary met him in the hall, her fingers fumbling in their hurry to tie the bow of her summer hat.

'Allow me.' Caine took the wide length of soft lilac satin. He liked tying women's hats. It was an overlooked courtesy that offered a chance for polite intimacy, an excuse to stand close, to look directly in the depths of a woman's eyes, to see every speck of colour in them.

Lady Mary's eyes were like smooth stones at the bottom of the running stream at home in the country, the quicksilver of her gaze a composite of greys, blacks and speckled earthy tones. He tied a loose bow and offered his arm, her maid falling in behind them. 'Shall we? I think we've managed to make every man in that room jealous.'

'Is that why you sent the roses?' she queried, perhaps starting to see his strategy.

'Maybe. Did you like any of them?' he asked seriously, part of him curious as to who would hold her attention and part of him envious that perhaps someone could. 'If there was one you liked, perhaps he just needs a little push.'

She thought for a moment, considering the question. He liked that about her. She was thorough in her responses. She had a sharp wit, but not a glib one, which made her barbs sting all the more. When she said something, it was deliberate. 'I did not *dislike* any of them, but that's not quite the same as liking them, is it? Liking should not be a default position.'

'No, it should not be.' He flashed her a smile as they descended the townhouse steps. At the kerb, he helped her up into the high seat of the phaeton and settled her maid on the back shelf before climbing aboard.

'Still, I think one must be careful about discounting them too soon.' She picked up the conversation as he steered the team into the afternoon traffic, heading towards the Cumberland Gate. 'It doesn't suit to scare them all off.' There was a warning there for him. While he'd not gone too far, he'd come close to it.

'Doesn't it?' he countered. 'If a suitor is frightened off because another outranks him or runs at the first sign of competition, it's probably best to know that now instead of later. That man is not going to stand beside you when there's real trouble to be faced inside your marriage.' He slid her a sideways glance, taking her measure, as he steered the phaeton through the gate towards the park's North-west Enclosure. 'That can hardly be the sort of husband you want.' It certainly wasn't the sort of husband Lady Mary Kimber, veteran of the husband wars, deserved after a long and mostly thankless campaign.

'No, but what I want does not change the fact that the sands are slipping out of the hourglass.' She met his gaze sternly, openly. 'I must choose one of them, regardless of my own hopes. There is always the chance I can bring them up to my standards later. We have a lifetime to spend together, after all.'

Was that the argument she made with herself? The argument that allowed her to find some consolation in her father's edict? His conscience couldn't let it go unremarked.

'If you would like advice from someone who has vastly more relationship experience, I would tell you this: people can change themselves. But we cannot change others. You could have two lifetimes and you could not reform a man who does not wish to re-form himself.' He clucked to the horses before add-ing, 'Women, too. Men do not have the exclusive on that. If you can't abide a man on your wedding day, you will not abide him any better five years in.'

She gave him a steely look. He'd threatened her shield, the one comfort she'd created in accepting her fate. She did not like what he'd done to that with his words. It was there in her silence. But she *was* pondering it. That was in her silence, too. The gate to the North-west Enclosure neared. 'Do you con-sider yourself a relationship expert, then?'

'How many relationships have you had?' he re-joined, knowing full well she'd not had any that truly counted.

'I'm not convinced quantity is the qualifier of ex-cellence in this case,' she replied smoothly. 'You've had a mistress every year for the last twelve years and countless dalliances in between. You've slept with married women. The affair with Lady Mores-tad is an open secret.'

'How does a lady—?' Caine began to say, but she interrupted swiftly.

'A lady only has to read the society pages to know such things. I may not have details, nor do I need or want them,' she clarified, making him laugh. 'But I know all about your patterns. When the bubble is off the wine, you're gone.'

'Those women don't expect anything more. One might argue, those relationships are a complete success,' he justified. He'd started this conversation to prick the bubble of her own naive understandings. Instead, she was pricking his. He set the brake on the phaeton as his tiger jumped down to the hold the team. He hoped the change of scenery would also change the topic of conversation.

'We'll go on foot from here, no horses and carriages allowed inside,' he explained to the maid. 'We won't be long.' He tossed the maid a coin. 'Treat yourself and my tiger to a glass of water if you like.' While he would treat himself to some private conversation with Mary.

They walked in silence past the sulphur stream and the woman selling glasses of the restorative water, neither of them wanting to speak until they were away from listening ears, even accidental ones. They reached a vista that allowed them to appreciate the keeper's house and its gardens, cattle and deer munching on grass nearby to add to the tranquillity of the scene.

Caine inhaled deeply and let it out slowly, peace settling on him. 'All of this space reminds me of home, at Willow Park. I miss the openness when I'm in town.' Which seemed to be always these days. Grandfather needed his eyes and ears more than ever now that age made travel a difficult burden for the old man. At eighty-eight, one had to budget the expense of exerting one's energies. They weren't as limitless as they'd once been, a reminder that time was passing, that Grandfather wouldn't always be there. It was not something he liked to think about.

'Willow Park has bridle trails, perfect for long rambles and long rides, meadows for gallops. There's no place in town for a real gallop.'

'I know.' She gave a long-suffering sigh. 'I don't even bring my mare up to town any more. I just rent a decent horse for the Season. I'm sure, though, that your new property outside Newmarket has some excellent rides.'

'I wouldn't know. I haven't seen it yet. Too much to do.'

'Aren't you curious, though? I must confess I'd have gone straight away to see the stables. Any excuse to get out of town.' Mary laughed.

'Perhaps I'll go after the Season. I have other commitments that take priority.'

'Like wife hunting? Or have you truly committed to setting it aside?' Lady Mary prompted.

'I have not decided about that yet.' He couldn't

fathom it really. 'How can I seriously hunt for a wife while my brother is missing?' Or while there was a traitor to hunt. Or knowing what sort of life he condemned a wife to and possibly children. But he said nothing of that last to her. It required too much explanation, too much exposure of himself.

'Should you decide to pursue a wife, we could help one another in that department. You could make me interesting, force some of those suitors who take me for granted to step up their game, as you've done today with your roses. In exchange, I could make you decent for a short time at least.' The last was said with a wry laugh and Caine smiled.

'Or keep the wolves at bay if the matchmakers thought I'd already set my sights on one match in particular.' Caine chuckled. It wasn't a bad idea and quite a surprising one coming from her. 'What do you think such a plan would involve?' It might just fit into his own larger plans quite nicely, creating an opportunity to be in her company, to be in her space. This could be the way to gaining access to her father's study and the potentially useful records he kept in there.

A bit of guilt twinged and he pushed it back. This plan was *her* idea, he wasn't the one designing an elaborate web for her to step into. Even so, Stepan was his brother. For him, it was worth doing whatever was necessary. There was always the chance he might discover nothing—if so, there'd be no harm done.

'I don't think it would involve much. Attending the same events, a few dances. Perhaps a few more lovely, expensive bouquets,' she teased. 'That bouquet made quite the statement. My mother tried to guess who sent it.'

'Will she be upset it was me?' Caine didn't want his little ruse to make Mary's life more difficult instead of less. He'd meant it to draw attention to her. Where one man saw a desirable woman, other men would follow. He hoped his attentions would bring the right suitor to her. If he could help her make a better choice for a husband, he would gladly do it in reparation for whatever damage he'd done her reputation, or might do in the future. He hoped that suitor might emerge soon. A husband's honour would help separate her from her father's scandal should there be one.

She laughed. 'I don't honestly know. The flowers impressed her. It will be hard for her to be angry over such lovely roses or for having her at-home be the talk of the *ton* for a few days. She does like the spotlight when it's for the right reasons. It will take the attention off the situation with Harlow and it might matter more to her than anything at present.'

Mary gave a sigh. 'Rumour has it that Harlow proposed to Miss Graylin here at the enclosure, right behind the big oak over there. A country proposal for a country girl. Harlow is a thoughtful man in that regard. He pays attention to others.'

Caine felt a brief tug of jealousy at the thought she might be mourning the handsome Duke despite her words to the contrary. 'Tell me the truth. Just between us, *did* you want Harlow for yourself?' She did not have to posture for him as she had that first night at the Barnstables' ball.

She shook her head. 'Not in that way. I'm just competitive. In the heat of the moment, I don't like to lose and I do prefer to please my parents. It keeps the peace at home. But I didn't want to keep him. We would not have suited over the long run. My parents felt I deserved him, as if I should have won him because I had good bloodlines and the best dowry. We were to be matched like two thoroughbreds. Harlow knew it, too.

'Despite that, he was always kind to me, always attentive. But it was clear it was only because manners demanded it of him. We were partnered for the archery contest at the house party and I don't think he saw a single arrow I shot that day. He couldn't keep his eyes off Miss Graylin, who, by the way, is an extraordinary archer. That day I knew with certainty that I hadn't a chance and, more importantly, that I didn't *want* a chance with him, not when he so clearly desired another.'

She stooped to gather some wildflowers and assemble them into a haphazard bouquet. 'But I suppose I do mourn the idea of losing him. I am competitive by nature. I don't like to be outdone, even if I don't really want the prize.'

'Now people are saying Harlow has lost Miss Graylin, that he may come calling again. Should I help that along?' It had been the latest gossip in the club last night. People had been laying wagers on what Harlow would do: go after Miss Graylin who had fled the city or redirect his bridal hunt. Something inside Caine twisted at the thought of that. He could not compete with the well-mannered Duke. He ventured another question. 'You were there the night Lady Elizabeth accosted Miss Graylin at the Duke of Cowden's ball.'

She plucked another flower. 'I regret that evening very much. Lady Elizabeth Cleeves is a devious young woman who will stop at nothing to get what she wants. I should have said something. I should have stood up for Miss Graylin. Perhaps I alone, with my own consequence, could have matched the viper tongue of a duke's daughter. But I stayed silent.

'Miss Graylin's Season, her marital prospects, her

future, were shredded in front of everyone. And Harlow's happiness, too. A broken-hearted man will not make Elizabeth Cleeves happy and he will not look her way now no matter what happens.'

That did not bode well for Kieran, Caine thought. He'd have to warn his brother, faux courting or not, that Elizabeth Cleeves was dangerous. 'And yourself? Would you have Harlow *now* if he called?'

She gave a little smile and tried to tease him. 'Are you trying to hedge your wager in the betting books?' Then she shook her head. 'No, I would not want him any more now than I did then. I doubt he'd call after his own contretemps with my father over the Prometheus Club. In my opinion, what he ought to do is saddle his horse and ride straight for Dorset. He won't be happy unless he does and the rest of society be hanged if they don't like it.'

'Spoken with great conviction.' Caine grinned, feeling the unexpected knot in his stomach ease at the knowledge he'd wouldn't have to deliver the Duke to her. 'Is that what you would do, Mary? Ride straight for love and the rest be damned?' Every day he was with her, a new layer was revealed. He'd not expected such passion, such rebellion to thrive beneath the genteel, well-mannered surface of her.

'I'd like to think so,' she replied resolutely. 'But

first, I'd have to find a man worth fighting for. What about you?'

'I'd like to think there was someone out there that would not only evoke such a response in me, but who was also deserving of it.' Not that he'd be able to act on that, but the thought was pleasant. They'd come to the place where the Serpentine flowed through the Enclosure.

'Said as if one has been hurt by that decision before.'

Well, hell. She'd picked up on that, had she? He'd not mean to give so much away. Caine scooped up a handful of stones, dusting each one on the leg of his breeches. He skipped the first one out over the water and they watched it bounce twice before sinking.

'A long time ago, when I was younger and perhaps less worldly, there was a young woman I aspired to. I won't offer you a name because she is still around and that wouldn't be fair. I was twenty-one and fresh home from university. I felt "finished" and sophisticated. But that didn't change the fact that I had no title, no prospects of a title, and no money other than the allowance my grandfather parcelled out to each of his grandsons. Those things mattered to the girl in question.'

That was when he'd started working for his grandfather, attending diplomatic events, helping with the effort against Napoleon. Effectively putting himself beyond marriage and the chances of heartbreak finding him again. A man in his line of work couldn't marry. The following year Kieran had come alongside and eventually Lucien and Stepan had joined them.

He skipped another rock.

'I am sorry, I didn't mean to dredge up difficult memories,' Mary apologised. 'Perhaps you might show me how to throw a stone? Mine always sink.'

It was a very nice peace offering and Caine accepted it. 'I think it's all about stone selection. The right stone matters.' He passed her one of his remaining stones. 'See how this one is flat and smooth? Try it, hold it in your hand.' He studied it and shook his head. 'No, it's too big. You need something that fits your palm.' He bent down and poked about until he found one suitable. 'This will be better.'

Mary laughed. He liked the sound of her laughter, so genuine, as if she laughed because something truly pleased her. 'I had no idea size mattered.'

He gave a wicked grin, unable to resist the opening. He leaned close and breathed her in as he whispered in her ear, 'Size always matters, Mary.'

'You are wicked,' she murmured, her cheeks flushing with knowledge.

'Yes, I am.' It was a promise, a warning of who she

was doing business with. He reached for her hand that held the stone and slowly closed her fingers, one by one, around its smooth surface, his voice low as he continued instruction. 'Hold the stone jagged side up. Now, this is where it gets tricky. Folks think the toss is all in the wrist and most of it is. We have to whip and release.' He let go of her hand long enough to demonstrate with his own stone. 'But it's in your stance, too. Bend at the knees to help with the backswing.'

He moved behind her then, encircling her with his arms, his mouth at her ear, his body spooned about hers as they bent together, her hand in his as they went through the motion of whip and release. The stone sailed out across the water, bouncing once, twice, three times. 'You did it,' Caine complimented, stepping back from the warmth of her before his own arousal became unconcealable. Not that he was embarrassed by it, he'd long ago comes to terms with his body and its functions, but because she might be and because erections could be complicated, especially with a well-bred girl.

The closeness had affected her, too. Her cheeks were still flushed and he'd smelt the beginnings of arousal mingled with the lily and vanilla of her before he'd stepped away. 'We should go, Mary. Your maid is waiting and I am sure your mother will be anxious to have you home.'

She took his arm although he sensed reluctance on her part to leave their bucolic surrounds. 'It's as if we're returning from a holiday and with every step we take reality gradually creeps towards us like an incoming tide.'

Yes, a very apt description. Too apt. Reality called. But they held it at bay, driving back in silence. Mary clutched her wildflower bouquet in her hands and he *might* have taken a less direct route.

At the town house, a footman was on the lookout for her and came down the steps immediately to assist her. 'Welcome back, my lady.' The gesture and words made it clear that Caine was to leave Mary at the kerb.

Mary slid him an apologetic look for the implied rudeness. 'Thank you for a wonderful drive. The fresh air has done me well, my lord.'

'Perhaps we'll do it again some time soon.' Caine mustered the appropriate response, suppressing a smile at the coy apology flashed his way, as if it were them against the world. She'd grown quite bold in their short time together, or perhaps she'd always been bold and he'd merely brought it to the fore the way a gardener coaxes a rose to bloom.

Guilt pricked at him. She would need all her boldness in the weeks to come if his concerns over her father bore out. He'd never so fervently wished to be wrong as he did now. She had enough on her plate with her own problems. She did not need him to add another. Nor did she deserve his betrayal. The more he encouraged her interest and indulged his, the more deceived she would feel if…if her father had betrayed his friends and in some ways his country and Caine was forced to be the bearer of that bad news.

Chapter Nine

Curiosity was one thing. Encouragement was another. Mary was in danger of overstepping that carefully drawn boundary. She could allow herself some private curiosity about Caine Parkhurst in the solitude of her bedchamber. But she should not encourage him in public.

Yet today had been spectacular. The ordinary had become extraordinary all because of a vase of flowers and a tool through the park—things she'd experienced many times over her Seasons. She was used to bouquets and callers, used to rides through the park and strolls with gentlemen. But nothing had prepared her for Caine Parkhurst's way of doing things.

She hummed a bit under her breath, twirling the little wildflower posey in her hand as she climbed the stairs to her chamber, the thrill of the afternoon still lingering. How dashing he'd been in the drawing room, pushing aside the protests of the Earl's heir with his words to establish his place at her side. She'd felt as if she was at the centre of a fairy tale, special, swept off her feet.

Normally, when a man looked at her, she could see him calculating the pound notes. When Caine Parkhurst looked at her, there was something else entirely in his eyes—secret promises, mysteries to uncover, decadence to explore and an invitation to traverse all of it together with an experienced guide beside her. What a temptation he posed against the backdrop of her current circumstance.

She must choose a husband, but they all seemed lacklustre when measured against Caine. None of them made her pulse race, her blood heat, her mind challenged. Yet she could expect nothing from him. He did not wish to marry, a wish he clung to so strongly that he was willing to forgo a hereditary marquessate. The universe was playing games with her again. Of course she was attracted to the one man who had no intentions of marrying when she must absolutely marry and soon.

'You're happy, my lady.' Her maid came up behind her, having stopped for a moment downstairs to exchange a word with a footman. 'Shall I take your wildflowers and find a vase for them?'

'No, no vase for these. I'll see to them myself.' Mary already had a container in mind for them.

Once inside her room, she took a clear glass jar down from a shelf and poured some of the fresh water from her washing ewer into it. 'There,' she pronounced, putting the flowers in the jar and setting it on her dressing table. Like magic and fairy tales, they wouldn't last long, a day or two at most. She would dry them and press them later to keep as reminder of the day she was a princess for an afternoon with a most inappropriate man and how she'd thrilled to it, how she'd felt alive perhaps for the first time.

'They're pretty, my lady...' Minton paused to appreciate them '...especially the deep pink ones.'

Mary studied the posey of Sweet William. 'Hmm, there's something missing.' She opened a drawer and pulled out her box of ribbons. She held up one length and then another, considering, before she settled on a dark rose. 'This one, I think.'

'Very nice, my lady,' Minton complimented. 'You've got so many interesting gentlemen.' She stepped into the wardrobe and Mary could hear her rummaging through the gowns.

'Just one interesting gentleman,' Mary replied absently, still allowing her mind to exist in the throes of the afternoon, replaying every word, every nuance of their conversation which had been as scintillating as last night's kiss. She'd never talked with a man the way she'd talked to Caine Parkhurst. 'The others in the drawing room were just the same as always.'

Minton reappeared with two gowns in hand. 'And the one coming to dinner tonight, my lady. Your father's special guest. Do you prefer the cream or the pale pink? There's the theatre to follow dinner, so perhaps the pale pink and the opal set. We can do your hair with the tiara.'

Mary hardly heard Minton's suggestions. Her mind was fixated on the first announcement. Her father had a guest for dinner? Just one. There was no one else invited. It was the first she'd heard of it. The implications were unnerving. A single man coming without his wife meant only one thing: he was being invited explicitly to meet her. Going on to the theatre with them meant he was also being encouraged to spend time with her. This man was meant to be one of her father's candidates for her hand. The realisation was horrifying.

She pressed a hand to her stomach and calmed her breathing. Horrifying,yes. Unexpected, no. He'd warned her and she knew he'd make good on his word. It was all suddenly just so *real*. She might be sitting down to supper with a man who would become her husband in a few short weeks.

Mary gripped the edge of her dressing table and

sat down. 'The pink will do, Minton.' She tried to sound as if the fairy tale she'd surrounded herself with last night and today hadn't come crashing down. 'What do we know of our dinner guest?' Right now, she needed information, not panic. Lady Mary Kimber was a cool, self-assured debutante, not a woman given to flights of fancy. But there was no denying that the tide she'd held back this afternoon was now fully in.

Caine's roses in their magnificent Bohemian crystal vase had been removed from the drawing room. Mary noticed their absence immediately when she appeared downstairs at twenty minutes to seven. Her parents and their guest were already assembled. But Mary had wanted some time to herself, arguing that she didn't want to appear over-eager and give the impression of waiting on their guest's arrival. She hoped the roses hadn't been thrown out, but perhaps they had been once her mother had realised who had sent them.

'Mary, dear.' Her mother swanned over, meeting her at the door and taking her arm, the gesture designed to draw the gentlemen's eyes to the new arrival. 'There you are, looking lovely.' Under her breath she said, 'Isn't your father's friend handsome? And young? He's so eager to meet you.'

'Where are my roses?' Mary replied sotto voce, offering their guest a polite, demure smile at a distance.

'In the music room. They were too ostentatious to leave out here in the public rooms. Showiness is so gauche. One can always tell a gentleman by the flowers he brings.'

They approached her father and their guest, her father making the introductions. 'Your Grace, allow me to present my daughter, Lady Mary Kimber. Mary, this is His Grace the Duke of Amesbury.'

Amesbury, blond, blue eyed and sleekly elegant in dark evening clothes, reached for her gloved hand and pressed a brief kiss to her knuckles. '*Enchanté*, Lady Mary. I've hoped we might meet for a while.'

'How is it that we have not, then? It seems everyone in society knows everyone.' But she did not know him. She was sure of it. Mary carefully retrieved her hand with another polite smile. A third duke and something of an unknown. She wasn't sure how that made sense in the social circles of London. An unmarried duke did not escape scrutiny for long.

'It's a bit complicated,' Amesbury demurred, which only intrigued her more. Where in the world had her father unearthed a duke?

'We have time before supper.' Mary offered her arm. 'Take a turn with me about the drawing room and tell me, the short version at least. I love puzzles.' Amesbury could not refuse, not in front of her parents and certainly not if his claim to wanting to meet her was to be believed. The offer pleased her parents who exchanged a knowing look as Amesbury took her arm. Perhaps it made up for driving out with Caine.

'Once London gets wind of you, you will be quite popular,' Mary began the conversation. 'How is it you've managed to escape social attentions until now?'

'I was never expecting to be found, if I may be blunt?' He raised a polished, practised blond brow in enquiry. 'My cousin, the Duke, died in an accident a few years back, leaving no heirs, very unexpectedly. I was abroad and it took a while to determine who the heir was and then time to locate me.'

'I am sorry,' Mary offered.

'As am I. Being a duke is a lot of work.' He gave a short chuckle. 'Between transferring the title, mourning, going through the paperwork and figuring out the estates, there has been no time for socialising.'

'But now all is in order?' Mary asked as they stopped before one of her father's prized Constable paintings.

'Yes, all is in order so that I might begin to set

up my town house, responsibly sit in the Amesbury
seat in the House of Lords and set up my nursery, of
course, to ensure that such a disaster does not happen again.' So, the man was wife-hunting.

'How do you know my father?' That seemed the
next logical question. If the man had truly been buried in paperwork, how had her father found him?

'We have a few mutual investment interests. We
met at a shareholders meeting, actually.' He smiled
to reveal straight white teeth. The Duke of Amesbury was certainly well appointed, which was all
to the good. He would turn heads and mamas still
reeling over losing Harlow for their daughters would
be more than appeased by this consolation prize.

'My mother and I would be more than happy to
make introductions for you. We can begin tonight
at the theatre. If you'd care to share some of your
interests, I might be able to make some suitable rec-
ommendations.' The sooner she could deflect his
attentions, the sooner she would not have to endure
him. There was something too sleek about him, too
perfect, as if she could not quite see behind and
beyond the mask of all that perfection. That made
her nervous. Caine was honest and blunt. He didn't
put on airs. He walked through a ballroom as God
made him.

Amesbury placed an overly familiar hand atop

hers and gave another chuckle, eyes smiling with a facsimile of kindness. 'There is no need for that. You do surmise correctly that I am wife-hunting. But the hunt is over. I have already settled on the woman I want.' A frisson of ice snaked down her back. She did not miss the unspoken implication that the woman he'd decide upon was *her*.

Mary steadied herself against the shock of the realisation and the subsequent shockwaves that followed. When a woman was settled on sight unseen, it meant only one thing. This had been arranged between him and her father. *Without* her consent. This was the height of male arrogance and egoism.

'And the woman in question? Has she settled on you?'

'I am sure she will.' He smiled easily, his eyes teasing as if this were all a grand bit of humour, as if they both knew who the 'she' was and both of them had agreed to the arrangement. 'We'll have a few weeks to get to know one another, but even so, we'll have a lifetime to discover each other.' A lifetime in which there would be no choice to leave if that 'knowing' didn't turn out favourably. That sounded ominous, *not* optimistic. It called to mind Caine's advice that a person could not change another person.

'How can you be so sure?' Even a man was

trapped, although to a smaller degree, by marriage. 'Sometimes we learn unsavoury things. It would be unfortunate if something unpalatable came out once it was too late to turn back.'

He laughed and leaned close for a moment, invading her space. It was not at all a pleasant sensation to have him so close…yet she'd enjoyed such a gesture when it was Caine Parkhurst leaning in. 'That's what asylums are for, aren't they?' He gave her a wink as if they'd exchanged a joke. But Mary knew such things weren't joking matters. A woman could be put away on grounds of the least provocation as long as there was a doctor's concurrence.

Then he sobered and patted her hand. 'I know a very nice place up in the Yorkshire Dales. My wife would have the best of care. But I don't anticipate that would be a problem. My wife will be biddable and loyal.'

Of course his wife would be those things if she knew the consequences that awaited her rebellion. Mary felt another shiver crawl down her spine. Amesbury embodied a different kind of boldness. A comparison arose organically in her mind, the afternoon still a vivid recollection, and the man she'd spent it with. Caine Parkhurst was bold because he gave a woman a choice—the chance to choose him and what he offered. But the Duke of Amesbury, whom she knew by title only, was bold simply because he believed no one would stop him.

'By the way, Lady Mary, you are all your father said you'd be and more. Quite impressive, actually. I am looking forward to the theatre tonight, are you? I am told Blackmantle's *The English Spy* is quite intriguing.'

'I have seen it before. It's a farce, so I think intriguing might be overstating it a bit,' Mary said coolly, casting a swift look towards the doors. She'd never wished so fervently for the butler to announce dinner. Surely, it would be any minute now.

These had been the longest fifteen minutes of her life and perhaps the most frightening.

'My mistake,' he said affably. 'I can see I will need your guidance as I enter society. *I* will appreciate *your* expertise in this particular matter.' This optimistic cheerfulness of his set her nerves on edge. While his words might *sound* congenial, she sensed a darker message lurked beneath—the innuendo of a barter: that she might guide him in the matter of the play's storyline and, in exchange, he would guide her in other more intimate pursuits, as a husband with experience might guide an untried bride. There was much not to like about the insinuation, not least of all the subjugation they implied. There was nowhere to run. She was trapped in her own home.

Panic began to well. She fought it back. She would not let Amesbury see her falter, see her fright. He would feed on it, use it to dominate her. She forced her mind to work. She had nowhere to run to, but perhaps there was someone to whom she could run? 'If you would excuse me for a moment? I'd like to collect myself before supper.' Lady Mary slipped away before he could protest. She'd only have a few minutes. Upstairs, she scribbled a note with a trembling hand and rang for her maid.

'Minton, I need your utmost discretion.' She folded the paper. 'This must be delivered to Parkhurst House. Can you send a footman who won't be missed while we're at supper? And if not, can you manage to go yourself?' She thought for a moment. 'In fact, the latter would be best. I won't need you for hours yet and you won't be missed.' The fewer who knew a note had left the house, the better. Secrets among many were hard to keep.

'I can go, my lady.' Minton looked worried. But there was no time to explain. Caine had suggested he'd stand as her friend. Tonight she needed an ally, perhaps someone to dissuade Amesbury's interest. More than that, tonight she needed the presence of a friend. She was still reeling from the realisation that her father had sold her in marriage, that her home had become a prison where her wants held no sway and she sensed this was only the beginning. She'd not hit bottom yet.

Chapter Ten

'Bottoms up!' The old barman's toast went around the drawing room of Parkhurst House in a raucous chorus of male voices followed by, 'To Westin! To the bridegroom!' Parkhurst House was bursting at the seams tonight, full of soon-to-be fully inebriated gentlemen giving Lord Westin a manly send off before his nuptials in the morning.

Someone slapped Caine on the back as he drank to the toast, slopping brandy on his coat. 'Your place is better than White's or Boodle's combined, old chap.' Caine reached for a handkerchief to mop up the spill. Thank goodness his coat was dark. He spied Kieran standing with Westin, a friendly arm draped about Westin's shoulder, giving the man advice, no doubt. The thought of Kieran offering marital advice was almost as humorous as the thought of someone being desperate enough to take it. Once

Westin was sober, he'd realise Kieran had no idea what he was talking about.

To the unsuspecting eye, it was business as usual at Parkhurst House, the drawing room acting as a de facto club for those who wanted something more private. It was only half past eight, but the card tables had been busy tonight, the liquor flowing. People had been in high spirits. Someone had even played the pianoforte. Soon, the crowd would thin. Men would move off to join their wives at the theatre, at a ball or a much tamer card party or musicale than what was on offer here. And he would have to hunt for his information elsewhere, Caine thought grimly. There'd been nothing of use gleaned from conversations over cards tonight or a private drink in the corner with those who would be most likely to let something noteworthy drop.

Noteworthy these days included any news of bodies washing up on the shores of the Thames, persons without their memories admitted to hospitals in the surrounding areas, anyone who might be Stepan in need of help. Caine had extended his net of surveillance into the villages and hamlets that lined the waterway of the Thames. Noteworthy also included any hint of who might have hired the explosives expert. If only the fellow hadn't died before Caine could have extracted answers from him. It would have given him the next link in the chain.

Kieran left Westin to his friends and joined him. 'Come drink with us. It looks like you're sulking at your own party,' he ribbed him, then Kieran dropped his voice. 'It feels wrong to me, too, to be celebrating something, anything, without Stepan here, but we must keep up appearances. Come drink with us. Westin wants to thank you for the party.'

Movement at the drawing room door caught Caine's eye. His brow furrowed as the footman accepted a piece of folded paper. 'I'll be there in a moment,' he told Kieran. 'Let me go see what this is about.' Hope began to race as he crossed the room. Was this news at last?

Caine stepped into the hall where it was moderately quieter and less crowded, the guests there too busy with their coats to pay him much heed. He unfolded the note, scanning its short message, disappointment quickly warring with distress. This was not about Stepan. This was from Mary. He slipped down the hall leading to his study, wanting to take a closer look. Messages offered more than words to read if one took the time.

He spread the note on his desk and turned up the lamp, rereading the words:

The Royal Theatre, nine o'clock. I need a friend.

With any of his other women he'd know exactly what this was—an invitation to a little risky public dalliance. That was not what Lady Mary Kimber was after. The note was short. No explanation. The writing somewhat unsteady. It had been written in haste or in desperation or a bit of both. He folded the note and put it in the inner pocket of his evening jacket.

Mary was in trouble and she'd called on him, taken him up on his offer that night in the library. The trouble must be concerning indeed if she thought her best ally was a rake. He checked his pocket watch. He'd never make nine o'clock sharp, it was nearly that now. But he would go straight away. He'd be there in time to assist her at the intermission.

The need for assistance was obvious the moment Caine stepped into the Caryses' box. Lady Mary's attentions were being commandeered—there was no other word for it—by a tall, blond man who had her cornered in the front row without her permission. Could the man not see from the rigidness of her posture, or hear from the shortness of her responses, that she'd rather be anywhere but there, with anyone but him? Or did the man know and simply not care? That last made Caine's blood boil. Where was her mother? Why didn't someone come to her aid? But of course, there was no one. She'd known there wouldn't be. That's why she'd sent for him.

'Lord Barrow.' Lady Carys stepped into his path. 'To what do we owe this honour? We were not expecting you tonight.' Unspoken words crackled between them.

We did not expect you because you've already sent our daughter flowers and driven with her in the park. You've already done too much, none of it welcome.

'I've come to see Lady Mary.' Caine side-stepped around her with years of practice in eluding mamas. At the sound of his voice, Mary's head turned towards him, relief flooding her features.

She rose and offered her hand when he reached her side. 'Lord Barrow, how *good* to see you.'

'How good to see you, my lady,' Caine replied before introducing himself to this man who made Mary uncomfortable. He was a rake and a marquess now, he could break whatever rules he wanted. He was definitely not going to make her introduce this unwanted interloper to him as if the man was a valued acquaintance instead of what the man really was: someone importuning a young lady while society looked on and did nothing all in the name of keeping the marriage mart thriving.

'I'm Barrow, who might you be?' If the civility could have been more congenial, so be it. Best to let a man know where he stood with you from the start.

The abruptness did take the man by surprise. Breaking rules usually put someone on their backfoot. They didn't know how to respond. 'I'm Amesbury. The Duke of, in case you're wondering.'

'I wasn't.' Caine gave the man a cold, dismissive smile while his mind filtered through names. He couldn't place the man, but the name was somewhat familiar. Where had he heard it? But that was a secondary consideration. Mary was the primary concern. He understood Mary's cry for help. Carys was duke-hunting for his daughter again and she didn't like it, perhaps because she knew this time she'd have no choice. Introductions achieved. Now for the next step: extrication. He needed a moment alone with Mary.

'Lady Mary, you seem a bit pale. Please allow me to take you out for a breath of air.' He offered his arm and she took it rapidly, held on tightly, as if he'd become an anchor.

Lady Carys offered a feeble resistance Caine quelled with a look before she spoke a word. 'Lady Mary needs air,' was all he said as he guided her past the guests in the box, the whispered comments starting to fly behind fluttering fans. He led Mary through the intermission crowd in the saloon to a space by one of the big windows overlooking Bow Street. This was the most privacy he could afford short of risking scandal for her.

'Thank you,' Mary breathed. A waiter came by, circulating with a tray of iced champagne. Caine took two.

'Take it, you look like you need it.' Caine handed her the glass and grinned to put her at ease. He clinked his coupe against hers. 'Have a few sips and then tell me what has happened.' She was definitely pale. Whatever this was, it was more than her father dredging up another duke. That might be unpleasant, but it was not unexpected. She'd known such a move was coming. Something else had surprised her, shaken her.

'It's all been arranged between them,' she whispered, clearly conscience of being overheard. 'I am to marry Amesbury. In August, before the Season ends. Likely, my parents think to make the wedding the last big event of the social whirl.' There was real anguish in her eyes and Caine's sense of protection surged. 'It was decided without me. I was simply reassigned as if I were an interchangeable piece in the machinery of society.'

'Caine studied her over his coupe. Her outrage was in line with what he knew of her, with what she'd revealed to him that night in Carford's garden. She valued having a sense of choice. But he did not think this was the entire source of her distress. There was fear beneath her outrage.

'So, your distress is about the principle of the arrangement?' He pressed the issue gently, aware that the longer they stood here, the more notice they attracted. He wished there was somewhere better to take her, somewhere they could be alone to talk at will. This was not a conversation to be rushed, but it must be because of who they were and what society would think.

'Yes, and no.' She shook her head, the little opals at her ears dancing. 'Yes, I am outraged that my father would treat my marriage so cavalierly. I'd expected an array of suitors and from that array to make a choice. Not this…forcing. I thought there'd be at least a facsimile of choice.' Exasperation was evident. 'I thought I might at least know the gentleman in question to some degree, slight as it might be.'

Her eyes dropped, embarrassment flushing the pearly sheen of her skin. 'I am being married to a stranger who doesn't even know me.' Her gaze flicked up to meet his, her voice shaky. 'And he is vile.' There was something more to that, but Caine would explore that later. He knew enough for now and time was ticking.

He pressed her hand, letting his touch steady her, comfort her. 'What can I do?' He gave a nod to cue her. 'Quickly, your mother and Amesbury are making their way over and your father has emerged from wherever he went visiting.' He felt her tense and wished he could take her away from here. What did it say of her family or her situation if she was safer with a rogue?

'Do you know him? Can you find out about him? Perhaps there is something in his past that would turn my father away from him.' She spoke rapidly, unfurling a fan that matched the blush rose of her gown.

'Yes.' His own gaze narrowed as Amesbury approached. Perhaps, too, there was a reason her father had chosen Amesbury for his daughter, sight unseen. What did Amesbury have that the Earl of Carys wanted badly enough to trade his daughter for it? Society would say it was his title. Carys *had* been adamant about wanting a duke for her. But Caine wondered if it might be something more.

'There you are, dear.' Lady Carys fixed a false smile on her face, much like the one she'd worn in the drawing room this afternoon. 'The second act will be starting, we must return.'

'I am glad you are feeling better.' Amesbury offered his free arm to Mary, but Caine took Mary's arm in a bold move.

'Lady Mary has convinced me to stay for the second act.' Caine gave a feral grin, holding the other man's eyes with his own. 'And I've accepted her gracious offer.' The saloon lights dimmed calling everyone to their seats. 'Lady Mary, shall we?'

There was a wealth of meaning in those two words. *Shall we.* Shall *we* take London by storm as we cross the saloon to the box? As *we* take our seats and earn more attention from the opera glasses than the second act? It was a delicious fantasy to play along with as Caine steered their course, the muscles of his arm taut and evident beneath her fingers. In reality, she knew better. There was no 'we'. There was just *him*. Well-bred young ladies strove to be invisible, to demurely avoid avid, overt attention. But Caine Parkhurst attracted attention wherever he went—even when there was a play to watch, he upstaged it.

She was envious of that and the freedom he had to be so bold, the freedom to draw attention and not live to regret it. Some day she wished to possess the confidence he did, to walk across a room knowing everyone was looking, everyone was commenting and not give a fig. For now, it was enough to walk beside that boldness, to feel his muscles flex with confidence and strength in the confines of his coat and revel in the knowledge that he had come for her when she'd called. Whatever he felt he owed her, the debt was paid.

At the entrance to their box, she slid him an appreciative glance. Good heavens, she could look at him all night and never tire of that face with its strong lines, long, straight nose and dark eyes. 'Thank you,' she managed to whisper, noticing for the first time that while he'd come for her, he'd not come dressed for the theatre. The realisation was both flattering and uncomfortable.

She cleared her throat. 'Especially if I am taking you away from something else tonight.' Or someone else, she thought belatedly. In her desperation, she'd not thought about where or how her note might find him or who he might be with. Had he been at Parkhurst House or had the message gone on to somewhere else? Guilt and curiosity pricked at her, along with something strongly akin to jealousy. Had he been with someone else? One of his mistresses perhaps? Or a *ton*nish widow?

'Let's allow the others to enter ahead of us,' he

murmured at her ear, dropping his hand to the small of her back, his touch warm and steady, unlike her pulse, which was just warm. 'And, no, I was not doing anything I couldn't leave,' he said quietly as her mother and Amesbury moved past them.

At the seats, Amesbury allowed Mary's mother to precede him and then took his seat, tossing Mary an expectant, almost predatory smile as she came down the short aisle of the box, Caine's hand at her back lending her strength. With Caine beside her, she could tolerate Amesbury. She made to step into the seat and felt Caine's hand press at her back in warning. 'Perhaps you'd like to sit on the aisle, Lady Mary?'

She smiled, picking up on the reason for the unorthodox suggestion. He would sit beside Amesbury. He would be a buffer, much to Amesbury's evident chagrin.

'I thought Lady Mary would want her seat back.' Amesbury's politeness bore a steely edge. Caine would defend her, she knew, but she could also defend herself.

'I am fine on the aisle—thank you for your concern, though,' Mary said sweetly, making it seem as if Amesbury had done her a favour. After all, if it was a favour, there was nothing to argue over.

She'd effectively taken away any reason for him to be angry.

Mary gratefully took the aisle seat and sat back, relaxing. Caine would be her shield. It was more than she'd expected. She took a deep breath and then sniffed again. He didn't have the usual scent about him. It was tainted with something. 'Are you sure I haven't taken you away from entertainment?'

'Just a bridegroom's final hours of freedom drinking in my drawing room.' He gave her a wide smile. 'Someone's drink spilled on my coat and I didn't stop to change it.'

The envious knot in her stomach eased. He'd not been with one of his mistresses. Not that she should care. But she did care. He'd kissed *her*. He'd made her burn, made her yearn for things she hadn't even known she wanted. And she'd thought in the moment that he had burned, too. She didn't like the idea of him burning with someone else. Did that make her wanton? She felt a blush creeping up her cheeks at the thought. How wicked she'd become since Caine Parkhurst had waltzed literally into her life.

The theatre went dark. Caine leaned close to her ear. 'A penny for your thoughts, Minx. They must be quite decadent to put a blush on your cheeks.'

She gave a throaty laugh. 'If so, maybe they're worth more than a penny.'

'Maybe they are,' he whispered. 'Enjoy the play, you're safe as long as I am with you,'

'But you cannot always be with me.' Although how wondrous it would be to have such a champion.

'Can't I?' He chuckled. 'We'll see about that.' The curtain went up and she felt Caine's hand slide around hers in the privacy of the darkness. For the first time since coming back from the failed house party in May, she felt safe, which was ridiculous, because Caine Parkhurst was anything but.

Chapter Eleven

Caine escorted Mary to the Earl's carriage under the glowering gaze of Carys himself whose countenance made it clear he would have preferred it if the Marquess of Barrow had made his goodbyes at the box. But Caine was determined to stay with Mary as long as possible and to offer her all the assurances of safety he could, including the promise of calling on her the next day. He helped her into the carriage with a covert squeeze of her hand while the Earl glared over her head.

'If you do call tomorrow...' the Earl said coolly once the women and Amesbury were inside.

'*When* I call tomorrow,' Caine corrected with a wolfish smile, prepared to go on the attack. He'd been waiting for Carys's warning since the moment he'd arrived.

Carys cleared his throat and then proceeded with his customary sternness. 'As you say, *when* you call tomorrow, I would appreciate a conversation. In private, Barrow.' It was probably all the politeness he would get from Carys. That was fine. He wasn't looking to be friends.

'I would welcome it,' Caine returned with a steely gaze to match Carys's tone. For many reasons. He would bring his persuasion to bear any way he could to champion Mary's cause of freedom, or at least freedom from Amesbury's attentions. It seemed that the modern world had not moved on from medieval arrangements when it came to marriage. Such arrangements were alive and well and just as barbaric as ever.

Oh, he wasn't an idealist by any means. He didn't think the aristocracy would stop marrying for money and power any time soon. They couldn't afford to. But he *had* thought the arrangements were made on slightly more amicable, consensual grounds, that blatant force had dropped out of the equation. Mary's case suggested otherwise. This was outright coercion. Subtly managed, certainly. Mary would have no case to plead. Society would say Carys was doing what any good father would do: finding a suitable match for his daughter who'd been out several Seasons.

No one would think marrying a daughter to a duke and all the benefits that came with it was coercive. But Caine had seen the look in her eyes at the theatre tonight, felt the tightness of her grip on his arm, seen the trembled construction of her words in the short note she'd sent. Amesbury frightened her—a woman who did not frighten easily. That was intolerable in Caine's estimation. Yet the duality of his own situation was growing intolerable, too. Soon he'd have to act on behalf of the Horsemen and that would possibly change everything.

You've become quite invested in Lady Mary Kimber's situation, more so than your own circumstances warrant, his conscience nudged. *Remember why you started this: To repay her for a social debt, long before you suspected Carys's involvement in the Greek business. But now that debt is paid and you need to think of your own cause. You need entrance to Carys House for Stepan.*

Tomorrow, he'd get a first-hand look inside Carys's study, which would be useful for conducting a more in-depth look through that study later in the hopes of finding paperwork that might connect Carys to the sabotage. Or perhaps in hopes of not finding anything at all even if meant they would be back to step one in finding the saboteurs.

His own carriage pulled to the kerb at last, having made its way through the post-theatre traffic and Caine gave instructions to go directly to Parkhurst

House. He wanted to talk to Kieran. Between the two of them, perhaps they could figure out who Amesbury was.

For a man like himself who lived in town more often than not, it was strange to run across someone so entirely new. Even newcomers had reputations that preceded them so that they were known, expected, before they arrived. But Amesbury had materialised as though from thin air.

Lights stilled burned in the drawing room windows of Parkhurst House, but the tenor was much more subdued than when he'd left. Westin's party had moved on and only a few men remained, playing a quiet game of cards at a corner table, Kieran keeping them company. Jackets had come off; sleeves were rolled up. Caine recognised the men, all of them involved in some level of diplomacy. Such men came to Parkhurst House often. It was a place where deals could be unofficially discussed, information unofficially learned and passed.

It was moments like this when Caine felt the loss of Stepan even more keenly. Stepan was usually the one who saw to the guests in their drawing room club, who signalled for more drinks to keep a man talking or a fresh pack of cards to keep men playing. When men were enjoying themselves, tongues loosened intentionally or unintentionally. Kieran looked up and caught his gaze. Caine gave a jerk of his head, indicating the study down the hall before he disappeared, knowing his brother would follow.

'Well, how was the theatre?' Kieran drawled, sprawling on the leather sofa in the study and accepting a tumbler of brandy. 'Good enough for drinks, eh?' he joked.

'It was enlightening. Worrisome.' Caine took the chair opposite his brother and rested his feet on the fireplace fender. 'The good news is that I have been asked to have a private word with Carys tomorrow at the house.'

'Let me guess.' Kieran swirled his brandy. 'The bad news is the reason for it?' He took a long swallow and let out a satisfied sigh.

'Lady Mary's situation is untenable. Which makes me suspicious. She is an attractive, intelligent, well-dowered, titled young woman. She does not need to be manhandled—for lack of a better word—into a marriage. There are plenty of suitors she could choose to make an appropriate match with. I saw them first-hand. The drawing room was crowded with them. Yet, her father is forcing the Duke of Amesbury on her.'

'So you're wondering—' Kieran took up the thread of thought '—why does he need Amesbury badly enough to override his daughter's desire to choose a match from an acceptable, well-vetted pool, which would meet both their needs.'

'Yes, exactly. Surely you and I are not the only ones to see how this situation could be remedied amicably with both parties getting what they want. Yet Mary says her father has already decided on Amesbury.'

Kieran studied the liquid in his glass. 'She is entirely opposed to the Duke? It's not just stubbornness because he is a duke? Perhaps she's feeling a bit rebellious after the last two.'

Caine flashed his brother a strong look. 'I believe her words were, "he is vile".' There'd been no time for details, but her words and the way they were delivered had raised Caine's hackles to be sure. Had the man importuned her in some way in her own home? Had he spoken to her crassly? A man's vocabulary indicated much about his thought patterns and behaviours.

Kieran grimaced. 'That bad. Hmm.'

'Do you know the name? Amesbury? I have to admit the man was a stranger to me.'

Kieran shook his head and sat up. 'I don't know, but *Debrett's* will.' He set aside his glass and strode to a bookcase. 'And Lucien would know, of course, but he's not here.' The brothers exchanged a look of mutual concern.

'Father's with him, helping him sort the library.' And, no doubt, helping Lucien sort his feelings, his grief along with it. Father was good at things like that. He knew how to come alongside a person in their time of need with a story or a piece of advice. 'I miss him, too. It's been a long time since it's just been the two of us.' He gave Kieran a rueful grin and swirled his own brandy. 'Thirty-four years, in fact.'

Kieran laughed. 'Do you remember the time we bundled up Stepan and took him sledding? It was only the second time we'd ever seen snow ourselves, but we were convinced we were experts.'

Caine nodded. 'We sent him down the hill behind the stables all by himself. He must have been…four? But he had no fear. He laughed the whole way down. He was still laughing when we pulled him out of the snowbank at the bottom. I thought Mother was going to kill us. But Stepan just wanted to go again.'

'I remember looking up at the nursery window and seeing Lucien glaring at us. He hated being left out even when he was a toddler. He could hardly wait to join us.' Kieran returned to the sofa, book in hand. 'I wonder if he feels that way still?'

'Once a Horseman, always a Horseman. He knew the commitment and the risk,' Caine said gruffly, although it had galled him that Lucien hadn't stayed in town with them to see it all through—the titles, the marriage agreement that went with them, the search for Stepan, and the search for the traitor. Instead, Lucien had decamped.

Kieran flipped through the pages, coming to the listing for Amesbury. He turned the book so that Caine could read. '"Born, 1783; Died, 1823". The fellow wasn't incredibly old.' Old was Grandfather in his eighties. 'He died without a direct heir, though. There's no spouse listed. He'd not married.' Caine thought for a moment. 'Perhaps that's why we haven't heard of this new fellow. He's a distant cousin.' So distant, in fact, that no one had heard of him. Yet.

'It might be nice to know how the previous Duke died,' Kieran posited.

Caine agreed. 'Seems to me that a man who hadn't married was either irresponsible with his duty or hadn't planned on dying. The latter means his death was likely an accident. I think I'll call on *The Times* archives tomorrow morning. I'd like to know before I see Mary and Carys.'

Kieran gave a low chuckle. 'That's the second time you've called her by her Christian name in this conversation. It's not Lady Mary?'

Caine tried to dodge the probe. 'You know I'm never one to stand on ceremony.'

'When you're seducing,' Kieran amended. 'Is that

what you're doing here? Do you intend on seducing the most proper Lady Mary Kimber? I didn't think virgins or ruining them were your style?'

'It's not.' Caine infused the two words with a tone of finality, resisting the temptation to argue in his defence that Lady Mary was not helpless or quite as proper as she made out. She'd turned docile propriety into an excellent façade over the years. But he was staunchly a gentleman who kissed, but did not tell. News of his exploits always leaked out from the female quarter, never his.

'Then what are your intentions?' Kieran queried, only half joking. 'Don't tell me they're the same as mine with Lady Elizabeth Cleeves because she's not sending me notes begging for my attendance at the theatre or asking me to rescue her from unwanted suitors. Nor am I buying out florist shops' worth of red roses. It seems like this has gone beyond a useful attraction.'

'I owed her for deserting her on the dance floor at a very inconvenient time for her,' Caine deflected.

Kieran raised a disbelieving brow. 'I should think the debt paid by now. But perhaps interest rates are higher than I understood.' He gave a shrug of his shoulder and rose, preparing to depart, but Caine knew how to read his brother. Kieran wasn't done informally probing. Caine braced.

'She wouldn't be the worst choice for a wife if you mean to fulfil the King's bargain. I mean, she does ride, after all. She'd fit in with the Parkhurst clan if she ever let her hair down, although I'm not sure how we feel about the Earl of Carys as an in-law.'

'You have that horse well ahead of the cart, Brother,' Caine cautioned. 'You know I'm not exactly wedded to the idea of marrying to save the title.'

'But you do like to save people, Caine.' Now it was Kieran cautioning. 'Whatever you're doing with Lady Mary, make sure it's for the right reasons.'

'What other reasons would there be?' Few people could put him on the defensive, mostly because he didn't give them the chance to get close enough, but Kieran was one of them.

'Atonement. You feel guilty you couldn't save Stepan, so you think to save her instead. Only, now you might not be able to. Her family's business is *her* family's business.'

'Unless her family's business *becomes* my family's business and right now there's a possibility the two may intersect,' Caine answered smoothly.

'If Carys is not involved in the sabotage attempt, you will dissociate yourself from Lady Mary, then?' Kieran was not shy in his argument. But they both knew the situation with Mary was not solely about investigating her father.

'There is no crime in helping a damsel in distress,' Caine countered.

'Until you help her right into your bed, then neither of you has choices no matter your intentions.'

'Weren't *you* going to bed?' Caine speared his brother with a look. Kieran saw entirely too much. And he was right. Should Carys turn out to not be connected to the sabotage effort, Caine would not abandon Lady Mary to Amesbury's affections, such as they were. And he knew very well where that could lead. But that was a bridge to cross another time. For now he was still collecting puzzle pieces.

He collected that first piece the next morning, up early for a ride on Argonaut in the park and a breakfast that lasted long enough for him to see that his attendance at the theatre in the Carys box had been noted by many under the guise of lines like 'it seems the new Marquess of Barrow is taking his responsibilities seriously when it comes to courting...' followed by a chronology of his efforts—dances, roses, now the theatre, and competing with a duke for the dukeless Lady Mary. Well, he'd expected as much. He did not think the article terribly damning to her since he'd been able to keep the focus on him. She was merely the victim of his attentions. It could have been worse.

He was at the front door of *The Times* the moment it opened, the receptionist rising nervously at the sight of him striding in, great coat flapping at his legs, and stammering an anxious, 'If you're here about the article…'

'I'm not here about the article,' he dismissed the concern abruptly. 'I need to find an obituary. Is there a staff librarian or an archivist who can assist me?'

Relieved, the receptionist was all brisk helpfulness. 'Yes, my lord, right this way.'

It turned out to be a relatively simple process as he had the date of death, which narrowed down the newspaper issues that would have carried the notice. 'A carriage accident?' He glanced at the archivist, a small slim man with spectacles in a dark suit. 'Is that all we know? It's not very descriptive.'

The archivist gave a frown of disdain. 'My lord, obituaries are not gossip columns.'

'Because gossip is for the living?' Caine couldn't resist the jab. 'Is there a story? Was there news coverage of the accident? It seems like a duke dying in an accident in town would be newsworthy.' Certainly gossip worthy, although he dare not say as much.

The archivist was chilly. 'We can look. We'll check the issues up to two weeks after the accident.'

'And prior,' Caine suggested, earning a stern stare. He was not making friends here.

'Why would we do that?' the archivist questioned.

Caine offered a meaningful stare in return. 'Sometimes accidents are not accidents.'

He managed to shock the starchy slim man. 'You don't mean to imply the Duke met with…misadventure?' The man clearly couldn't bring himself to say the other 'M' word—murder. Or heaven forbid, suicide.

'The Duke died in an accident. He most certainly met with misadventure.' Caine chuckled at the man's ridiculousness. 'The question is what kind of misadventure, self-inflicted or otherwise.' There were a hundred things Caine would like to know about that carriage accident. Had it been a race? Had the Duke been driving? Was the Duke a regular racer? A reckless driver in general?

All he found was a short story that mentioned Prince Baklanov of Kuban had pulled the Duke from the water too late to save him. Caine smiled to himself. He knew that name. He made a few notes, tucked them into his coat pocket and said farewell to the archivist, mentally checking off another item from his task list. Next stop, the florist's, where

he'd send a note with the roses: *Wear a riding habit.*
Then, over to Mary's. Thanks to that one name, he
knew how they'd spend their afternoon.

Chapter Twelve

The afternoon with Caine would be her escape and Mary was ready for it. She'd spent the morning tolerating her mother's lectures on her behaviour last night at the theatre, how she'd treated poor Amesbury, their guest, and the remarked attentions she'd shown 'the rake'. She'd parried the comments as best she could with reminders that the 'rake' was a marquess; surely such attentions were required when one sent floral arrangements of such magnitude and wasn't she supposed to be on the lookout for a high-ranking suitor?

That last was said in an attempt to provoke a confession from either of her parents that a match with Amesbury was *au fait accompli*. But the most she got from her mother was that her father favoured Amesbury and had the highest of hopes *this* time and didn't the two of them look well together? Wasn't Amesbury a witty conversationalist? To which Mary replied, 'Only if one thinks it's funny to joke about locking one's wife away on a mere whim.'

The newspapers hadn't helped. She'd expected it, had known her decision to associate with Caine would attract notice. But the notice fuelled her mother's dislike, which was only marginally mitigated by the arrival that day of another gorgeous display of red roses and a card that had Mary announcing, 'I need to change.' He wasn't just calling; he was going to take her out. Away from here. She didn't care where. It would be out of this house, beyond her mother's gaze and her father's glare.

Mary took a final look in her chamber's long mirror, smoothing the lines of the plain blue riding habit over her hips and tugging at the jacket. She had fancier habits—the pink habit with its black frogging and decoration, for instance—but such an ensemble was for a quiet ride on the paths of Hyde Park where the goal was to be seen and she did not think that was Caine's intent. He was taking her *riding*, real riding. Where or on what horse she had no idea and the mystery only added to her excitement.

She fiddled with the white stock tied at her throat, trying to still the butterflies in her stomach. Caine Parkhurst, one of society's most notorious gentlemen, had planned an afternoon for them. For *her*— proper Lady Mary Kimber, who never put a foot wrong, who never strayed outside the lines. Once again she was reminded about what happened when she *did* step outside those lines…a rake was calling—one her parents could not outright refuse because he was also a marquess. Life was suddenly exciting. The butterflies in her stomach now were far different than the butterflies that trembled at the thought of Amesbury.

Yet what was she stepping outside the lines for? What could or would become of this unlooked-for friendship—if that was even the right word for their relationship—with Caine? What did this gain her? He wasn't the marrying type. Not even the reward of a hereditary title was enough to entice him. She had to keep reminding herself of that, which was difficult to do when she thought he would make quite good husband material if he chose to apply himself.

He *was* a rake, that was not in argument. However, he was not without compassion, or without heart. She saw how he mourned the loss of his brother, how concerned he'd been for her reputation on numerous occasions, how he'd come to her rescue when she'd called. That spoke of loyalty and honour. Such a man would defend his family. Protect them, care for them, provide for them. Put them first. A woman could not ask for much more than that, except perhaps for love and fidelity.

But weren't these characteristics a type of love? There would be passion, too, he'd demonstrated his capacity for that as well. A low heat began to burn. Would he demonstrate that capacity again today? She wouldn't mind if he did, although she ought to know better than to encourage it. They were on a path that led nowhere.

Ultimately, they would reach a place where their lives would be incompatible and they would reach it soon. In a few weeks when she would be married to…someone. Hopefully not Amesbury, but someone whom she could tolerate, and Caine would go on searching for his brother. But until then, perhaps she ought to enjoy the journey and not worry over the destination.

Minton quietly opened the door to her chamber and poked her head inside, ready to depart with her. 'My lady, Lord Barrow is here.' The butterflies started all over again. She could hardly wait to be off. Mary stuck a final pin in her hat and hurried downstairs. Her father was not home at present, delayed by a late-morning meeting that had run long and she did not want *her* outing postponed by his sudden arrival. He could have his conversation with Caine when they returned.

She found Caine in the drawing room with her mother, praising her wallpaper and decor. 'I must consider your choices when I decorate at my estate outside Newmarket,' he was saying, 'Your sense of colour is exquisite, my lady, so very tasteful.' Then just to add a bit of salt, 'I see my roses have found pride of place. I am honoured. Perhaps I should send two arrangements next time, one for each end of the mantel, one for each of the beautiful ladies of the house.'

Mary stifled a laugh. He pulled off the line so effortlessly yet he had to know how much it would gall her mother to put two such bouquets on display and know that she could not choose to do differently. He would call and expect to see them. When her mother said nothing, he persisted with easy charm, 'Perhaps you do not prefer roses. What *are* your favourite flowers, Lady Carys?'

'My mother's favourites are tulips.' Mary stepped forward into the room and made a small curtsy. 'Good afternoon, my lord.' These pleasantries felt as if she were in a play, all of them actors speaking required lines. She and Caine would discard those lines as soon as they left the house.

'My maid and I are ready, my lord.' She communicated a sense of urgency with her eyes although Caine seemed unbothered by the need to make a quick exit. Drat him. He was probably looking forward to speaking with her father. Caine felt himself the equal of many men and the superior of most, such was the attraction of his confidence. He was not afraid to meet a man toe to toe. She would love to be the proverbial fly on the wall during that discussion.

'We are riding today,' Caine announced his intentions to her mother as if their attire had not confirmed it. He was dressed in tight-fitting buckskin breeches that showcased the muscles of his thighs rather well. Too bad he wore a coat. The tightness of those breeches might showcase some other parts, too, if they were but visible. 'At Prince Baklanov's school in Leicester Square.'

Amid her own excitement engendered by Caine's announcement, she watched her mother's expression soften further, the dislike of Caine Parkhurst melting under the barrage of decor compliments, personal enquiries, and the casual mention that he knew a foreign prince. It wouldn't last. Her mother was fickle that way, but for the moment, it would make an impression. 'How wonderful.' Her mother fluttered her fan, overwhelmed. 'Have a good time. Mary misses riding when we're in town.'

'I do miss it,' Mary interjected, wanting to move this along. 'Thank you for thinking of me with this singular treat, Lord Barrow.' Mary offered her arm.

'We should be off. We wouldn't want to keep Prince Baklanov waiting.'

She didn't let herself relax until they were in the carriage. Only then did she give herself fully over the excitement of the outing. 'Are we really going to Prince Baklanov's?' she asked as they pulled away from the kerb. He had an extraordinary reputation that had reached legendary proportions among the horse set.

'Yes, we are and we are really riding there, but we're also going for some business I have with the Prince. Your business.' Caine gave her a serious look, the easy charm he'd displayed in the drawing room put away to use another time. 'Last night you asked me to look into Amesbury. Is that something you still desire?' His dark eyes held hers and her pulse quickened at being the recipient of such intensity.

'Yes,' she breathed, hope blossoming. Had Caine found something that might be her way out? 'What did you learn?'

'Not much yet. The former Duke died without a direct heir.'

Mary nodded. 'Amesbury told me the same last night. He said it had taken a bit of time to locate him.' Lord, Caine Parkhurst had a beautiful mouth. She ought not stare at it. It was hard to concentrate on his words when all she wanted to do was remember the feel of that mouth on hers. In truth, she wanted more than the memory. She wanted to feel that mouth on hers again.

'The former Duke died in a carriage accident when his vehicle plunged into the Thames. Prince Baklanov was on hand. He and his friends tried to save him, but were unsuccessful.'

Why did she care about this? It was hard to think when so many of her thoughts were busy elsewhere. Caine reached for her hand. 'It's not much, but I just thought you would like to know why Amesbury had come out of what seems like thin air. Baklanov could shed some light on that, perhaps fill in some details. Meanwhile, you can ride a splendid horse.'

Baklanov's riding school did not disappoint. The Prince had bought up several lots on Leicester Square and turned the mews into town stables and a beautiful riding arena where he gave lessons to the *ton*'s finest young ladies and hosted riding showcases. Mary stood in the doorway of the stables, closed her eyes and breathed deeply, inhaling the scent of horses and hay—a clean smell, a country scent in the middle of the city.

'This smells like home.' She let her breath out with a long sigh. She turned to Caine, an uncontrollable smile on her face that stalled only at seeing the expression in his gaze—dark and intense and absolutely riveted on her as if he were looking into her very soul and seeing the depths of her. Her breath caught. 'Thank you for bringing me.'

He laughed, low and private, just for her. 'We just got here. You haven't even ridden yet.'

'It doesn't matter. This is everything. The city has disappeared.' Dear heavens, he was so very good at creating intimacy out of nothing: his laugh at her ear, his hand at her back as if it had been made to belong there, as if he'd been made to touch her and she to be touched...by him. Just him. How had she gone so long without knowing it? And now, she *craved* it. How would she live without it? For surely this interlude of acquaintance with him would come to an end. Caine Parkhurst wasn't a forever man and her own time was running short.

'I am glad.' He gave a nod. 'Here comes our host, Prince Baklanov, and his wife, Klara.' Mary noted Klara was wearing riding breeches. She hadn't even been introduced and she already knew they'd be friends.

If she wasn't so smitten with Caine Parkhurst, she would have found Prince Baklanov undeniably handsome with his long dark hair and piercing eyes. He had a strong, commanding presence that made it

easy to believe the few rumours she'd heard about
him—that before being exiled from Kuban, he'd
been in charge of the Kubanian Tsar's cavalry.

'I am so glad you're dressed for riding,' Klara said
after introductions were made. 'We have the arena
all set up for jumping. Lord Barrow indicated in his
note that you're an accomplished rider. Come with
me, let me show you the horses, you can pick one
out and we'll meet the gentlemen in the arena.' She
tossed her husband an unmistakable look of flirtation. 'I was thinking we might have a jump-off,
women against the men, once everyone is properly
warmed up.'

Baklanov crossed his arms. 'And the prize?' His
eyes engaged in a private, intimate exchange with
his wife that made Mary warm to witness. She ought
to look away, but there was something honest and
entrancing in the exchange that required her attention. There was a lesson for her in this. *This* was
what it *should* be like between a husband and a wife:
the teasing, the private knowing of one another even
in public, the way Baklanov touched his wife with
his eyes—*We are lovers, partners, we are each other's warriors.*

Intuition whispered through her: it would be like
that with Caine. He would love fiercely, protect

fiercely. The woman who could claim such affections from him would be lucky indeed.

Klara's eyes glowed with competition and with love as she answered, 'The prize shall be a forfeit of the winner's choosing to be named at the winner's discretion.'

'Carte blanche?' Caine's eyes sparked with devilish humour, resting on Mary with their own private message that stirred a heat low in her belly at imagining the forfeit he might claim, or the forfeit *she* might claim. 'I rather like the idea of that. Baklanov and I accept. Go find Lady Mary a horse equal to her ability while we take care of our business.'

Three-quarters of an hour later, Mary found herself on a gorgeous thoroughbred mare with a glossy coat and her blue riding habit exchanged for a pair of Klara's riding breeches, which felt enormously freeing. 'She moves beautifully!' Mary called to Klara, who was putting a splendid white mare through her paces.

Klara drew the mare alongside. 'Would you believe we rescued this lovely girl from the kill pens three years ago?'

Mary patted her mare's shoulder. 'She looks healthy and sound, I would never have guessed.'

'You handle her well. The Marquess did not exaggerate your skill,' Klara complimented. 'Here come the men now.' She smiled as Baklanov and Caine walked their horses into the arena. Klara flashed her a grin. 'They're handsome, but their good looks aren't going to save them from our skill.'

Jove save him. Caine could not take his eyes off her. Mary Kimber in breeches was a sight to behold. Those breeches clung to her curves and put the athletic grace of her body on naked display. Mary Kimber in breeches *and* jumping a course of brick walls and three-foot fences was positively breathtaking. Her concentration, her confidence, her focus on the needs of the horse beneath her, was evident in every choice she made. It was a good quality in a rider to put one's horse's needs first. It spoke to having a selfless spirit, a conscientious awareness.

She approached the last fence, garnished with flower boxes on each side designed to distract the horse, and Caine held his breath. All three of them had struggled with this jump. Baklanov had missed it entirely and had to wheel his horse around for a second try. It had cost them the lead against the women and, oh, how Caine wanted to win the competition. He knew exactly what he'd claim as forfeit on the carriage ride home. But as much as he wanted that forfeit, he wanted a safe, clean ride for her more.

She was coming in fast and sharp. Caine worried she wasn't giving the horse enough room to take the jump. He would have come in wider, taken the jump from a straighter position. She launched and Caine didn't exhale until she and the horse landed safely on the other side.

'You were concerned.' Nikolay nudged him, their horses putting their noses together. 'You like her. This trip wasn't strictly business.'

Caine slanted him a look. 'I do like her, but I also didn't want to explain to her parents what she was doing when she fell off her horse. Now, thankfully, I won't have to.' He could imagine how her mother would take the news her perfect daughter had been riding astride when she fell off.

They applauded as Mary walked her horse over to the edge of the arena, letting it cool off. 'That was too much fun!' Mary was breathless with the exhilaration of the ride, the colour in her cheeks high. She unfastened her helmet and removed it. She shook down her dark hair and Caine felt arousal stir, deep and primal, an arousal that was not merely a reaction to her attractiveness, but a reaction to seeing her completely given over to pure enjoyment.

She was in her element here and it was intoxicating. It seemed a shame to him to stifle all that by confining it to ballrooms and gowns. It also seemed a shame to take that joy from her with the news he'd learned from Prince Baklanov.

'Mary's was the last ride,' Klara announced, 'and it was clean. That means the ladies win.' He and Baklanov had both knocked a rail in a rare misstep for them both and Klara's horse had spooked at the flower box, needing a second try. Only Mary had ridden entirely clean. And on an unknown horse as well. It was impressive on all fronts.

A groom came to take the horses and Klara took Mary off to change. Caine watched her breeches-clad derrière walk away until she was out of sight. Damn, but he'd miss those breeches. When she returned a short while later, she was all proper Lady Mary Kimber again in her blue riding habit, hair pinned up, not a strand out of place. No one would guess she'd spent the afternoon wearing breeches, riding astride and jumping neck or nothing.

He smiled as she neared. That was the whole point of the clothes, the hair, the manners, wasn't it? That no one *did* guess what lay beneath. If they guessed, they might discover the real Lady Mary Kimber was too much for just any man to handle.

They made their farewells to the Baklanovs and Caine handed her into the carriage that would carry her back to her other life. It seemed as if he were escorting her back to her cage. He'd prefer to stay here with her a bit longer. 'You rode spectacularly today. No wonder you miss the country so much.'

'I could say the same of you,' she demurred at the compliment. 'If not for that one rail at the end, you would have gone clean. Baklanov, now, that's different. He was reckless on his approach. No excuse for it.'

'He was showing off for his wife. They do that, show off for each other.' Caine chuckled. 'Surely he can be forgiven. No doubt his wife is claiming her forfeit and putting him through his paces as we speak.'

He watched her blush at his indelicate reference, but she did not turn away from it, did not lower her gaze. 'I imagine she is. It is very…intimate…to be with them. They hide nothing,' she ventured. 'Least of all their feelings, their passion.'

'No, they do not. They are lucky to have married for love. He had nothing when he came to England, just his skill and his horse, the one he rode today. He was a prince, but not here. He worked as an instructor at Fozard's, trading on those skills.' He watched her fingers pleat her skirt, watched her eyes lower even though he knew a thousand thoughts were coursing behind them. He hoped one of those thoughts was not about what he'd learned today on her behalf.

'That's quite a story,' she said at last. 'I envy them their confidence in one another. They are certain that no matter what life throws at them, they'll have each other. It is not their money or their titles they protect themselves with, but with each other. I think that's rare in the *ton*.' She lifted her grey eyes, two silvery pools of thought that would suck a man into their depths if he looked long enough. 'Is that why you are not keen to wed despite your circumstances? Because you think you'll not find that?'

'Is that why *you* have not wed?' he parried.

'I asked you first.'

He did not answer. She cocked her head and let the silence drag out between them. 'You hide it well, Caine Parkhurst.' She gave a throaty laugh that had him rousing all over again. Did she have any idea how sultry that laugh was? How it made a man think of beds and dark rooms?

'What exactly am I hiding?' he teased with a hint of seductive playfulness, but in all seriousness, the list was getting quite long where she was concerned and he regretted that for them both.

She leaned forward and tapped his knee. 'You, sir, are a romantic. Despite your affairs and opera singers, *you* seek true love.' A lightning bolt to the chest could not have been more shocking. He was not used to being seen so clearly. Most women saw only what he wanted them to see.

'That is a bold claim, Mary.' He let his gaze rake her lips, signalling that perhaps he was more interested in seeking something else at the moment.

'None the less, I think it's true. Don't worry. Your secret is safe with me.'

He believed that. If she pledged herself to someone, she would be unfailingly loyal to them. He sensed her friendship and affections were not given lightly. In all of their interactions, she'd been honest and forthright. Secrets *were* safe with Mary Kimber. Even his, but that didn't mean she'd thank him for sharing them. Secrets could be powerful; they could bind people together or they could be burdens. His secrets, including what he'd learned from Prince Baklanov today, fell into the latter category.

He shifted in his seat, wanting to move to a topic that wasn't a probe into his own romantic yearnings or into his meeting with Prince Baklanov. 'And your forfeit? Have you thought about what it will be?'

A coy smile took her mouth, her grey eyes sparkled, and Caine felt his body's arousal heighten in anticipation. 'If Klara is putting her husband through his paces, perhaps I should put you through yours.' She moved across the carriage and lifted her skirts, revealing slim calves and silk stockings. She was feeling bold, no doubt the thrill of the competition was still thrumming through her, urging her to a delicious recklessness. He did like a bold woman.

Caine shifted his body to accommodate her, revelling in the feel of her derrière against him as she straddled his lap as if he, too, was a thoroughbred she would ride astride. She wrapped her arms about his neck, her bottom wiggling against his groin as she settled. He moved his hands to her hips, to steady her, to steady himself. He knew instinctively that this was the real Lady Mary Kimber. She was putting her true self on display for him and for the first time. She was both bold and vulnerable in these moments. It was his privilege to be the first to see it and it was positively decadent watching this woman come alive in front of him, for him.

Her words were a whisper against his lips. 'For my forfeit, I claim you.'

His whisper was a growled invitation deep in his throat. 'It would be my pleasure.' He would ensure that it would be hers as well.

Chapter Thirteen

Pleasure was indeed the word of the moment. Her body trembled with it, vibrated with it. Mary pushed her hands through the depths of his midnight hair, stealing a look at him from beneath half-lidded eyes as her lips played with his, exchanging soft nips, gentle, lingering busses, noses rubbing, mouths melding.

He was beautiful, she realised; the sweep of his dark lashes against his cheek offering a soft juxtaposition to the hard strength of him as his mouth made love to hers until the experiment in claiming burned hotter than their playful busses could tolerate. She might have begun it, but it was his mouth that was doing the claiming now. When had she lost control of her forfeit?

'You're a thief,' she murmured against his mouth, eliciting one of his private chuckles, his eyes glowing like polished obsidian. 'This was supposed to be *my* kiss.'

'It was.' He laughed against her lips. 'And now it's mine.' She felt his hands move from her hips to the curves of her bottom and draw her taut against him so that she felt him: the heat and muscle of him; the dangerous passion of him that always seemed to simmer so near the surface, dancing in his eyes, and underlying the provocative words that fell from his lips; most of all, she felt the tangible masculine proof of his desire rising hard and insistent against her belly.

A sinful smile curved on his lips, his eyes agleam with wicked intent. 'Do you feel what you do to me? You're a temptress in hiding, Mary.'

Something courageous and confident leapt within her. He would never know how much those words meant to her. To be beautiful, to be desired for herself and nothing else, was a pleasure that transcended any kiss, any touch.

A moment later, when his warm hand slid up her leg, past silk stockings to rest on the bare skin of her thigh, she was re-evaluating that claim.

'What? I can see the laughter in your eyes. I'm missing a grand joke,' Caine teased and this, too, was a revelation—to laugh, to play amid what she'd once thought of as the serious, formal business of seduction. She'd not once imagined seduction as casual, comfortable, *easy*, where one was not in a constant state of awkward self-awareness. She was barely aware of how his hand had got there. She was only aware that it was there now and she more than liked the feel of it.

'I was just thinking about your words, about desiring *me* and how much that meant. I don't think I've ever been desired simply for myself,' she confessed. 'And that such a feeling was grander than any touch could be. Then you slid your hand up my leg and I had to re-evaluate that.'

He laughed against her mouth and his hand moved higher, discovering her little secret. 'Mary, you're not wearing drawers,' he drawled.

'No, I dressed in haste. They seemed…expendable…at the time.'

'A very fortuitous choice.' He was all wicked grins and dancing eyes that drew her in, that made her feel the extent of a seductress's power. How wondrous and new this realisation was. She had a power that was uniquely hers to wield simply because she was herself and that pleased him.

And yet, when he slid a finger between her legs and traced the private seam of her until he found the little nub beneath its hood, all she could think of was surrender, complete and abject surrender to the stroke of his hand, to the pleasure his touch sent shooting through her, although pleasure was much too tame of a word for the sensations he roused within her now.

She moved against his hand, a gasp escaping her. Her hands tightened in his hair as she pressed into him, against him, her body blindly searching for something, reaching for something to make the sensations stop. Stop? No, that couldn't be right. Why would she want this to stop? But she wanted *something*. Her body was gathering, preparing for that something. She gave a moan of want, of frustration, rocking against him.

'It will come, pleasure *is* coming, Mary. *Claim it*,' he encouraged her with a voice as raw, as exposed, as she felt, proof that this pleasure was a pleasure for them both to give and to receive. Then she was there at the place she'd blindly been seeking and it seemed to her that the world behind her eyes exploded into fragments of new sensations she'd not felt before, an intensity she'd not imagined existed. She was in his arms, her head lying against his broad shoulder, her own shoulders heaving with release. The only thought that came to her as the world began to settle once more was, 'I didn't know.'

'Of course not. You're not supposed to know. What would happen if young, innocent girls did know what their bodies were capable of? Everyone would be riding around in carriages all day.' Caine laughed and she laughed with him.

'You are truly wicked.'

'Because I have shown you the truth? Given you knowledge of your own body?' He was only half teasing.

'I am sure this is exactly how the serpent tempted Eve, with arguments just like these.' How could logic be wicked? How could logic lead to wrong conclusions? How could logic be immoral? She was only half teasing, too. Had the serpent held Eve against a broad chest, a strong arm about her as she rested? Created a cocoon she didn't want to leave for the life that waited beyond it? If so, it was easy to see why she'd eaten the apple. Mary didn't want to step foot out of the carriage, didn't want to go back to Carys House and all that waited there.

They rode in silence, Mary savouring the feel of Caine's body against hers, her mind running through a thousand questions, most of them stemming from what had happened in the carriage. Familiar blocks came into sight. They hadn't much time left if she wanted to ask them. Perhaps she'd start with the most obvious. 'Is it like that every time? Can anyone do that?' She looked up at him, wanting to watch his face, wanting to ensure that he told her the truth he proclaimed to value.

'Technically, I suppose the answer should be yes, the parts involved don't change, but it's not like that all the time. I think it matters who the partners are. It is important that we are with people with whom we can entrust our bodies as well as our emotions.' Caine paused, considering. 'Does that disappoint you, Mary?'

'No,' she replied, pushing back a tousled lock of his dark hair—tousled from *her* efforts, she might add. 'I would not like to think just anyone could make me feel this way. Pleasure should be my choice. Someone should not be able to take it from me, wring it from me.' As pleasurable as the experience was, she didn't want it to be common, generic. She wanted it to mean something, she wanted to control whom she shared it with, whom she came apart for. Even if it meant this was something she could have with only one man whom she could not hope to keep for ever.

The carriage stopped before Carys House and she could hear the step being set. The adventure was over. 'Thank you for today, for all of it.' She spoke the words in a desperate rush.

'There's always tomorrow, Mary.' Caine smiled, his eyes lingering on her as if he, too, was making a mental picture of these last moments before the world intruded. She'd like to think that was the case, that this had meant as much to him as it had to her. 'I'll come in with you. Your father had asked to talk.'

She gave a gasp, suddenly remembering. 'I didn't ask you about your meeting with the Prince!'

He lifted her hand to his lips, his eyes still warm with the remnants of their passion. 'We had better things to do. It will keep for later, Mary.'

'Will there be a later? My father may not allow it. He can be most determined.' She should not have voiced her fear out loud. It would seem silly to him, a reminder of the vast gulf between her life and his. A reminder, too, that she was not like his glamorous women. She was tied to the strings of familial obligation while Caine was tied to nothing he did not choose.

The door opened and Caine exited first. He helped her down, his voice at her ear where it seemed to naturally belong, saying, 'He doesn't get to decide anything unless we let him.'

She wished that were true. How easy he made it sound. To have what she wanted, all she had to do was simply choose it. But Caine was a man. He could do such things and not have to consider the repercussions.

In the hall of Carys House, a footman stood ready to greet them. 'Lord Barrow, Lord Carys is waiting to receive you in his study.'

Most men would not smile in the wake of those words. But Caine merely bent over her hand once more, in a proper farewell this time, and turned to the footman. 'Yes, he had indicated an interest in conversation. Lady Mary, thank you again for a delightful afternoon.'

Mary watched him disappear down the hall with the footman and wondered if she would see him again. It wasn't that she didn't think Caine could handle her father. He probably could. It was the question of whether or not he thought she was worth the bother. After all, he'd more than fulfilled his self-imposed obligation to her. At some point, he'd simply give her up. There was nothing to keep him with her, certainly not the promise of a future. Which prompted again the question: what did he want from her? What did he get out of this?

She touched her fingers to her lips. Even now, it was something of a wonder he'd gone to all this effort for her. The only explanation she had was the sight of him in the carriage today, his face rapt with desire and his body flush with it. Or perhaps desire, too, was different for a man?

Lord Carys was no different than any other man. His office was proof of that—decorated with all the trappings of his importance: the big desk made of imported mahogany and polished to a high sheen, the Moroccan leather chair behind it, the matching wing-backed chairs set on the other side, the Aubusson carpet, the bookcases filled with exquisite leather-bound editions that had likely never been opened. Lucien would think that a grave sin. The carved walnut mantel adorned with male accoutrements: a set of brass scales, a captain's telescope the man had probably never used. The art on the walls consisted of an old map of the world, and an oil painting matched the seagoing theme, perhaps courtesy of Lady Carys's decorating efforts. There was likely a safe behind that oil painting.

Lord Carys did not rise to greet him, but stayed behind the big desk and gestured for the footman to pour drinks. 'Thank you for your time, Lord Barrow. It seems we have reached a point where some discussion between us is necessary.' Carys took his drink from the footman without even a nod of acknowledgment before dismissing him. There was a message in that. *Things* were important to Carys. People were not. People were, in fact, disposable, items to be used for further material gain, even his own daughter. The other message was that appearances were everything. Carys *wanted* people to *see* his control, to *feel* it in the way he treated them.

'I agree, I am eager to speak with you as well.'

Caine took his drink from the footman and nodded his thanks in direct opposition to Carys's behaviour. Carys would not miss the gauntlet being thrown down. He had the pleasure of watching Carys's jaw tighten a nearly imperceptible fraction. He'd been obtuse on purpose, knowing very well what Carys would think. Men wanted to speak to fathers of eligible girls for only one reason. Carys did *not* want a proposal from him despite him being a marquess and perhaps the only real suitor of Mary's to rival Amesbury in rank. He decided to push Carys's discomfort a bit further. 'I find Lady Mary to be a singularly attractive, intelligent, woman.'

'I must stop you there, Barrow. I would save you the indignity of a proposal,' Carys cut in. 'I am not entertaining any further offers for my daughter's hand. We have accepted an offer from the Duke of Amesbury, whom I believe you met last night.'

So it was true. Mary had not exaggerated the situation. Caine held Cary's gaze, careful not to give away the disappointment Carys was hoping to see. Carys wanted the upper hand back. 'Has Lady Mary offered her approval to the match as well? I do not recall seeing an announcement in *The Times*.'

'We have not announced it formally yet, but we will soon.' Carys gave a falsely benign smile and steepled his hands on the desktop. 'You are new to your rank, Barrow. Allow me to give you some fatherly advice as a man who was *born* to his title. When a gentleman is met with the news a woman he aspires to is now off the market, he retreats politely. He does not question the nature of the arrangement and argue with the woman's father. It is not how these things are done.'

'Is forcing one's daughter to accept a match also how it is done these days? I thought we'd left such things behind with the Middle Ages.' Caine levelled a hard stare at Carys. 'Lady Mary does not want this match.'

'Does any woman know what she wants? Or what is even good for her?' Carys chuckled. 'She is playing coy and teasing you, Barrow. Perhaps she delights in arousing a bit of chivalry from you. You of all people should know how women are with their games.'

Caine also knew how men were. This one deserved a drubbing for treating his daughter as a pawn on his own personal chessboard and then speaking of her as if she were a merry widow revelling in casual affairs or a woman of even looser virtue still. 'Those are harsh words to which I take offence on Lady Mary's behalf.' He'd not fought a duel for two years, although he'd nearly challenged Creighton on his sister's behalf last year before they'd wed. One did like to stay in practice.

'You are not her protector. You have no right to level such accusations at me.' Carys was on edge now, perhaps remembering that Caine was known for his prowess with a pistol and his short fuse of a temper when it came to those he cared for. Carys was a seaman, not a marksman.

Caine tried another tack. Carys was nothing if not self-centred. 'Perhaps I ask for your own benefit, too. What do you know of Amesbury beyond his title?' He'd learned some interesting things about the former Duke from Nikolay Baklanov this afternoon and circumstances suggested it was possible the new Duke had followed in the former's footsteps. The question was whether or not Carys knew and was involved. The latter seemed highly possible given how Carys's Season was unfolding.

Carys stiffened and stilled. 'Is there something you think I should know?' Caine noted the defensiveness. Carys felt there was something to defend, something to protect. A secret relationship, perhaps? A covert business deal? Something he didn't want exposed? Or was it merely that Carys was protecting his choice, not wanting to look the fool?

'The former Duke was involved in an ammunitions scandal. He involved himself with a covert arms dealer by the name of Cabot Roan who sold arms and munitions to whichever side was buying. Furthermore, the bullets were faulty. The machinery used to produce them was not always accurate, thus up to an estimated twenty per cent of the bullets misfired. The factory knew this and did not spend the necessary monies to make the correction.'

Carys's gaze had gone hard. 'Where did you hear such a thing? There was nothing of the sort in the newspapers when the former Duke died.'

'From Prince Baklanov, who was there the day of the carriage accident. He indicated the cause of the accident and the reason for it were tied to the factory scandal. Being a duke, there was a desire to keep much of this out of the papers in order to save face for the family. I have met with Baklanov and he assures me he is more than happy to meet with you to discuss the scandal.'

Caine kept his gaze steady on Carys, watching carefully as the man's restraint faltered. He could tell it was taking all of Carys's willpower to not squirm or leap over the desk and plant him a facer in an attempt to silence him, a sure sign that he was getting to him. He was close to something, although Carys was unlikely to admit it. Perhaps that meant he was close to culpability, but that meant nothing if Caine couldn't prove it.

'I thought you should know. My concern, of course, is for *your* family and for Lady Mary's reputation.' It wasn't entirely false flattery. He was indeed concerned for Mary and that concern had grown considerably this afternoon. Roses were hardy blooms that could survive under myriad conditions, but that didn't mean they didn't deserve better.

'If you were concerned for Mary's reputation, you would not have danced with her,' Carys said through gritted teeth.

'You're the one marrying her against her will into a family tainted by scandal. I sincerely think my crime is not the biggest one here, Lord Carys.' Caine spread his hands in a gesture of peace. 'But perhaps there is nothing to worry about and the scandal will not touch the new Duke. We can always hope it will remain buried.' Unless, of course, the reason for the scandal had never truly died and the new Duke had taken up his predecessor's hunger for money as well as the man's title. War was a lucrative business and there was always someone to fight if one wasn't particular about the side they fought on.

'Thank you for your time, Lord Carys. I will see myself out. I will enjoy seeing you tonight for the musicale your wife is hosting.' Caine rose, knowing that his decision to end the meeting would irritate the other man to no end. Carys was a man who decided when his meetings were over, not the other party. He would not like that petty power usurped. It was beyond time someone did some usurping. Carys was too used to getting his way and too used to having no one gainsay him.

Even if the news today had been a shocking revelation and Carys had truly known no more about Amesbury than that he was young, unmarried and had a title, it didn't change the reality that Carys was a tyrant in his own home and was forcing his daughter towards a marriage she did not want. On those grounds alone, Caine would gladly teach the man a lesson. On the grounds of ensuring Mary's freedom from such tyranny he found himself willing to do much more—a realisation that was quite sobering for a man who insisted he couldn't and wouldn't wed.

Chapter Fourteen

Mary was still on his mind hours later as Caine dressed for the evening. In the span of an afternoon things had become infinitely more complicated. He rooted about in his trifle box for the round diamond cravat pin he preferred for this evening and fastened in the dark folds where it winked like a single star in a midnight sky, or perhaps a single beacon of hope in circumstances that might quickly be coming to a head.

Caine did not relish his task tonight—to find the final connection that would link Carys and perhaps even Amesbury to the sabotage attempt. If he found that link, it would put him one step closer to avenging his brother, but it would also put him another step closer to ruining Mary. After this afternoon, he knew how that step would look to her. It would look like betrayal and *he* would look like the worst of deceivers. One did not allow an innocent to find pleasure in one's arms, promise them hope and the illusion of friendship and then turn around and destroy them.

He would be entirely guilty of everything she accused him of. He should have known better and he should not have let things go as far as they did, not only because he was the more experienced party, but also because he knew what was coming. Yet she'd been irresistible in her excitement, her passion. He'd wanted to show her the possibilities of pleasure—real pleasure, to show her what she deserved. And heaven help him, he'd wanted to experience those things, too. With her. Before it was too late and harsh reality intruded for them both.

A knock at the door interrupted his mental flagellation. Kieran let himself in, already dressed for the evening. They'd discussed his meeting Baklanov when he'd returned and Kieran had taken some time since then to sift through all of it. He knew his brother would want to talk one more time before they split up for the night.

'We have a valet.' Kieran looked him up and down. 'You should use him. Your cravat is crooked.' Kieran strode towards him. 'Let me help. Cravats are a two-person job.'

Caine lifted his chin and let Kieran fuss. 'Yours looks fine.'

'Phineas, our *valet*, helped me with mine and he should help you with yours.' Kieran removed the diamond pin as he scolded. 'It hurts his pride that the Marquess dresses on his own. He feels as if he can't do his job.' Kieran re-inserted the pin and smoothed the folds. 'That's better.'

'I'll make it up to him tomorrow when I need a shave. Tonight, I needed time to think.'

Kieran made a sympathetic noise. 'You're worried about what you might find in the Earl of Carys's study tonight.' They'd decided the sooner they knew the better and this evening's musicale provided the perfect opportunity to be in the Carys town house without having to break in. All he needed to do was find a moment to slip away to the study. It would be a quick search. The Earl would either keep important documents locked in his desk or in a safe behind the nautical oil painting.

'Whatever I find or don't find will be a disappointment at best and disastrous at worst. If I find no connection between the sabotage and the Earl, we're back to square one in our search for the saboteur, or I find something damning and become the instrument of Lady Mary's ruin.' She did not deserve that. Dread settled in his stomach. If he did find something, he wouldn't have a choice. England and his brother had to come first.

Kieran gave him a considering nod. 'I think that depends on how you define ruin. If the Earl is connected with the sabotage attempt, it will all be handled privately. Grandfather isn't going to go public with this any more than he's gone public with our other work.' Which meant none of it. London society had no idea what the Horsemen got up to outside reckless rides and wild wagers. 'The shipment was private,' Kieran went on, 'only the investors knew about the incident in Wapping and they certainly don't want that to go public for political reasons. All anyone in the general public knows about Wapping is that an unknown man died after being apprehended by Stepan and Stepan is...missing. Grandfather does not want a front-page story in *The Times* about an arms deal double-cross involving an earl.'

And what Grandfather wanted, Grandfather got. 'If a tree falls in the forest and no one hears? Is that your reasoning?' Caine rummaged for his onyx and pearl cufflinks.

'Something like that.' Kieran shrugged. 'The point is, Lady Mary will not be ruined by an arms scandal. That won't even come to light.'

'No, she'll be ruined by the fact that she's lost a third duke.' Caine could just imagine the frenzy that would throw the gossips into. If Carys was implicated, Amesbury would not want the marriage.

'You'd be saving her, not ruining her. I thought you said she didn't want to marry Amesbury?'

'She doesn't. It's just the thought of what it will do to her. Society will think it's just another piece of matrimonial gossip and she'll be affected badly by her father's crime.' She couldn't win—she faced scandal on one hand and a dangerous, disappointing marriage on the other. Hadn't she suffered enough? She needed a middle path.

'You could marry her,' Kieran put in. 'Why not? You need to marry for your title's perpetuity and a marriage would deflect talk about her.' That was *not* the middle path he was thinking of.

'That's a horrible idea, and an impossible one.' Caine stared hard at his brother. 'Do you actually think she'd even look at me once she realises I'm to blame for all of it? That I betrayed her father?'

'Oh, I see.' Kieran couldn't quite suppress a grin. 'It's not the ruining of her that has you worried, it's the ruining of you and her together that bothers you. You don't want to lose her.'

'Not like that, I don't,' Caine said sharply. 'Even if she would forgive all that, have you forgotten I am not a marrying man?' The idea of wedding Mary, who'd matched him jump for jump in the arena, who'd straddled him in the carriage this afternoon and moaned her pleasure against him, was not unpleasing. But it was impossible. He might actually fall in love with that woman and that folly would risk her doubly.

'Have you thought what it would mean to a woman to be married to one of the Four Horsemen? I think she'd be unpleasantly surprised to learn that we're a bit more than rakes. Rakes might be reformed if they so choose, but once a Horseman, always a Horseman.'

'So you're allowed no happiness of your own?' Kieran countered.

'What happiness would there be if I could not be happy knowing my family was potentially in danger because of me?' Caine snapped his pocket watch shut with a sense of finality. He did not want to have this discussion with Kieran with the feel of Mary still imprinted on his body.

'So you will choose for her? You will decide who she gets to love? What would she say to that?' Kieran pressed, stopping to check his own cravat one last time in the mirror.

Caine knew what Mary would say, assuming she had good feelings for him at the time of decision making. He could hear Mary's voice in his head arguing that a woman would want to make the choice, that she would not want a man to decide for her who to love and how to love. But how could she know what such a choice meant? But he *knew*.

Grandfather had made it clear when he'd recruited them that this was a life *and* a lifestyle, that there was no ready exit from either. One could retire, but that did not ensure one's enemies would forget them. Families and wives became leverage. Caine would not ask a wife to risk herself in a relationship with him. It was selfish to do so. These had not been considerations when all this had begun, proof of just how complicated things had become.

A footman knocked on the door to alert them the coach had arrived for him and a cab was here for Kieran. He smiled at his brother. 'Time to go.'

Kieran gave a nod. 'You'll be safe? Do you want me to come? I could act as a lookout. I don't like the idea of you in Carys's study alone.'

'It will be fine.' He gave a chuckle at Kieran's worried frown. 'We've successfully done far more dangerous things than pilfer a puffed-up lord's study.'

'I know. It's just that I've lost one brother on this mission and I don't want to lose another,' Kieran said soberly.

Caine shook his head. 'Do not think like that. If we perceive we have limits, then we do and that's when we make mistakes. Stepan is out there, alive, somewhere, I know it. I *believe* it, every day I get up. If we can find the saboteur, we are closer to finding our brother. Those two missions are intertwined, inseparable, now.' He would do whatever it took to see that mission completed.

'I would say "be careful"...' Kieran laughed '...but I know you won't be.'

Caine drew his brother into a quick hug. 'Don't worry, but I know you will. Have a good evening, Brother.'

Mary was *not* having a good evening. Her evening was, in fact, a study of opposites compared to her afternoon. Her afternoon had been wildly thrilling on horseback and off. A night of music sung in a language she did not understand would not approach anywhere near even mildly thrilling. The same could be said of the company as well. Caine Parkhurst was an *excellent* companion. He encouraged her to claim her own passions. The Duke of Amesbury was not, taking every opportunity instead to remind her in subtle and unsubtle ways that he meant to claim her—something that was growing increasingly alarming because of his persistence in mentioning it and in her parents' refusal to deny it.

Mary waved her painted fan in the vain hope of creating any kind of significant breeze in the drawing room, but despite the French doors being thrown open to the gardens, a cooling draught remained elusive. Amesbury had gone for lemonade and she hoped he'd be a while. Her mother's musical evening was a positive crush. Apparently, the Italian soprano engaged for the evening was quite popular on the Continent and it was counted a social coup for her mother to have got the woman for a private engagement.

Although, Mary wondered just how private it was if it seemed that half of London was here. Except for the one person she wanted to see the most. The venue might be tolerable if Caine were here. If he were, she could imagine them sneaking off to a quiet, dim room to sit and sip. She would have port instead of lemonade. She would hear the news from his meeting with the Prince. Then she would share the disturbing conversation she'd had with her mother this evening as she'd dressed. She could still hear the words in her head.

'Wear something new and pretty tonight, my dear. I think this evening might be very exciting for you.'

One didn't have to be a fortune-teller to know what her mother referred to. Her mother thought Amesbury was about to propose. Perhaps she knew he would. Her mother had smiled and patted her hand, pleased over the development. This solved all their problems, all the tension that underlay their little family. But what seemed ideal to her mother seemed ominous to Mary. It was not the end of trouble, but the beginning of a life without hope, without escape, without pleasure.

Tonight, she'd forced herself to imagine behaving with Amesbury, doing with Amesbury what she'd done with Caine. She simply could not do it. To make a comparison required there be some level of sameness between the men and there was not. Caine had encouraged her. She could still hear Caine's voice at her ear.

'Pleasure is coming, Mary. Claim it.'

It had all been for her, although she rather thought Caine had experienced his own pleasure in watching her claim her own. Amesbury would never be so selfless. Any pleasure to be had would belong first and foremost to him. Caine might be the rake, but Amesbury was ruthless.

Mary glanced around the room, hoping to catch sight of Caine, that somewhere in the crush she'd spy his dark head, his broad shoulders, his black attire standing out from the black and white uniformity of the other men. Perhaps he was just late.

'You won't find him here.' There was a light, sophisticated feminine laugh at her side. The elegant woman perched on the chair beside her smiled, blue eyes full of worldly knowledge to match the elegant sophistication of her striking dark blue and silver gown. Diamonds dripped from her neck, sparkled at her ears and in the depths of her raven's wing hair. A bracelet to match encircled her gloved wrist. 'I'm Lady Morestad.'

'Lady Mary Kimber.' Mary smiled politely, wondering why this woman would seek her out.

'Oh, I know who you are, my dear.' Lady Morestad gave a practised flick of her fan. 'It's hot tonight. Too many people, really. Such events need to be exclusive to mean anything. But here we all are.' She leaned close in assumed familiarity and Mary caught the scent of expensive perfume on her. Everything about this woman was expensive and calculated for maximum impact. Quite successfully so. The woman was beautifully turned out, making the most of all her assets despite her age, which must be nearly thirty-five.

'All of us except Parkhurst, of course, the one man we'd all like to see. Or Barrow, as I suppose we should call him now.' The beautiful Lady Morestad fluttered her fan in a languid motion. 'Musicales aren't for him. The only thing he likes about Italian sopranos isn't their voices.' She arched a slim dark brow and gave a throaty laugh.

'I wouldn't know.' Mary found the woman's au-

dacity too much. She felt defensive on Caine's behalf. He wasn't here to protect himself from this
woman's barbs. But perhaps he wouldn't mind. 'Nor
am I sure why you think I would *want* to know.' She
suddenly wished Amesbury would hurry with the
lemonade. His reappearance at least would require
Lady Morestad to vacate the seat. It was very much
a case of the devil one knew. She knew Amesbury.
She hadn't the faintest idea what Lady Morestad
was playing at.

'No, you wouldn't know. You are far too innocent and definitely not Caine Parkhurst's usual type.
But perhaps you're the new Marquess's type?' Lady
Morestad's eyes narrowed. 'Perhaps he's interested
in such an innocent because now he has a title that
allows him to marry far above his anticipated prospects. The daughter of an earl would be quite the
catch for him, something he could never have aspired to as the son of a third son.'

She gave a smug smirk. 'Don't think for a moment that marriage will tame him. I feel sorry for
his bride, whoever she'll be. He'll wed her, bed her
and move on from her. I doubt his fidelity will last
beyond the honeymoon. After all, they don't call him
and his brothers the Four Horseman for the ruin, but
for the rapture.'

Mary might have only partially guessed at the reference, but she fully understood what the woman wanted now. It was on the tip of her tongue to say, 'Is that what he did to you?' But she would not lower herself to this woman's cattiness. This woman was here because she was jealous, because Caine had turned his sights away from her and she wanted them back.

'I think you should go. This is an unseemly discussion.' Mary summoned all her coolness to dismiss her. This woman was jealous and in that jealousy she was lashing out. She couldn't possibly know how close her remarks came to the vulnerability Mary carried deep inside, the wounds those arrows threatened to reopen. Wasn't that her greatest fear? That she was desired not for herself, but for what she brought to the table?

Lady Morestad waved her fan and made no move to leave. 'I don't mean to upset you, Lady Mary, just to warn you. He's absolutely audacious in his pursuit and unrepentantly wicked in his conquest. That's the part he enjoys most. Once he feels you've been conquered, he's ready to move on.' She gave Mary an assessing look. 'Of course, as long as a woman understands what the arrangement is, he can be quite a pleasurable experience. Our poor husbands can't compete and I do think a woman deserves one good lover in her lifetime.'

Mary fixed her gaze straight ahead as the musicians took the stage and began to tune up. 'I am not for the conquering, Lady Morestad. Thank you, though, for the warning. I know what Caine Parkhurst is.' But it hurt to hear it out loud, to see one of his lovers face to face and have to admit to the truths in her head—that what he'd done with her today, he'd done with countless women before and would do with countless women after her. She was simply here and now for him, the woman he was with at present.

Lady Morestad made a sound of false empathy. 'He's got you thinking, like every other woman he's seduced, that this time it will be different, that you can change him, that you can make him stay. It's a delicious fantasy and he plays the part so well. All that...' Her gaze strayed to a point over Mary's shoulder and a hungry, predatory light shone in her blue eyes. 'Well, wonder of all wonders, the Marquess of Barrow at a musicale.'

Mary turned, her heart leaping at the sight of Caine in his usual black evening attire, tousled hair combed into temporary submission, a round diamond pin winking as it held his cravat in place. His dark eyes had never looked so dashing or so dangerous as he bowed. 'Ladies, good evening. You both look lovely.' Mary didn't *feel* lovely in her soft rose-coloured silk next to the elegance of Lady Morestad's blue and silver silk. She felt young and untried despite knowing that to not be quite the truth. But it was on her that Caine's eyes lingered.

'I'd ask to what we owe the honour of your attendance, Barrow, but I understand the attraction of the musicale better now, I think,' Lady Morestad said coyly. 'There are new pigeons for you to pluck now that you're a marquess.' At her words, Caine's gaze shifted to Lady Morestad, perhaps the response Lady Morestad had intended, but the gaze that passed between them was ladened with daggers and just as sharp. This was the way former lovers who'd parted badly looked at one another. Mary was distinctly uncomfortable.

'If there's anyone who knows about plucking pigeons, it would be you, Lady Morestad. I bow to your experience,' Caine replied smoothly. 'Lady Mary, I have seats in the back near the door where it is cooler. Perhaps you would join me?'

Amesbury chose that moment to make his appearance, too late to be of any use in fending off Lady Morestad's indecent conversation, but in plenty of time to exchange strong glances with Caine. 'Lemonade, my dear.' He handed her a sweating silver cup with an overt show of proprietorship in the gesture. Mary's temper flared. He did not own her. Not yet.

'Barrow, perhaps you might share your seats with Lady Morestad.'

Lady Morestad beamed. 'What a splendid idea. I would love a seat,' she said smoothly, offering Caine her gloved hand as the Italian soprano took the stage and a little bell rang calling everyone to attention as Mary's mother mounted the dais to make introductions.

'I hope you didn't have to suffer the two of them unduly. The refreshment table was a battleground on account of the heat,' Amesbury groused as he settled into his seat. 'Good riddance to Barrow and Lady Morestad. I haven't the foggiest idea why she'd want to talk with you. I'll have a word with her and let her know the association isn't appreciated. She won't bother you again. I was afraid we might be stuck with them for the duration. They're both odious. They deserve each other.'

That was very much what Mary was afraid of— that this was what her life would be like, with Amesbury picking her friends and deciding who she could and couldn't speak with. As the soprano began, Mary fought the urge to look back at Caine and Lady Morestad to ensure they were in their seats. She would never be able to explain such a glance to Amesbury. But when she and Amesbury walked past their seats at the intermission, Amesbury whispering that he wanted to go somewhere and talk, the seats were empty. Her heart sank, each and every verbal arrow shot by Lady Morestad finding their target. The very real fear rose that Caine and Lady Morestad were indeed, off somewhere, 'deserving' one another, and she with her inexperience was already forgotten.

Chapter Fifteen

Mary had forgotten the cardinal rule for any young unmarried lady at an entertainment: never be alone with a man. Perhaps it was because the entertainment was in her own home or perhaps, and more likely the case, she was too caught up in her own head about Caine and Lady Morestad. Whatever the reason, she found herself with Amesbury in a sitting room at the back of the house.

'Your mother has excellent attendance tonight,' Amesbury said, stopping at the sideboard to help himself to her father's brandy. He didn't offer her any. He turned, tumbler in hand. 'But a crush can be wearying. I find it is difficult to have a decent conversation or an extended one of any quality. I want to have such a conversation with you tonight, Mary.' He nodded towards a chair. 'Won't you sit, my dear?'

Mary shook her head. She would meet her fate

standing up. She would not relinquish any source of power she had and right now that might only be her height. She would not let Amesbury tower over her, as he proposed. He did not strike her as an on his knees sort of fellow. Certainly, that was where this conversation was heading. It wasn't going to be a conversation at all.

'As you prefer, my dear.' Amesbury smiled, teeth gleaming. He reminded her of a sleek, blond tiger and he was stalking her. 'Let me begin by saying, you are a treasure, Lady Mary. In the time we've recently had together, I've come to the conclusion that you are indeed all that I hoped you'd be. You are exactly the sort of woman I need by my side. I've never been in society until now, I know no one, but you do and that will pave my path going forward.'

Mary's heart was in her throat. How could she put him off? Her best strategy, perhaps her only strategy, would be polite belaying. 'You flatter me, Your Grace. Perhaps it is too soon to make these decisions. I hardly know you and that is true for you as well. You do not know me outside of a few balls and a couple of at-home calls. I would like for us to have time to know one another better.'

Amesbury seemed to give the suggestion some thought and for a moment she dared to hope her ploy had been successful. 'What is there to know? I've been on the Continent, conducting family business.' He gave a laugh. 'You know, the sort of business a great family tasks its less important relatives with. Minion work, I call it. Nothing exciting enough to tell you about, my dear. And then the mail caught up with me to inform me that I'd inherited. I do agree with you, if the circumstances were different, time together would be ideal. But we both know time is of the essence. Your family is eager to see you wed and I have my own exigencies given the sparsity of males in the Amesbury line. It suits me to wed sooner than later.'

He stepped towards her, a hand raised to stroke her cheek. She clenched her jaw against his touch. 'You tremble, Lady Mary.' His tones were deceptively silky. 'Is it because you're such an innocent? Or because you are thinking of another's touch?'

'If I tremble, Your Grace, it is because it is too great of an intimacy between strangers.' Mary didn't bother to disguise the contempt in her voice. 'As you say, you are new come to society—perhaps you need a refresher on the rules. We should not be alone. You should not touch me in such a familiar way. You are to treat me as a lady, not as a possession.'

He gave a cold chuckle and stepped back, his eyes a blue steel, hard and unforgiving. 'You have some fire to you, Lady Mary. It will be a pleasure to tame

you to my hand. I think it is you who need reminding of the rules of this particular game, however.'
His tone was chilling.

Taming. As if she were an animal on par with
his hound or his horse. Mary swallowed and took
a breath to calm herself, aware of just how quiet,
just how alone they were. One could barely hear the
drawing room crowd from here. 'You speak as if
we have an understanding but you and I do not. We
have never even spoken of one. You have intimated
only that you have chosen a wife.' She was fencing
with words now and they were a dull blade indeed.

He gave her a look that sent a shiver down her
spine. 'Dear Mary, I thought the nuance of our exchange that evening was clear. The woman I have
chosen is you.' He gave a low laugh.

'But *I* have not chosen *you*. I have not consented,
nor have I been asked.' She was feeling trapped.
Amesbury stood between her and the door, the fireplace was at her back. Too bad the andirons were
on the other side. A poker would come in handy
just now.

'You do not need to choose, Mary. Your father has
consented on your behalf.' He gave an evil, smug
smile, his voice conversationally matter of fact. 'You
are mine, Mary. Your father and I finalised it earlier
this evening. Your mother would like to announce

the engagement tonight at the end of the musicale and we will wed as soon as possible.' He reached a hand once more to stroke her cheek. 'So, you see, your rules are satisfied. No one will care if we're alone and it is perfectly respectable for me to touch you like this, or even in other ways should I desire it, since we are to be wed.'

'I won't marry you.' Mary wondered if she could push past him, if he would let her go. If she could get out of the room, she could run, back to the entertainment, the light, the crowds. Until then, she was on her own.

Amesbury offered a look of feigned perplexity. 'You would shame your father? Ruin your family?' He gave a harsh laugh and she knew she was seeing the totality of Amesbury for the first time. He was not merely arrogant and obtuse in his privilege, but cruel as well. 'You cannot refuse, even if you had the legal right to do so. *You* are his payment, Mary.'

He gave a sigh, more play-acting in his tone of false sincerity. 'I had hoped it wouldn't come to this, that we wouldn't start our married lives with this knowledge hanging over us. I had wanted this proposal to be nice for you. Every girl wants to remember the moment a man chooses her.' He shook his head and her disgust with him grew. She had to escape this room. 'But you've made me say hard things, Mary. Your father owes me a debt he cannot pay. He hovers on penury, but I have generously offered to take you instead of currency to settle that debt.'

'You lie!' Mary spat at him. Her world reeled with the revelation. Surely that could not be true? An earl could not be impoverished. Her father, upstanding to his core, could not be in league with a man as disreputable as the one who stood before her. 'You speak filth! I will not stay in this room a moment longer. I will go to my father.'

She used her anger to fuel a rush past him, but he had no intention of letting her leave. He grabbed her as she passed, his hand an iron band about her arm, and the full force of her fear raced through her. He had no intention of letting her leave this room without having garnered her consent to the marriage one way or another. This was his end game, she realised. She kicked at him, pushed at him, fought against him with all her strength. She let out a great scream and then another. Would anyone hear? Would anyone come?

Caine had forgotten how much he abhorred Italian musicales and especially how much he abhorred the manipulative, self-serving Lady Morestad. But it had all come rushing back when he'd seen her talk-

ing with Mary. He didn't even need to imagine what
Lady Morestad had imparted to her. He *knew.* He
wished he could say it was all lies, but it most likely
wasn't. He'd regretted that affair the moment he'd
started it. He'd been quite happy to concoct a reason to desert Lady Morestad shortly after the con-
cert had started in order to rifle Lord Carys's study.

Caine softly shut the study door behind him and
turned up a lamp as much as he dared. Too much
light and it would seep out below the door and draw
the attention of a vigilant servant. But too little light
meant searching would be more difficult and time
mattered. He had only until the intermission to find
what he was looking for. He'd start with the nautical oil he'd spied this afternoon.

He crossed the room and lifted the painting, smiling. A safe. Just as he thought. Carys was indeed
predictable. It would be the most logical place to
hide any incriminating documents. He went to work
and had it open in short order. People were far too
confident in their securities. Grandfather would be
proud.

Inside, his eyes shoved past the requisite stack of
coin and pound notes and lit upon a stack of what
might be deeds and papers. That's what he was looking for. He took them to the desk and riffled through
them, scanning quickly. There it was, tucked be-

tween deeds to estates, the partial title to a munitions factory located in Belgium. His eyes halted on the other signature on the page. *Amesbury.* The Duke had indeed carried on with his predecessor's business. His blood went simultaneously hot and cold, his mind racing at what this meant and what it *might* mean.

It meant the ducal money came from arms sales. It meant Carys had invested with Amesbury. In and of itself, that was fine. Many gentlemen might invest in munitions factories. It was the circumstances of that ownership that concerned him and the timing. He tucked the deed into a pocket, put the other items back in the safe and re-locked it. It would help clarify those circumstances if he could find some confirmation of Carys's financial status. It was one thing to have a working hypothesis, it was another to have proof. Evidence acted as powerful leverage.

He sat behind the desk, pulling at drawers until he found one that was locked. This lock was easier than the safe and he soon had it open. Ledgers. From down the hall in the drawing room, he could hear the soprano moving into her first act finale. Time was running out and ledgers had to be read. They couldn't be taken and hidden as easily as a single sheet of paper. They'd be missed sooner, too.

Caine rapidly flipped through pages, searching

for dates—something from the within the year or the past five months. Good heavens, from what he could tell at a glance, the man was bleeding money. He reached March and ran his finger down the column. There was a large pay out to the munitions factory in March and then in April, a single infusion of cash from Amesbury that temporarily balanced the books. And then, more withdrawals upon withdrawals.

The sound of applause reached him. The soprano was done. Caine gave himself a few precious minutes more. People would take a while to get up from their chairs and mingle. But then, anyone might come down the hall. Carys himself might decide to make a quick visit to his study. There were mysteries to decipher here and no more time to do it. There was nothing for it. In a neat motion, Caine ripped four pages from the ledger and folded them into his coat pocket.

He returned to the drawing room, hoping to seek out Amesbury for a little conversation. But Amesbury was nowhere to be found and neither was Mary. Likely they were in the garden where it was cooler, but he couldn't dismiss the tremor of concern their absence raised for him.

He was thinking about the possibility of posing as a potential investor to draw Amesbury out when he heard the scream, a sound just loud enough to be heard amid the general hubbub of a hundred conversations, and it was blood curdling. Caine had heard enough screams to know the difference between a cry for help, a cry of startlement and the cry of someone who was merely overloud in their enjoyment. This was most definitely the sound of the former.

There was a second cry. People were starting to look now, breaking off from their conversations. Caine pushed through the crowd, following the sound. He called out to Carys who showed no sign of responding, 'Come on, man. One of your guests is in trouble.' His instinct told him that guest was Mary as he raced down a dimly lit corridor and the trouble was Amesbury. There was every urgency to reach Mary. She should not be down here alone with the man. But she literally didn't know better. She didn't know what he'd learned from Baklanov and she certainly didn't know what he'd discovered tonight. To her, Amesbury was just an arrogant suitor. But he was so much more. He could not be handled with the usual feminine off-putting.

Dear God, let me be in time.

He reached the sitting room, aware of Carys on his heels, taking action at last, and his anger spiked. 'Mary!' Violence surged in his blood at the sight of her actively fighting, struggling against Amesbury, her gown torn, her alabaster cheek reddened. The bastard had hit her! By God, what sort of man hit a woman during what he guessed was a marriage proposal? But Caine knew the answer to that: a man who would joke about locking that same wife up in an asylum for disobedience, a man who didn't take no for an answer.

Caine let out a roar and charged, throwing his entire, and not inconsiderable, weight against Amesbury. They went down, Amesbury gasping for air, Caine on top and taking advantage. He felt the hands of several gentleman on him, trying to pull him off Amesbury, trying to restrain him. A few others attempted to pull Amesbury free. A melee of arms and legs separated them. Caine staggered to his feet with a snarl, pulling free of the would-be restrainers, his first thought for Mary.

She stood pale and shaking against the wall. He staggered towards her, gathering her in his arms, not caring who was watching and appalled her mother or father weren't already there. 'Are you badly hurt?' he murmured against her hair. 'You'll need ice or a steak for that cheek.' His voice was low, just for her. No one else needed to hear. He could feel her breathing in and out against him, each breath shaky as if she'd run far. He gave her a moment, using the breadth of his shoulders to shield her from the room. He felt her hands clutch at his back, holding him to her. 'You came,' she managed the words.

'I heard you call out,' he whispered.

'Get your hands off her, let her go.' Carys approached in high dudgeon, making a bad scene worse. Caine's mind was firing at top speed now, attempting to mitigate the situation.

'Clear the room, Carys,' he growled. 'Where is her mother? Your daughter has been assaulted; she needs time, privacy.'

'Assaulted?' Amesbury struggled to his feet, sputtering in his anger, blood on his cheek from a split lip. 'She is my fiancée. I should call you out for such an insult.'

Caine turned, putting Mary behind him. He glowered at Amesbury. 'Is that a challenge? If it is, please know that I am more than happy to meet you on the field of honour and let my pistols do the talking.' An ominous hush fell over the room. 'Carys, didn't I tell you to the clear the room? Out, I want everyone out!' If Carys wouldn't clear the room, he damn well would. People began to move, Carys finally galvanised into action. Mary's mother made her way to her daughter's side and ushered her to the sofa.

When the room was empty, Carys shut the door.

'Now, let's sit down and discuss this rationally. There seems to be a misunderstanding.'

'I think the misunderstanding is on the Duke's behalf.' Caine took up a position behind Mary, unwilling to leave her unguarded in a room surrounded by people who ought to have her best interests at heart, but did not. The only friend she had present was him. He would do his best for her although she might not thank him for it. 'When a woman says no, she means no, Amesbury.'

Amesbury took a chair opposite the sofa and, despite his bleeding lip, he crossed a leg over his knee with all the casualness of a man who owned the room. Caine felt his ire, which had not cooled by any means, rise again. This man should not be allowed to stay in the same room as Mary. He could only imagine how Mary felt to have her attacker remain in the same room and to have the whole incident classified as a misunderstanding by her father, no less.

Amesbury sneered. 'I think *you* misunderstand, Barrow. She doesn't get to say no. She is mine. Her father has given her to me in payment of debt.' Caine watched Carys pale at the unpleasant truth being spoken aloud.

'Tell him, Carys, about our deal.' Amesbury gave a smug grin, perhaps thinking he controlled the room. He certainly controlled the Earl. They were not partners in this deal. 'How you wanted a duke for your daughter and I was happy to oblige, along with forgiving your considerable debt in exchange for you helping me ease into society.' Caine thought about the ledger pages tucked in his coat pocket—the loans he'd seen there, the accumulated debt. He and Kieran had been right about this part of the hypothesis at least.

'Father, say it's not true?' Mary cried, but Carys did not deny it, only stared at her with pale stoicism.

'It's time for you to earn your keep, Mary. He's a duke, it's a good arrangement. You could not hope for better,' was all he said.

Caine disagreed. 'I think she could do much better than a man who hits her when he doesn't get his way.' He had solved half the puzzle tonight—Mary's half. He'd not solved Stepan's half. There was still work to do and now he had the clues to do it with. He still had to link Carys and Amesbury's munitions factory to the sabotage. That would be his next step, but he could not leave Mary here among her enemies. Tonight's debacle would make tomorrow's papers and that was just the beginning of the disaster for her. Society would feel she had no recourse for her reputation but to marry Amesbury who would make it plain that he *wanted* to wed her.

Any resistance was on her part alone. This time her reputation would not recover. Assuming she'd be allowed to refuse. Already, her mother was making soothing noises and plans. 'Don't worry, Mary. Amesbury can see the archbishop tonight, wake him up if need be. We will have a quiet ceremony at the house tomorrow, maybe something in the garden by the fountain. You like the fountain. You can wear one of your new gowns and Minton can do your hair up with wildflowers. Cook can make some of your favourite little cakes.'

Amesbury tossed Caine a smug look over the women's heads. *See, I win.*

'Mary, is that what you want?' Caine broke in, ignoring Amesbury's look. 'Your mother is right; a quiet wedding will make tonight's contretemps go away.' But it would not erase what her father had done, nor the potential scandal to come if Caine found the link to the sabotage. Did Mary think she had a choice? Did she believe there was an option? He gave her the only option he could.

'If you don't want this, Mary, I will take you out of this room tonight and keep you safe.' At least he hoped he could keep her safe. That last bit was bold given that he'd not been able to keep Stepan safe. Perhaps his offer of safety wasn't worth what it used to be. Still, he had to try. This was her moment, her choice, and it would decide so much more for her than she knew, yet she had to decide and, Caine reminded himself, he had to abide by that decision. If she chose to stay, he would have to abandon her to her fate, something that would be more difficult to do now than it would have been a few weeks ago. A most disturbing thought indeed.

Chapter Sixteen

The choice was hers and it could very well decide the trajectory of her life—a most disturbing thought, given that the choice must be made on the fly. Mary sat up a bit straighter and edged away from her mother's dubious comfort, aware of Caine's presence behind her, the heat of him, the strength of him. He'd come for her, he'd *fought* for her—the sound of his roar, the sight of his muscles unleashed in her aid still played through her mind. No one else had come to her defence, not even her own father.

The result of Caine's efforts was this moment laid before her. Her father had bartered her to another. Caine offered to take her away from honouring an agreement she'd not consented to. Take her away to where? To what? She didn't know. That was the chance. Caine would set her free. Where she went from there was anyone's guess and she could not delay in her answer.

Her father was rising. 'You cannot take her from this house.'

She felt Caine bristle, could imagine the thunder in his face, the storm in his dark eyes, his anger a palpable thing. '*I* am not forcing her to do anything. I am giving her a choice. You cannot say the same. If she leaves, it will be of her own free will.' It was the unspoken argument in his words that decided her. By extension, if she stayed that would be by her own free will as well. It would be as good as consenting to the match with Amesbury. Although it took all of her courage, Mary stood. 'I will go with you. There is nothing for me here.'

Shouting broke out: her father incensed, Amesbury spewing furious epithets, her mother gasping. She was only conscious of Caine's hand closing around hers, tugging her after him as he strode to the door. 'I'd hurry if I were you,' he growled. 'I'd rather not have to shoot anyone while we're in the house.' There was more shouting in the hallway, her father calling out to servants. Dear heavens, would he really bar the way?

'Take the back hall then, it lets out into the garden and there's a gate to the street,' Mary instructed, lifting her skirts to run. A deeper fear came to her for the first time. If she were caught now, she'd be locked in her room and let out only for a wedding.

Caine scuffled with a footman at the door and then they were free, Caine pushing her ahead of him into the garden as they sprinted for the gate. They were nearly there when the shot rang out, passing so close to Mary that her hair lifted. She screamed in shock and looked back to see Amesbury at the door. The man had fired at them—at Caine or at her? Thank God he'd missed in the dark.

'Go, Mary! The latch!' Caine yelled, forcing her to refocus. She fumbled with the gate and they were through, running in the night, Caine in the lead now, her hand tight in his as they headed straight for his coach. 'Hurry, take the road to Sandmore,' Caine commanded the coachman as he bundled her inside and climbed in behind her, the coach lurching into instant motion without hesitation as if escaping from social events was a usual part of the coachman's evening.

'Are you hurt, Mary? The bullet didn't graze you?' The breathlessness in Caine's voice was not from exertion. His hands were at her temples, searching her face, her hair in the dark, feeling for blood, she realised.

'I'm fine, it just lifted a few hairs as it passed.' She gave a shaky laugh. It must have passed close indeed if Caine was concerned. 'He shot at me.' She began to tremble as the words gave life to the final moments of the brief chase. 'The man my father wants me to marry shot at me.'

Caine's hands framed her face, his own face close to hers so that she could see the stern set of his features, the dark anger of his eyes. 'Set it aside, Mary, as best you can for now,' he instructed in earnest. 'It will only paralyse you, overwhelm you if you let it, and you must absolutely not let it. You must be alert and brave for me, for yourself. Can you do that for me?'

She swallowed hard and gathered herself. 'Yes.' He was absolutely right. The horrors and betrayals of tonight were staggering if she dwelt on them. There would be a time for that, but this was not it.

'That's my girl.' Caine smiled his approval and she felt an irrational surge of pride that she'd pleased him.

'Where are we going?' Mary asked.

'To my grandfather's. We should reach Sandmore by morning.'

'Do you think they'll follow?' Mary asked as Mayfair fell behind them. She didn't let herself think what would happen to Caine if they were caught on the open road in the dark. With no witnesses, Amesbury might dare anything.

Caine gave a non-committal shrug. 'Hard to say. They'll lose a lot of time harnessing a coach and they're not sure where we're headed.' He reached beneath the seat and pulled out a wooden box. 'If they do, however, we'll be prepared.' He lifted the lid to reveal a pair of pistols. 'Can you shoot?'

Mary met his gaze over the box, solemn and grim. 'I can if it's not too far.' And she would if it meant keeping this man safe from the likes of Amesbury. Tonight, Caine had stood up for her. He had been her champion. If needed, she'd return the favour and be his. But she hoped it wouldn't come to that, at least not until she had a bow and arrow in hand and could do it justice.

Caine reached beneath the seat again and pulled out a blanket and flask. 'The blanket is for later, once we're certain we're not being followed. The flask is for now.' He passed it to her. 'It's whisky. Sip it. It will burn going down, but it will settle your nerves and I dare say they need it after the night you've had.'

Mary took a brave swallow, thankful for the instruction. It *did* burn. It was definitely not port. But it helped. As the warmth spread through her, she felt her fear ease, replaced by something more powerful, more exhilarating. She'd taken control of her future, whatever it might be. In the morning, that fact might scare her witless, but for now, in the dark of the carriage with Caine beside her, she'd revel in it and let the realisation make her strong. No matter what the morning held, she was going to need all her strength.

Morning light streamed through the carriage windows, limning the curve of Mary's jaw, turning the cream of her skin to a delicate pearl as she slept, wrapped in the blanket from beneath the seat, her breathing soft, slow and even. Somewhere in the darkness, she'd found peace while he kept watch throughout the long drive.

It was difficult to believe someone in possession of such elegance, such delicacy, was also in possession of such iron and steel. She'd found the strength of character to stand up for herself, to fight for what she wanted. The only other woman he knew in possession of such tenacity was his sister, Guinevere, whom he admired greatly and who had married the Duke of Creighton, one of Mary's intended suitors.

Mary had nearly died for that tenacity tonight. While Caine was fairly certain Amesbury's bullet had been meant for him, his aim had put that bullet in Mary's way instead. Amesbury's actions tonight certainly did nothing to dispel Caine's instincts that the danger of Amesbury was more than that of an unwanted suitor. He'd shown himself to be not only a violent man, but also a man who used that violence often enough that it had become a choice of first resort; a man who defended his claims and got his way through violence was a dangerous man indeed.

He would not soon forget the sight of Mary at Amesbury's mercy tonight despite her best efforts. Nor would he soon forget the feeling that sight had engendered in him; primal anger had taken root deep within him. Not because Amesbury was physically assaulting a woman, although Caine would have come to any woman's aid in a similar situation, but because it was Mary.

Those feelings ran beyond a sense of responsibility and general protection towards her. Perhaps it was because of the recency of the intimacy they'd shared that afternoon, and perhaps it was something more, but those feelings were real. There was a logical explanation for it, of course. In the past few weeks, they'd become friends.

Friends who climaxed in carriages against your hand?

His conscience was having none of that argument, which prompted another argument: what were his intentions in regard to Mary? Did those intentions stop at protection? What constituted protection? *How* was it achieved? Did he owe her more than that? After all, she'd walked out of a life it would be difficult to return to at best and impossible to return to if Caine's other suppositions bore out.

The coachman called down, 'One mile to Sandmore.' It was time to wake Mary and brace her. She was about to walk into the heart of the Parkhurst legacy and it wasn't going to be what she thought. Sandmore was not the usual bucolic country house of an earl. It was imposing both in its architecture and its atmosphere. Secrets trod its halls, people arrived at all hours of the day and night with messages for his grandfather. The walls fairly vibrated with intrigue. One could not be at Sandmore and remain oblivious that all was not as it seemed.

Caine leaned over and gently shook her. 'Mary, we're nearly there. You've slept the night away.' A sign, perhaps, of how exhausting the evening's events had been for her that she'd slept so long and so soundly in a rocking carriage. She raised her head, her dark hair falling down from its pins, her eyes drowsy.

She met his news with a soft smile of relief. 'We're safe, then. They didn't give chase.'

Caine only smiled in reassurance, something inside him responding to that small, powerful word 'we'. But it was a misnomer. *She* was safe. For the moment. But he was never safe. He'd left safe living behind years ago. She'd learn that soon enough at Sandmore.

Caine braced himself as well as they turned on to the long oak-lined drive. He'd never brought a woman to Sandmore to meet his grandfather or to meet his own secrets. He watched Mary's quick fingers work some feminine magic fashioning a hasty bun for her hair. He reached for her chin in a gentle gesture and turned her cheek towards him, wincing at the bruise left by Amesbury's palm. 'That will hurt for a while. I am sorry we didn't have anything for it.'

She touched it gingerly. 'Does it look awful? Perhaps we can find some rice powder to cover it up.'

Caine shook his head. 'You needn't worry about covering it up. Do not be ashamed. It is your badge of courage. You fought honourably.'

She plucked at her dress. 'I look a mess. People will wonder what you've dragged in.'

'We'll take care of you. There will be dresses and hot water and rice powder if you desire it.' Guinevere would have left gowns here and Grandfather was always well stocked for all nature of emergency. The wheels crunched on gravel and Caine felt protectiveness surge. He ought to warn her. But about what? About himself? Or perhaps she had enough to worry about and a disclosure, did her no favours.

How ironic that in his attempt to protect her, he had to risk exposing himself. But not now. Not yet. He said simply, 'We're here', and handed her out into the bright early morning light to meet his grandfather's piercing gaze.

The Earl of Sandmore stared down at them from the top stair of Sandmore's front steps, leaning on his walking stick and looking fresh and alert for dawn's early light—a sharp contrast to how Caine felt in rumpled evening clothes and dark stubble on his chin.

'You've driven all night. My outriders spied you the moment you hit the village.'

Caine nodded. Of course his grandfather knew. Grandfather knew everything, some of it even before it happened. 'I come with urgent information.' He ushered Mary up the steps.

Grandfather raised a white brow in correction, 'You've also come seeking sanctuary.' His gaze indicated he was not entirely pleased.

'This is Lady Mary Kimber. There's been developments with Amesbury.' Caine met his grandfather's disapproval evenly with his own gaze. Grandfather valued his privacy. Mary was not a welcome guest, but he knew Grandfather wouldn't turn her away on the power of his word.

Grandfather's gaze moved to Mary, taking in the

bruised cheek, the torn dress. He gave a curt nod. 'Then you'd best come in. I'll have my maids lay out something for you. You can wash and rest.'

'You are too kind, my lord.' Mary smiled and Caine watched his grandfather soften.

'I am not kind, Lady Mary, merely practical. I can't send you away without putting you and other important matters at risk. Grandson, we'll talk after you've had something to eat.'

Caine found his grandfather in his office, the same office in which his grandfather had shared the letters patent a few weeks ago. It seemed a lifetime ago now. He pulled out the papers culled from Carys's study and put them on Grandfather's desk. 'Amesbury is indeed continuing the family business of munitions and Carys is definitely in bed with him. There's a deed with both of their signatures on it for a munitions factory in Brussels. And Carys owes Amesbury money. There are ledger pages that show some losses, a decrease in income since his expulsion from the Prometheus Club, and two loans from Amesbury for which he likely used the promise of a marriage to Mary as collateral based on the events that transpired last night.'

His grandfather's eyes were dark. 'From the look of her, I take it Amesbury's proposal wasn't met with resounding joy.' He picked up the pages and took his time to read them. 'Tell me what you think, Caine. Your instincts are usually good. What do you think is happening?'

'I *think* Carys invested with Amesbury under the belief that they'd win the Prometheus Club's bid for supplying arms to Greece. When they didn't, Carys ran into money problems. He couldn't cover some of his debt, hence the first loan from Amesbury. Then, there was the social contretemps between Carys and Cowden and when Amesbury suggested they sabotage the shipment in order to force the Prometheus Club to buy arms from them on the second go round, Carys saw it as a chance to get his money and his pride back. He traded on that, to his detriment.' A detriment he was likely unaware of. In his desperation, he'd tied himself to an event of political sabotage that could have had far-reaching implications for Greek democracy and he'd tied himself to the potential death of the Earl of Sandmore's grandson.

His grandfather thought for a moment. 'Are you of the opinion, then, that Carys doesn't know how deep Amesbury's treachery goes?'

Caine had grappled with this very question during the long night. How much *did* Carys know? How much was he a willing party to or an unsuspecting one? 'I don't think he knows that the munitions are potentially faulty if the Brussels factory is following the same production as the previous factory here in England did. I don't think he knows that Amesbury will sell to anyone who has money to buy regardless of what that party is fighting for. And I don't think he knows or perhaps believes that the Amesbury family could still be connected with the arms dealer, Cabot Roan, who was tried and escaped sentencing a few years back on the power of the Amesbury name.'

That was the connection he didn't have proof for, it was supposition only, but it made sense. Why would the Amesbury family have manipulated the justice system to get the man off of charges simply to let him disappear? 'Carys is facing financial ruin. He is a desperate man looking for one big payoff to restore his coffers.' That he would barter his daughter to get it did not make him likeable. Caine had known plenty of desperate men in his time and they were always dangerous because they had nothing left to lose.

'Knowingly or unknowingly, Carys has put himself in a horrible position. He is ruined in more ways than finances.' Grandfather tapped his fingers on the desk's surface, thinking. 'Does Lady Mary know any of this?'

'Only that she's been promised in marriage in exchange for debt forgiveness. She thinks it's a social swap. Her connections to pave the way for the new Duke of Amesbury, who hasn't been out in society, for her father's financial stability.'

'She'll have to be told for her own safety and her own plans.' Grandfather met his gaze steadily. 'I do not relish you the task.' Caine didn't relish it either. What she knew already was bad enough. Telling her that her father was likely connected to his brother's disappearance would…well, it would drive a wedge between them. She would feel entirely alone, betrayed even. He'd certainly dragged her into the lion's den without warning.

'What are her plans? Does she understand the ramifications of coming here?' Grandfather asked, then added shrewdly, 'Do you?' He gave a short chuckle. 'I take it that her father's involvement isn't all she doesn't know.' He gave him a knowing glance. 'Seems like you will have some explaining to do.'

Caine nodded. 'I just hope I don't have to do it all at once.' And that when he did tell her, she wouldn't regret her choice.

Chapter Seventeen

Reality—not regret—she would *not* use that word—
was starting to settle in as Mary strolled the gardens
at Sandmore. She did not regret coming here or her
choice last night. She had only to touch her cheek or
to look at her face in a mirror to know that the regret
would have been in staying behind. Caine had offered her a way out—a way out of a dangerous marriage, a way out from a life that had lost its lustre for
her. But now that she had achieved a way out, where
did she go from here? Where did the way out lead?
There was freedom in the thought of remaking herself in her own image, but there was fear, too.

She had no money. The clothes on her back were
borrowed, she was in residence at a stranger's home
with nothing to call her own. The only items of value
she possessed were the pieces of jewellery she'd
worn last night. Not even her name would stand
her in good stead. By now, rumours would be cir-

culating about last night, the gossip pages would have reported the incident, every drawing room in London would be speculating.

She could imagine the sordid cast the story would take. No one would focus on how Amesbury had struck her or on her father's marriage deal with him. The focus would all be on how she had run out in the middle of her mother's musicale with Caine Parkhurst, the rakish Marquess of Barrow. It was further proof as to how unfair life was for a woman. She was ruined because she'd stood up for herself, because she had claimed her freedom, because she had protected herself the only way she knew how. And for that, society had thrown her out. There was no going back.

No going back to a closet full of more dresses than she could wear.

No going back to the well-appointed estates that were her luxurious prisons.

No going back to the pressures of the marriage mart.

But that also meant no going back to other things, too.

No going back to summer house parties with archery competitions and picnics by lakes.

No going back to Christmas parties in evergreen-strewn manor houses, tables groaning with food and tradition.

No more taking hedges in the field on the back of her mare, Mathilda. She would miss that the most. She hoped Mathilda would understand, that she would go on and bring joy to someone else. Her eyes stung at the thought of her horse.

All those things were lost to her now as well as those things she wanted to be so desperately rid of. To give up a life meant to give up all of it. It could not be done half-heartedly and she grieved for those losses as she walked the pretty gardens. The Earl of Sandmore had a good eye for Italian topiary. There was a giraffe, a lion and a stag among the menagerie of shapes interspersed with soothing water features, all of which held her interest and helped keep the grief at bay.

She reached the edge of the garden where the Earl's dominance over nature ended. The manicured verge giving on to the green of untamed grass running down to a lake. Un-curated, raw and natural, like her life now. Mary closed her eyes and lifted her face to the sun, letting its warmth bathe her as she put her sadness aside. The future was hers to chart. She was starting from scratch.

She laughed out loud to the sky and held her arms out wide. She was indeed starting from scratch. One did not get any more 'from scratch' than she. Once, she'd dreamed of doing such a thing and now she'd done it. Finally. After years of trying to make others happy, she'd done something for herself.

'Mary!'

She turned at the familiar shout to see Caine crossing the garden, a basket on his arm. He was without his coat, his shirt sleeves rolled up, the summer breeze playing with the waves of his hair. 'Your grandfather has released you.' She wondered what they'd discussed for hours behind closed doors. Surely it hadn't all been about her.

'Yes.' He was smiling and the sight of that smile made her thoughts grow bold. Here was something else she might claim for herself before she went out into the world. She wanted Caine to finish the lesson he'd started in the coach—was that only yesterday? 'I thought we might picnic down by the lake and take a quiet moment.' He held up the basket in illustration and offered his free arm as they left the garden. 'What were you laughing at, just then?'

'Not at, in. I was laughing *in* celebration of my freedom.' She smiled up at him, letting a moment's euphoria spill out. It was better than crying. 'I might go anywhere, be anyone, do anything.'

He answered with a grin, 'That sounds ambitious, Mary. But you needn't go tomorrow. Or the next day,

or even next week. Take your time, stay a while.
There is no hurry.' It was kind of him not remind
her she had nowhere to go, or that she needed to wait
until it was safe to leave. There *were* loose ends to
settle. 'How are you otherwise, Mary? I am sorry
I could not come to you sooner. Grandfather and I
had much to discuss.'

They reached the edge of the lake and they shook
out the blanket, laying it on the ground. 'I am well,'
she said sombrely, sitting down. 'I am coming to
grips with last night. It's a lot. Just when I think
I have an understanding that makes sense to me,
there's something more, like ripples on a pond.' She
reached for the basket and began to help lay out the
food. 'The worst should have been Amesbury's...
attack.' The word was still hard to say. 'But as awful
as it was, it isn't the worst thing about last night.'

She set down a loaf of bread and held Caine's
gaze. 'The worst was that my parents simply didn't
care, not about what he did and not about what I
wanted, and it wasn't the first time. They've never
cared about what I've wanted. I was to accept the
proposal and move on to be a dutiful wife, a dutiful
duchess just as I've been a dutiful daughter. Dutiful
and beautiful, that's what they say about me behind
my back, isn't it?'

She laughed at the uncertain expression on his

face. 'Did you think I didn't know? It's all right. It's true and it's not the worst thing to be called.' She sat back on her heels. 'Oh, my, look at all this food. How long did you think we'd be out here?'

Caine stretched out beside her, his head propped in his hand. 'I don't know. Grandfather has guests for supper tonight.'

'So, we should make ourselves scarce? Is that it?' Mary laughed. Being with him, here, out of doors, focused on the moment, she could forget all her other cares. 'Won't they see us from the garden?' She glanced back over her shoulder at the house in the distance.

'No, Grandfather's guests aren't the garden strolling type.' Caine assured her. 'Although they'll miss a spectacular sunset. We have the best view of it from right here. The sun goes down over the rim of the lake.' He pointed to the horizon. 'When we were boys and we'd come for summers, we'd camp out here and sleep beneath the stars. Sometimes we'd have a bonfire, but most of the time, we'd just stay awake, looking up at the sky. Grandfather taught us our constellations that way.'

She studied him, trying to imagine him as a young boy. 'I bet you were precocious.'

Caine laughed. 'I was, but so were my brothers,' he said as if that excused their antics. He plucked a strawberry from its bowl. 'Here, eat. Grandfather's gardener grows the best strawberries. It's something to do with the soil he uses.' He popped it in her mouth and she bit into the most delicious berry she'd ever tasted.

'You're still precocious. And you're trying to distract me with berries.' She chose a berry for herself. 'Tell me a story from your childhood.'

'All right.' Caine grinned and shifted on the blanket, settling in. 'Do you see that little island in the middle of the lake? We would have swim races out to it. Last one out there had to do the other's school lessons for a whole week.'

Mary squinted, gauging the distance. 'That's a long way.'

'It is and that's why Lucien is by far the best of us at Latin.' Caine laughed.

'Who won most often? Did you?' she prompted, liking this glimpse into Caine's past.

'Most of the time until we were about sixteen and then Stepan started to outpace us, even though he was four years younger than I. But he loved the water, he was born for it. The rest of us just tried to dominate it, whereas he was one with it.'

Caine's eyes sobered. 'We were having a relay race—Stepan and Kieran against Lucien and I. Lucien raced Kieran and I raced Stepan, but in the middle of the race, I got a cramp. I couldn't swim, I couldn't tread water. I was too far from shore to go back and too far from the island to go forward. I might have drowned if it hadn't been for Stepan. He came back for me, got an arm about me and found the strength to swim me to shore. No mean feat for a twelve-year-old given that I outsized him in every way.'

Mary gave a wistful sigh. How wonderful it must be to have brothers. She could hear his love for them in his words—his grief, too, because a person could not have one without the other. For all their rakish ways, the Parkhurst brothers were close, the family was close. Caine was close even with his grandfather. Despite his grandfather's displeasure at their sudden arrival, there was something about the way the two men had spoken with each other, the way they simply were with each other when they shared space, that indicated a respect and love that transcended disagreement. So very different from her home, her family.

Caine looked off into the distance and she sensed he was remembering a different swim now, one much more recent and more deadly. 'He was younger than I, but always protective of me, even though it was my job to be protective of him.'

Mary smiled softly. 'You hate that, don't you? Allowing others to take care of you.'

Caine cocked a dark brow. 'I dislike others doing my job for me. I am the oldest, it's my job to look out for them, all of them, whether they like it or not.' As he'd looked out for her, whether she'd asked him to or not. He'd certainly gone above and beyond what she'd expected of him. What an interesting dichotomy that offered: a rake with a soul, a conscience. It was something to hold up against Lady Morestad's claim of inconstancy.

Caine's voice dropped and his words came slow and deliberate. 'That night at Wapping…'

He chose each word with care, perhaps so as not to open himself up to grief.

Heaven forbid the great champion Caine Parkhurst be vulnerable, she thought, even as she found herself leaning forward, not wanting to miss a word.

Here was another secret she might add to her treasures.

'We were on the dock and he said to me, "If it comes to swimming, you let me go in." And he hasn't come out. Yet.'

She reached for a strawberry, aware of the silence around them. One could hear the night birds begin their evensong, the gentle susurration of the lake water against the shore. She ought not probe, a young lady should avoid indelicate conversation, but perhaps that did Caine a disservice. Perhaps here, with the privacy of dusk settling around them, where no one could hear, it would be a kindness to ask the question, to give him a chance to talk about something that obviously troubled him deeply.

'What happened in Wapping, Caine?' Why had Stepan Parkhurst jumped into the water at midnight? What had been so urgent to call a gentleman away from a ball? What had been so dire it could not have waited until morning or even a few minutes?

'Business for Grandfather.' He held up the jug of lemonade, silently asking if she wanted more. It was an attempt at distraction. But she would not be diverted.

'You can tell me, Caine. You *can* trust me. I've kept your secrets,' she offered the reminder softly.

He set the jug aside and touched her good cheek with a gentle caress that sent her blood pounding. 'It's not that, Mary. Some secrets are not made to be shared.'

She would not get more than that from him. He was withholding for her sake, not his. He was protecting her again, this time with his words. He could not tell her because the secret was too big, too much of a burden. That was perhaps more frightening than whatever it was he felt he needed to hide.

'You're a complex man, Caine Parkhurst,' she murmured, 'I don't think you're all that London says you are.' There were too many contradictions for that to be true.

'Oh? And what do you think I am?' Caine's eyes glinted with amusement.

'I think you are more, much more.' She selected another berry. This one she held up to his lips, miming his earlier gesture, and watched his eyes go obsidian black, watched them drop to her own lips and linger. Her mouth went dry.

'Mary, what are you doing?' Caine's voice had become a seductive rasp.

She wet her lips, her breath catching at the sight of desire stealing over him, naked want in his gaze. 'I am claiming my forfeit.' Her own voice was a sultry husk she hardly recognised, but then again, she was hardly herself these days; she was a new person since she'd met him.

'Minx,' he growled, taking a slow bite of the strawberry that left juice on her fingers. 'You've already claimed your forfeit.' His gaze held hers, hungry and hot. He took her wrist and drew her fingers to his mouth, licking them one by one, his tongue a wicked caress against her skin. Mary felt the heat of want and desire rise in her cheeks, stir low down in her belly, until she was boiling with it.

She swallowed hard, finding the words to answer his challenge.

'The forfeit was to claim *you*, but as I recall in the carriage, you were the one doing all the claiming.' And quite honestly, that had been fine with her. His mouth, his hands, had wrought all nature of wicked pleasure, but that was not the forfeit. Would he even allow her to claim him? This man who protected others but would not permit others to protect him?

'Mary, do you know what you're asking? Wanting?' he warned, his eyes meeting her in a clash of onyx and lightning.

'Yes, I know exactly what I'm doing, Caine, and who I am doing it with.' She wanted this moment, this night, to take into a new world with her new self, to hold against all the other nights to come— empty ones, lonely ones. 'Tonight, I want to know pleasure, Caine, and I want to know it with you.' She raised her arms, feeling deliciously exposed as his eyes followed the motion of her body, and reached for the first hairpin, just to be sure Caine knew she meant business.

Chapter Eighteen

The first length of hair fell over her shoulder, a silken walnut skein shimmering in mauve twilight. Another length fell and his body answered with a primal bolt of arousal, searing him at his core even as his mind launched its best defence. He should say no. He knew better—he should *not*, under any circumstances, *particularly these circumstances*, induct Lady Mary Kimber into the exquisite art of lovemaking on a picnic blanket beside the lake.

There were a hundred reasons why, beginning with she was vulnerable and her world had only just been upended—she was reaching out for something, for someone—and ending with he did not seduce virgins, with ninety-eight other salient points in between. But not one of those arguments singularly or taken together were a match for Mary taking down her hair with slow, deft motions one would think she'd deliberately designed to tease a man into insanity. Her grey eyes held his, making promises his body was more than happy to help her keep. How had this happened? How had he come to want her with a single-minded ferocity that drove reason into oblivion, that had him brawling with dukes in drawing rooms and racing through the night?

'Mary,' he growled her name in warning of his desire and in witness to it, as he lay back and drew her over him, her legs straddling his hips, his hands unerringly sliding beneath her skirts and resting on the warm, satin skin of her calves. His gaze was riveted on her, his eyes attuned to every detail of her face: the dusky sweep of lashes, the cream of her skin, the delicate length of her nose, the sensual bow of her mouth...the elegant column of her neck. He could not recall a time when the individual parts of a woman had roused him so thoroughly, fixated him so completely to the exclusion of all else. He raised a hand to her hair, pushing it back behind her ear. 'I am no gentleman, Mary.'

'I know. I would be disappointed if you decided to play one now.' She licked her lips and wriggled against his groin. His desire spiked in evident ways. 'I don't want the gentleman, Caine. I want the rake.'

He gave a groan between gritted teeth. She could not be ignorant of his desire now. 'I will ruin you.'

'I am already ruined. What you and I do here on

this blanket will not be worse than what society is already doing to me in their gossip columns and behind their fans. In fact, I am certain what we'll do will be a whole lot better.' Then she leaned low, her hair skimming his chest, her mouth finding his as she whispered the words that lit his body on fire. 'Shatter me.'

'Your wish is my fervent desire.' He gave a rough, raw laugh and rolled her beneath him. 'What would you like first, my queen? My mouth, my hands?' He watched her eyes go wide and dark at the prospect, her desire a palpable thing that pulsed between them, hot and strong and wild.

'Both,' she breathed. 'I want what I had in the carriage, I want that…again.'

'Then you shall have it and more.'

Caine had his mouth on her, trailing kisses up her leg, his mouth a deliciously warm, wicked and wonderful contrast to the gentle evening breeze blowing against her bare skin. She had thought nothing could match the pleasure of Caine's hand on her, his fingers within her, but what did she know? It was clear now that she'd simply had no bar for comparison. This was sheer heaven, this peaceful interlude that presaged the storm of pleasure to come. Her body tightened in anticipation of it, desire winding itself up hard and pulsing in the place between her legs, attuned and waiting for his arrival.

He pressed a soft kiss to the curls there and her body went wild, her blood thrummed, a moan of welcome purled up her throat. And then his mouth, his lips, his tongue, his teeth, went to work, putting the prior efforts of his fingers to shame as she arched into him, every nerve of her, every inch of her alive. His tongue gave a wicked lick at her seam, tracing the track his fingers had once followed, and she trembled with the delight of it, pleasure echoing through her.

He looked up, his gaze travelling the intimate distance of her to meet her gaze, a slow, sinful smile spreading on his face, his own breath ragged as he coached, 'Be a good girl, Mary, this is for you, all for you. Reach for it, get lost in it, take what you want and let it take *you*.'

To take what she wanted, to take what this man offered?

Yes, and yes again. How heady, how glorious to take instead of always giving, and this time she knew how to take, how to let go. Her body was hungry for him, it craved the release that waited for her, called for her with every press of his mouth, every stroke of his tongue. He'd found her secret place once more, this time with the tip of that wicked tongue, and she gave a gasp, turning her face up-wards, eyes wide open to the purpling sky.

She clutched at him, her hands buried in the depths of his dark waves, either in search of an-chorage, or in the hopes of control, that somehow she could prolong the pleasure, hold it, hold this mo-ment where she hovered on the precipice between pleasure denied and pleasure achieved for ever.

His hands tightened at her hips, a groan escaping him. The sound of his own pleasure racking him pushed her beyond the careful brink she'd wrought. She wanted to hover no more, she wanted the re-lease, wanted to shatter against him, wanted to soar to the skies and she was not beyond begging. 'Caine, Caine, Caine.' His name became a plea, a prayer on her lips that she sent up into the firmaments and the gods of pleasure took pity on her. She fractured, the skies swallowing her cries while Caine collapsed against her, his head on her belly, her hands knot-ted in his hair.

It was worth it. This was the one thought that flitted through her mind as she spiralled back to consciousness, her soul falling slowly out of the pur-ple sky as the moon rose in summer-gold splendour above her. Whatever happened next, this had been worth it. She would know the pleasure for ever— the feel of his touch at her most intimate places, the luxury of these floating, peaceful minutes that came afterwards. No one could take this from her. She had permitted this, given this to herself and she would dare a bit more before this was over.

'Caine,' she called his name softly.

He lifted his head from her belly, his dark eyes dreamy in the aftermath of desire. This was not a gaze Caine Parkhurst cultivated for public consumption. A warm heat stole through her at the thought that perhaps this look was for her alone. 'What?' Even that simple word was spoken as a seduction.

'Can I give you something…ah…similar?' For all of her newfound boldness she lacked a refined knowledge of what might be offered and how.

Caine crawled up her body and stole a kiss before rolling on to his side, head propped in his hand, wickedness returning to his eyes. 'You can, if you like,' he drawled, 'but you are not required.'

'I want to,' she murmured. 'I can use my teeth, my tongue, my hand?'

Caine growled. 'Do you have any idea what those words do to a man?'

She laughed. 'If they do anything close to what you just did to me, then, yes, I do.' She lay down alongside him, her head in the pocket of his chest where shoulder met torso, revelling in the warmth of him, the security she felt lying in his arms. This was another revelation—how intimacy could be passion, hot and wild, while it could also be closeness and comfort in the stillness of a summer night. But Caine knew. Perhaps that was part of his charm: he knew seduction's deep magic.

She sought him in the darkness, her hand reaching for him through his trousers and finding the length of him still aroused and hard against the fabric, against her hand. She let herself learn him, tracing him, marvelling at him. The hardness did not surprise her. She'd felt the press of him against her buttocks twice now, hard and hot and insistent. But the length, the size, *that* was a surprise. 'You feel bigger than I thought.'

Caine gave a low chuckle. 'I am not sure how to take that. I thought we'd discussed big men before.'

'But that was about dancing, not about...*this*...'

'Dancing is sex, didn't you know? That's why I like it so much,' Caine teased in low, wicked tones.

'You're incorrigible.' She laughed with him, wanting to be as bold as he. What freedom there was in boldness, to do and say what one wanted, when one wanted. To speak one's mind instead of looking for delicate ways to say things. She continued her hand study of him, feeling the tip and then tracing his length back to the root, her fingers fascinated.

'It's more fascinating to see in person,' he coaxed.

'Undo my breeches. Take it out, give it a proper introduction.'

She bit her lip in anticipation as she worked his falls. This, too, was something she'd not anticipated—the playfulness, the togetherness of love games. This was not the formal, perfunctory activity her mother had alluded to on rare occasion, an activity to be endured, over and done in a few minutes. She had him free of his breeches, her eyes taking a moment to feast before her hand could not resist the urge to touch.

Caine's hand closed about hers as they made a loose fist about his phallus, moving slowly up and down its length, then left her to find her own rhythm. She explored his tip, running her palm over it, finding the moisture there. She smiled as she spread it down his length.

'Does it please you that I rouse to your touch so thoroughly?' Caine lifted himself up on his elbows, his gaze following her hand.

'Yes, I suppose it does,' she admittedly somewhat shyly. 'I'm glad you like it.'

'I do like it.' He claimed a kiss, his voice a whisper against her mouth. 'Do you know what else I like? I like the scent of you when you're aroused, I like the sight of your hair falling down your back, the sight of your body claiming the pleasure I give you, the sounds you make when you shatter. I like the taste of you…'

A gasp of shock and new-born arousal escaped her. How could it be that she wanted more again, so soon? How much would be enough to satisfy her? 'You are truly wicked. I don't know anyone who talks like you do.'

Caine laid back down with a laugh. 'You know no one who says exactly what they think?'

'No one but you, apparently.' That struck her as all too true. She trusted Caine, had told him things she'd not voiced to anyone. In turn, he'd opened up a whole new world for her. To think this had all started with a dance. That night they'd talked and danced for the first time, she'd wondered what would happen if she stepped off the path of propriety. Where would other, less proper, paths lead?

This path had led here, to this moment, to her hand on him beneath the stars, her body replete with the pleasure he'd given her and yet somehow ready for more. The path had led her to decadence, certainly, but it had led her to more than that. Caine made her feel things she did not want to name for fear of becoming attached to them, to him, any more than she already was and then losing them, him. She'd lost enough in the past twenty-four hours, except for the one thing she'd like to be quite rid of.

'Mmm, that's good.' He sighed, his eyes half-lidded as he lost himself in her touch and she basked in the praise. 'Do you want to finish me off, or shall I do it?' He opened his eyes and she felt his gaze rest on her. He was waiting for her to set their direction. This was her moment, another chance to be seized if she dared.

'Perhaps you might finish us both off, instead?' Nervously, she wet her lips as she made her request. After all, it wasn't every night one asked a man for sex.

Caine looked startled. She flushed for a moment. 'I seem to recall you promised to ruin me.' She gave a breathy laugh. He was going to refuse and she would feel entirely embarrassed. She sighed and closed her eyes, taking her hand from him. 'Have I made a fool of myself?' Caine would tell her the truth even if she didn't wish to hear it.

He grabbed her hands, squeezing them hard. 'No, never, Mary. I'm quite intoxicated with your boldness, with *you*, if you must know.' His mouth was soft on hers, stealing a gentle kiss as he murmured, 'Wouldn't you rather do this in a bed?'

'No.' She smiled against his mouth. 'I want to make love right here with the moon watching and the night birds singing.' This would be her paradise, a place out of time where she had a lover who coveted her, cherished her, who saw a woman, not an earl's daughter with bloodlines and a dowry. She rose. 'But you'll have to help me with my laces. I can't get out of this dress alone.'

'I am more than happy to oblige.' Caine came to his feet and moved behind her, sweeping aside the length of her hair, his mouth whispering decadent words at her ear; how her skin was moonlight itself, her scent like a summer garden. His hands worked the laces at her back, warm and competent. His own desire pressed against her in promise of what was to come as her dress slipped to the ground. Oh, how her pulse sped with want and her thoughts raced with desire as her underthings joined her dress and he whispered, 'I'll make it good for you, I promise.'

She turned in his arms, pressing her naked body to him, arms wrapped around his neck. 'Make it good for both of us. I trust you.' She stepped away from him then.

'You are beautiful.' His voice was gravel and she rather enjoyed the power of having stolen *his* breath.

She sat down on the blanket and wrapped her arms about her knees. 'Your turn now.' He made short work of his shirt and his already open breeches and the moonlight did the rest, favouring the angles and planes of his body with its light and shadow. Although he didn't need any favouring.

He looked like a god as he came to her, his broad shoulders and arms corded with muscle, his torso a carved marble atlas of muscle, his hips lean, his thighs long, the perfect setting for what nestled between them. No, nestled was too tame of word. His phallus was too large for nestling; it *rose*, it *jutted*. It did *not* nestle. He fell to all fours in front of her, his eyes, dark and dangerous, holding hers as he lowered himself over her. She lay back in invitation, her arms reaching up for him, urging him to come onwards, to cover her in full. His phallus brushed her leg and heat rose in her, the wet, damp heat of desire. She wanted this man. Wanted him inside her. To know the feel of him for ever.

His own breathing was ragged. She sensed he was holding himself in check, keeping his own desire leashed on her behalf. 'You don't need to be careful of me, I won't break,' she encouraged, want outstripping her own sense of caution.

He nuzzled her ear. 'This moment is for savouring, not devouring.' And she understood. This was not to be frantic like his mouth at her nub. There was to be nothing cheap and hurried in this. This was to be a slow taking, a deliberate taking. Perhaps even a bridegroom's taking of his bride. Her heart swelled at the care, the courtesy he was showing her amid the surging passion when it would be easy for recklessness and individual need to hold sway, when it would be easy to devour, to sate, and she revelled in it, her body stretching languorously beneath him, hip to hip, leg to leg, as she tried to match his height with hers.

He held her arms over her head, gripped in a single hand. 'All the better to see your breasts, to kiss them,' he said and it was she who felt wicked as his mouth sucked at them, turning her insides to aspic, a slow heat building in her she could not contain, so that she was more than ready for him when he finally came into her, slow inch by slow inch, his eyes holding hers, both of them enrapt by the other's response. He filled her, a sense of having been joined intimately with another, with *him*, swamped her.

'Wait, there's more,' he murmured as he began to move within her. Joining turned to completion, and completion turned to climax, this time, a climax they both could share. They were headed to the great release together. The knowledge of that was heady. He'd be there with her when she shattered and she'd be there with him. That release was on them quickly, desire refusing to be held in abatement any longer. Her hips met his, she wrapped her legs about him, holding him close, her breath coming in gasps as he thrust once, twice more and then came the brilliant fracturing, of being at one with another while knowing that one's self was splintering into a thousand shards of feeling.

Two thoughts swept her at the last. *This* was the pinnacle of intimacy, the purpose and secret of life, perhaps even what made life worth living. And how would she ever move on without the man who could achieve it?

Chapter Nineteen

They had to move. They couldn't spend the night here on the ground with nothing more than a picnic blanket and themselves in their rather natural state. Caine sighted the moon through a drowsy eye. It must be past midnight based on the moon's position. They'd fallen asleep. No surprise, given their exertions.

He wasn't sure what had woken him, perhaps the hoot of an owl, or the cooling evening air on his bare skin, or perhaps, from the semi-roused state of his phallus, Mary had shifted in her sleep and nudged him into wakefulness. That didn't mean he wanted to move. Being awake merely meant he had no excuse to avoid taking the necessary next steps—getting him and Mary back to the house. He wondered if that included getting dressed? He didn't think he had the wherewithal to manage laces and corsets and he didn't give enough of a damn about who saw him in his altogether to bother with his own breeches.

If he had his way, he'd spend the night by the lake, wake to a sunrise with the woman he...*cared for*— he didn't dare call it anything else—in his arms and start the day with a slow bout of lovemaking. Beside him, Mary shivered in her sleep, gooseflesh standing out on her skin despite the borrowed warmth of his body's heat.

He curled around her, cradling her tight against him, wanting to keep her warm a bit longer, wanting to enjoy the peace surrounding him a bit longer, too. Peace was foreign to him. He did not inhabit a world that allowed for peace or for the safety that went with it. Safety and peace were contingent, one did not exist without the other. But tonight, for a few hours, he'd had both. Because of her.

He'd been with enough women to know that peace and safety were not guaranteed aftermaths of sex. Even though it had just been a few hours, he'd not slept beside a woman for this long perhaps ever. Usually, he left shortly afterwards, giving the excuse of a late-night card game or an evening meeting he needed to attend. And, usually, he was quite eager to go. Mystery and desirability wore off fairly quickly once the clothes were gone and people were left with only themselves.

That had not been the case tonight. Caine breathed in Mary's scent, all lilies and vanilla underlaid with the faint lingering musk of sex and arousal. She'd been a fascinating mix of boldness and innocence. *Wreck me.* Such potent words that had fired his desire and he'd done his best although he'd felt as if he'd been the one who was wrecked. His usual rake's detachment had not held fast tonight.

As much as he might want to frame the evening as instruction, the fulfilling of a forfeit or the continuation of a game they'd started in the carriage, tonight had been none of those things. Which was all the more reason he should have said no. It was one thing to play sex games with women who were looking for the same thing—a few nights, a few weeks, a few months of physical pleasure. But to *make love* with an innocent who knew nothing of such games, who knew only the honesty of her passion, was another.

It had meant something to her and it had meant something to him as well. She roused all his finer instincts. He wanted to protect her, wanted to make things right for her. Because he alone knew just how wrong things were going to be for her. And therein lay a host of other complications.

All evidence was pointing to the fact that her father had been involved in the incident that had led to Stepan's disappearance, an incident that had been intended to be violent, regardless, and was riddled with corruption. Even if nothing went public about it, the Earl would face ruinous consequences that would change his life and his family's. Those consequences had already started to change Mary's life.

You can save her. You can protect her with your name and your title.

The idea whispered in his head, a wispy ribbon of a thought that began to slowly take shape. He needed to marry to satisfy the King and marriage would separate her from her father's scandal should it leak beyond its immediate circles. Marriage would also put her beyond Amesbury.

A shooting star crossed the sky and he let himself dream a little. They would go to Longstead, the estate near Newmarket attached to the marquessate. There would be a house to keep Mary busy and stables for them both to enjoy. They could build a life in the horsing community there, ride with the hunt, sit on the board of directors for the racetrack, perhaps establish their own thoroughbred string.

The dream wandered down other paths, too, paths where there were dark-haired children with grey eyes whom he carried about on his shoulders and who rode ponies in the white-fenced paddocks, who learned to shoot pistols and bows. It was a vision of a life he'd long set aside, an impossible life because of choices he'd made. It was not the life of a Horseman. There were plenty of reasons to justify wedding Mary, but they were short-term reasons only. They did not outweigh the more significant consideration.

The dream dissolved first, followed by the idea. In the long term, there was no guarantee he could keep her safe. A Horseman's life was a dangerous life, full of unpredictability. One minute he was waltzing, the next he was trying to fish his brother out of the Thames basin. He could promise her nothing. Not even love. Loving her endangered her. If his enemies knew there was someone he cared for, he'd be vulnerable. He had to let her go. He sighed and held her tight. Well, it had been a nice thought while it lasted. Perhaps it was time to end this little fantasy, too. 'Mary, wake up, love, we have to get you to the house and tucked in your bed.'

The idea of trekking back to the house in the dark was met with little enthusiasm from Mary. Struggling into her clothes just to have to take them off again at the house was met with even less. In the end, Mary wrapped herself in the well-used picnic blanket, her clothes stuffed in the basket. Caine walked back stark naked, Mary pressed to his side. At the edge of the garden, he swung her up in his arms. 'No more grass,' he explained. 'The gravel will hurt your feet.'

'But you're barefoot, too,' Mary protested.

'My feet have calluses. Yours will be too delicate.' He laughed and kissed her, winding his way through the garden to a servant's door and up the back stairs to Mary's room. 'Shall I find you a nightgown before I go?' he asked, setting her down on the bed.

She reached for his hand. 'Must you go?' The blanket had slipped, revealing a smooth, creamy shoulder. Temptation roared.

'I must, Mary.' He held back the covers for her. 'I can't be here when the maid comes in the morning.' This was more to save her from embarrassment than himself. In all likelihood Grandfather probably knew already who was sleeping in whose bedroom and who had walked across his Italian gardens naked. He knew everything that happened in Europe, he certainly knew what went on in his own house.

'But you can walk across the grounds naked with a half-dressed woman in your arms.' She laughed softly. 'You have an odd sense of ethics, Caine Parkhurst.' She tugged at his hand. 'Please stay, just for a while. You can still slip out well before dawn.'

It was reason enough, and he was tired enough, to not fight it. He slid beneath the covers with Mary and blew out the lamp. Not only because she asked, but for the first time, he wanted to stay, Grandfather and the rest of the world be damned.

Grandfather was waiting for him in the breakfast room when Caine made his way downstairs the next morning shortly before nine o'clock. He'd left Mary sleeping just before dawn and returned to his own chambers to put in a couple of hours of work before dressing and facing the inquisition that likely awaited him over coffee. There'd been letters to write to the Prometheus Club and a letter to Kieran apprising him of developments, although the newspapers had likely done some of that for him.

'Sleep well?' Grandfather looked up from his own stack of newspaper, delivered from all corners of Europe, his expression bland, giving nothing away. But it was never just 'good morning, did you sleep well' with Grandfather. Even the most innocuous question was a probe for information.

'Yes, I did. First time in ages, actually.' Caine helped himself to coffee from a silver urn and a plate of eggs with a generous slice of ham. Grandfather insisted ham was healthier for a man than sausages.

'The country air agrees with you.' Grandfather nodded affably before returning his attention to his papers. 'Seems to agree with Lady Mary, too. She was out walking yesterday. Is she taking a tray in her room?'

'Probably.' Caine sat down and reached for a slice of toast from the rack.

'It was a good night for sleeping outside. The Perseids are starting. Did you see any shooting stars?'

He was just confirming for them both what Caine had already suspected. But Caine wasn't quite ready to discuss last night. He deflected. 'How were *your* guests, Grandfather? Did any of them stay over? Did you have a productive supper?'

Grandfather set aside his papers, satisfied that Europe wasn't going to fall into chaos for the moment, and fixed him with a serious stare. 'Last night's dinner was intended to verify your conclusions and I think we can safely conclude that your instincts were right once more. Creighton has written on behalf of himself, Cowden and the Prometheus Club to confirm that Carys had lobbied hard for Amesbury's bid on the arms. He'd been exceedingly upset when the club used another provider in order to avoid what they felt was a conflict of interest.' Grandfather gave a sly smile over his coffee. 'It is useful having a duke for a grandson-in-law. Your sister did well for the family when she married Creighton.'

Coupled with the ledger pages he'd taken showing the loans and the deficit indicating financial troubles, that certainly leant more credence to Carys's motives regarding the cargo than simply an act of revenge against Cowden and Creighton for supporting Harlow's membership. But good news for Caine meant bad news for Mary. Her father was now implicated at best in underhanded business dealings and at worst international sabotage. Caine slowly buttered his toast, thinking. 'Will the earl and Amesbury come here? It would save me a trip to town. I want a conversation with Carys.'

Grandfather raised a brow in interest. 'What sort of conversation would that be?'

'A conversation where Carys confesses his participation, filling in the gaps between our supposition and hard proof, and where he rolls over on his compatriots in order to save himself. With luck, he'll give up Amesbury, offer us the name of the explosives expert Stepan killed and help us figure out who Amesbury is working with or for, if anyone. This might just be a money grab for them.' Which would be more than a little disappointing to Caine. It all seemed too much to risk for too little return.

'You still don't think it stops with Amesbury.' It wasn't a question. Grandfather was eyeing him with sharp awareness.

'I don't. The damage done by this act of sabotage over a mere arms contract and money far exceeds the benefits the act would accrue.' This was the conclusion he reached even when he took away the emotion of losing Stepan to this ridiculousness. *If* his brother was dead, he wanted it to be for a 'good' reason, not because of a petty earl's pique.

Grandfather broke into a smile that even at the age of thirty-eight could warm Caine with pride in having done something that pleased his grandsire. 'Damn, but your instincts are the truest I've ever seen in this game. You are indeed right about that last piece.'

He leaned close, his voice lower. 'The Amesbury family *is* still in league with Cabot Roan. Falcon is on the Continent right now and sent word that Roan is at the munitions factory in Brussels. He's using an alias, of course. He might have escaped conviction a few years back, but not all justice is meted out through the legal system. Roan can't set foot in England and I am sure he has enemies in Europe, too, hence the alias.' He sat back, giving Caine a moment to take in the information.

Caine let out a low whistle. 'The question is whether or not Carys knows and simply doesn't care, or that he doesn't know about Roan at all.' He thought for a moment. 'This does help explain Amesbury's strong desire to wed Mary. With a title and a well-born bride, he'll have access to social and financial resources in England that Roan cannot access for himself. I'd wager Roan is setting Amesbury up to be his intermediary in Britain.'

'Do you think Carys knows all of it? Could he even give up a name beyond Amesbury? I don't know Carys well,' his grandfather said, 'but he's always struck me as a conservative man, a stickler for propriety and for following the rules, so I am hard pressed to understand why he'd turn against his fellow peers in the Prometheus Club, why he'd sell his daughter in marriage to a man she doesn't want and why he'd participate in an act that, if known about, many of his countrymen would find unpatriotic. Most folks support the Greek movement in at least theory.'

Caine finished the argument for him. 'All of that suggests strongly that he did not know the whole of it, which is why he allowed himself to be motivated by personal pride and financial issues; he simply didn't know there were larger repercussions.' He paused, a thought occurring to him for the first time. 'Do you think he even knew about the plot to blow up the ship? Amesbury could have told him an entirely different plan in order to persuade him.' Caine blew out a breath. 'I think talking with Carys is becoming a necessity even if he can't give us all I hope.'

'I have men in the village. If anyone is coming, we'll have warning. Make sure Lady Mary stays on the property, the closer to the house the better, and if she does go out further make sure you're with her,' Grandfather cautioned. 'Which obviously isn't a problem,' he added slyly.

Caine ignored his grandfather's barb. 'I had the archery butts set up for her down by the lake. That will keep her well occupied.'

But Grandfather wasn't done quite yet. 'If Carys is any kind of father, he'll want his daughter home. And Amesbury will want his leverage back. If I were you, I'd be thinking about what you can do to prevent any of that if she truly does not want to go back. I'd also be thinking that Carys may want reparation and it is within his rights to expect you to make an honest woman of his daughter.'

'Are you suggesting I marry her?' Caine asked bluntly.

'You must admit, marriage solves many problems for her. It restores her.' Grandfather reached into his stack of newspapers. 'The society pages have not been kind. But I am sure you *both* expected that when you brought her here.'

Caine scanned the page Grandfather had folded back and winced. Expecting it was one thing, seeing it in print was another. It was ghastly. He set it aside. 'I *have* thought about it, but you know I cannot offer myself in marriage. It is too dangerous for her. I'd be gone on Horsemen work for you and who knows what enemies might seek revenge by threatening her or any family we might have.'

Grandfather made a frown. 'So you've decided? You'll let the title die with you? That you will spend your life alone?'

'You disagree with my reasons?' Caine challenged.

'I think it would be a waste. I've watched you grow up. I've watched you build the bonds between your brothers. Not all brotherly relationships are amicable, especially among the peerage. It is more common to see brothers compete against one another. But you made a band of your brothers. You saw to it that your sister's business affairs were looked after in Italy when her husband died. You saw to it that Creighton came up to scratch for her when the time came. You are a man built for family, Caine. All of you boys are, but you especially.'

'I don't think it's fair to Mary to require she take on the danger of my life.' It had been bad enough seeing Amesbury's mark on her. It had stolen his reason for a moment. 'I couldn't protect Stepan. What makes me think I could protect a wife? Children?'

'Fair for her or fair for you?' Grandfather chuckled. 'Who are you really protecting with this argument, Caine?' He pointed to a portrait of Caine's grandmother on the wall. 'Your grandmother and I were married fifty-two years. Best fifty-two years of my life. Do you remember what she died of?'

'Pneumonia,' Caine said slowly, trying to anticipate the trap his grandfather had laid.

'That's right. Natural causes. She wasn't kidnapped, there were no gunmen hiding behind hedges waiting to waylay the carriage when she went out. All three of my sons lived to adulthood, married and led the lives they chose. None of them were kidnapped, although after some of their pranks, I often wished they might be.' Grandfather chuckled. 'Of course, I did take some precautions. There were always outriders with my wife and my children and we were very strict about who came to the house, who the boys met. But any man who loves his family is. One does not throw rubies to swine, after all, spy master or not.'

Caine played with his fork. 'I'd have to tell her about the Horsemen, tell her what I do. I'd have to tell her about Wapping, all of it.' It would also require him to tell her about her father. She might hate him for that. She might feel used, betrayed. She might feel that the proposal didn't come from an honest place, or even worse, that his own feel-

ings hadn't been true, that he'd put on a show to seduce her to gain access to the Earl and Amesbury.

'Yes, you will have to tell her all of that. But don't
you think it's about time?' Grandfather finished his
coffee and rose.

Caine rose with him. 'I think I'll take a swim.'
And sort his thoughts. Grandfather had pushed
him this morning, but he'd also opened a window
of hope. Was it possible to have the life he wanted
without giving up the life he had? The answer was
that it *might* be. If he was willing to take a chance.
He strode through the house and out the back doors
to the gardens and to the lake beyond.

At the lake shore, he stripped off his clothes and
dived in, letting the water cool his thoughts and
settle his mind. He broke through the surface of
the water and eyed the island in the distance before
striking out for it.

Nothing was ever simple when one was a Horseman. Most men proposed with a single question,
but a Horseman had to risk much more than that. A
Horseman had to be sure of his bride's answer before he even asked the question.

Chapter Twenty

Her arrow struck the centre of the butt sure and true with a satisfying thump, the tip sinking dip into the hay target. Mary was certain Caine had ordered the butts set up for her. What she wasn't sure of was what did it mean? Had it been the act of a thoughtful host? Or dare she read anything more into it? After yesterday, perhaps it was a subtext involving Cupid's arrow finding its mark?

Deep down, Caine *was* a romantic, but he was also a rake. Nights like last night were commonplace for him. Just like carriage rides, or games involving forfeits. He lived a far more decadent and experienced life than she when it came to such things. She was out of her depth here. Boldness without knowledge behind it could only carry one so far.

Mary nocked another arrow on to the bow and sighted the further target. What did it matter if it *was* romantic? It would be a short-term affair that ended when she left Sandmore. She let the arrow fly, satisfied with the shot just a hair off centre. She'd not shot since the archery competition at the Harlow house party. That party belonged to a different life, a different person.

She strode towards the butts to collect the arrows. That young woman would not have dreamed of taking a lover, of challenging the rules she'd been brought up to obey. That young woman would not have made love beneath the stars, or left home with no plan, no resources for her next step. She would not have discovered her inner strength, or her own power. Her own identity would have escaped her entirely given time.

She did not despise that young woman. That young woman had her own strength to be sure, a successful debutante didn't survive without it, but that young woman would have missed so much. It had been worth it. The refrain from last night still echoed today.

The poche at her hip refilled, Mary walked off the paces and scanned the gardens behind her for any sign of Caine. She'd not seen him since he'd laid down beside her in bed—the quiet eroticism of sleeping skin to skin with him was not something she'd soon forget.

He'd been gone when she woke and the breakfast

room had been deserted when she'd finally made her way downstairs. She'd been disappointed, but perhaps he was giving her time to be alone to think.

What did one say to someone after they'd spent the night exploring one another's bodies? Did one talk about it? Or did one say 'pass the toast, please' and carry on as if the night had never happened? Was that what Caine was signalling with his absence? It was to be business as usual between them? Although that business had its own murkiness to it. The lines between friends and lovers had been blurred nearly the entirety of their association. Still, Mary felt they ought to talk about last night—would it happen again? What did it mean, if anything?

Mary looked at the sky. The sun of yesterday had been replaced by heavy, cloudy summer skies portending a storm later today. Had Caine gone riding without her? That would be disappointing. She'd have liked to ride with him. Mary prepared to shoot again, a motion at the lake shore catching the corner of her eye. She turned towards the movement and her breath caught at the sight of him: Caine rising from the lake, water sluicing from dark hair, his body slick.

The arrow in her bow fell to the ground, forgotten. All her thought was riveted by the man—the *naked* man—emerging from the waters like a masculine rendition of the Birth of Venus. Neptune Rising. He looked even better in daylight than he had by moonlight. This was the man who'd strode naked through the gardens, who'd carried her to bed and slept beside her. She took a very long look.

Caine bent and retrieved a towel, offering her a glimpse of his buttocks in profile. Then he slipped his shirt over his head and the show was over. He nearly had his breeches fastened before he saw her. He raised a hand and waved to her, walking her direction barefoot, boots in hand. 'Good morning, Minx.' He kissed her cheek. He smelled of fresh lake water and summertime. 'How long have you been watching me?' he teased, his dark eyes dancing.

'Long enough,' she replied with a coy smile.

'See anything you like?' He bent down to retrieve her forgotten arrow.

'Maybe.' She couldn't stop smiling. Would she always feel this way around him? As if she could burst with life? He fairly vibrated with it—life, adventure, all rolled into one man, all the things the dutiful debutante she once was had been taught to stifle, taught to be afraid of, even. She put a hand on his arm and lowered her voice. 'I missed you this morning.'

He answered with a slow kiss that lingered at her lips, his eyes half-lidded. 'I had business with

Grandfather.' Before she could ask about that, he hurried the conversation on. 'How are the archery butts? Shall we shoot a little? I asked to have lunch brought down.'

They spent the next half-hour in a fun, spirited competition, Mary besting him in shooting. Caine was an adequate archer, but in his own words, he was 'much better with pistols'.

'Maybe you can teach me to shoot a weapon of your choice next time.' Mary leaned her bow against the little canopied pavilion erected for lunch.

'Perhaps I should. You should definitely know how to handle a gun.' Caine grinned, but she didn't miss the scrutiny in his gaze, which didn't match the teasing in his voice. It was not like him to prevaricate and he was not in the habit of mincing words, but he was hiding something now.

Did it have to do with last night? Did he think she expected anything as a result of it? Or had he heard from her father? Did it have to do with Caine's business with his grandfather? Had there been news about Stepan? Perhaps he needed to leave and follow a lead?

She assembled a small plate from the meat, cheese and bread laid out, but her attention was fixed on Caine. Something was on his mind. Had all the fun beforehand been a way of easing her towards it? Her stomach tightened as scenarios ran through her mind. Was he going to say last night was a mistake? That he was returning to town? That she needed to leave?

'Is that all you want?' Caine nodded to her plate. 'You're not hungry?'

Mary shook her head. 'No, I'm quite nervous in fact. You have something on your mind and I'm not sure I'm going to like it.' She sat down and set her plate aside. 'Perhaps we might just cut right to it because the suspense has killed my appetite.' And her hopes that there might be more lovemaking after lunch, that perhaps the little pavilion had been erected with a few purposes in mind, had been dashed as well.

'Well, if you're nervous, that makes two of us.' Caine knelt before her, grasping her hands in his. 'I had meant to go about this a little differently, but perhaps it would be better to start at the end and then work back to the beginning.'

Her pulse began to race. She knew a prelude to a proposal when she heard one and this one bore all the trappings. If there was one thing that would make Caine Parkhurst nervous, it would be marriage. She bit her lip, her mind sped. What to do? What to say? Nothing in her training had prepared her for this. This might be a proposal, but it was not like the proposal she'd refused from the Viscount in her first Season, or any of the other carefully curated offers where everyone knew their lines and the rules.

'Mary, I want to ask you if you would consider doing me the honour of being my wife, *if* you find the idea of marriage to me satisfactory after I share some things with you.' His dark eyes were holding her captive with his gaze, making any kind of thought difficult, let alone formulating a logical response.

'Why are you doing this? Is it because of last night?' She found her voice, found her logic at last. 'I expect nothing in that regard. You have no obligation.'

Caine chuckled, but did not let go of her hands. 'Did you not enjoy last night? I was under the impression you did. *I* did. One might say I'd be interested in having last night every night. Last night was a pretty good audition for marriage in my opinion. We had some other successful auditions, too.'

'Oh, hush! You're wicked.' She blushed, but she smiled as she said it. 'One needs more than that to make a marriage.'

'Yes, but it's a start. A good start. There're worse ways to begin than with sexual compatibility.' A seductive smile teased at his mouth.

'It won't last, that sort of thing never does, not when that's all there is. It's not enough to hold a man who can find that excitement elsewhere,' she cautioned.

'Says who?' Caine challenged. She bit her lip, not wanting to say. But Caine guessed anyway. 'Is that one of the scintillating and valuable pieces of advice Lady Morestad imparted to you at the musicale?' He shook his head. 'Philomena Morestad is not someone anyone should take marital advice from.'

'I expect fidelity, Caine. You don't have a reputation for such.' It would indeed cut to the quick to know he was doing with another woman what he'd done with her.

'Don't I? Perhaps you might consider measuring fidelity with markers other than dalliances with opera singers and *ton*nish women of low morals, where fidelity was never asked for.'

Another thought occurred to her. 'Is this because of the condition of your title? I am to be an expedient solution? Or is this because you want to protect me from the scandal that is currently making its way through society?'

Caine sat back on his heels. 'Careful, you might walk yourself into a contradiction, Mary. A few minutes ago you were questioning my ability to be faithful and now you're holding my fidelity against me.

You can't have it both ways. Either I am faithful to you, or I am not.' He laughed. 'This proposal isn't going well. All I asked is if you wanted to marry me.'

Mary gave a coy smile. 'Let me reframe the conversation. I will ask you a question. Why do you want to marry me?'

It was his turn to feel uncomfortable. She'd already shot down the reasons he would have offered: to stop the scandal and to satisfy the King's requirement, because if he had to marry it should be to someone he trusted. 'Because I care for you, Mary. I care what happens to you and I can affect that in a positive way. And, yes, there are secondary benefits that make it a practical solution. I need to wed and you need to wed to escape social ostracising.'

'Do you love me, Caine?'

Damn, but she knew how to ask hard questions. Would she be able to handle even harder answers when he gave them? 'I don't deal in love, Mary, because I can't. That's what I wanted to discuss with you.' He'd meant to lead with that, with his life as a Horseman, lead into her father's potential involvement with the sabotage in Wapping and then give her the choice. But the worry in her eyes had derailed him and he'd leapt straight to what had become the most salient point of the conversation—the proposal. 'The Four Horsemen, my brothers and I, we do unofficial diplomatic work for my grandfather.'

'You're diplomats?' Mary tried to follow and couldn't piece it together.

'Not per se. We prevent undiplomatic things from happening so that diplomatic things can. The *ton* thinks the Four Horsemen are about being rakes. But it's really about preventing disaster from striking. We stand between destruction like war, death, pestilence, famine.' He gave her a moment, watching her head nod slowly.

'That night in Wapping,' she said slowly, 'that was for your grandfather?'

'Yes.' He reached for her hands again. 'There was a ship carrying cargo meant for an important military engagement on the Continent.' He tried to be as specifically non-specific as he could be. Secrets were burdens. 'There was an attack planned on it. We foiled it.'

'At the expense of your brother,' she said softly, squeezing his hands in commiseration. Good Lord, this woman could break him with the simplest of gestures, each of them full of sincerity. Here before him sat a *good* person who would truly care about him if he'd let her. He did not deserve such goodness, should not drag such goodness into his world, tarnish it with the moral ambiguity of a Horseman's life.

It took him a moment to respond, knowing that his response would shake her world, and his, perhaps to their foundations. 'There's more, Mary. It will be hard to hear.' He felt her hands tighten on his as if he were her anchor. 'Amesbury is responsible for arranging the attack. Our visit to Prince Baklanov confirmed that the Amesbury family is still in league with an arms supplier named Cabot Roan. They sell arms to any who is buying. They're rich, successful, powerful and entirely corrupt, devoid of any ethics.'

He could see dread growing in Mary's grey eyes. 'Did he think to use my family as social connections?' Her mind was racing, trying to figure out the last piece.

'Yes, I have reason to believe Roan wanted Amesbury to be his dealer in England since Roan can't step foot on English soil. As a duke, Amesbury would have connection and resources in the most powerful nation on the planet. He'd need a bride of your quality and not everyone was interested. The current Duke is from a very thin branch of the Amesbury family tree, not like Harlow who is a direct descendant.'

'But my father was interested?' Mary had begun to pale.

'More than interested. He is involved. Your father is part-owner of the munitions factory and he owes Amesbury a small fortune. His finances are in tatters, Mary.' He explained the failed attempt to win the arms bid from the Prometheus Club. 'Being exiled from the club will only further impact your father's finances negatively. Amesbury is the only thing keeping your father afloat at present.'

Mary began to shake. He hurried to mitigate the damage. 'All this is true. What I don't know is what your father knew. Does he know Roan is involved? Does he know the long-standing effects if that shipment had been destroyed? We simply don't know.' He hated defending the man, but he *would* be fair.

'You have proof?' Mary asked after a while.

'Yes. The night of the musicale, I entered your father's office, found the deed in his safe and tore pages from his ledger. Other sources corroborate the documents and what they indicate.'

'By other sources, you mean the people here for dinner last night?' There was an edge to Mary's voice. She was overwhelmed and anger was a defensive response to feeling that things were beyond one's control. Caine had dealt with that reaction before, but never with someone who tugged at his heart, someone he didn't *want* to hurt, someone he cared for.

'Yes. I will not lie to you, Mary. We have proof and the dots all connect. Your father is either involved and knows what is going on or he oblivious to the further-reaching implications. If the latter is true, he is in danger because as long as he owes Amesbury money, he can be manipulated. But either way, *you* are in danger. If Amesbury has you, that is another string that ties your father to him, that ensures Amesbury has the entrée into society he and Roan need.'

'So I am supposed to wed you in order to put myself beyond the danger?' Her tone was cold, her grey eyes stormy as waves of realisation crashed in her mind. 'But who will protect me from you, Caine Parkhurst? That night at the Carfords' ball, I thought you asked me to dance for the sake of an apology, but that was after Wapping.' She was running the timeline in her mind and coming to the conclusion Caine did not want her to reach.

'You bastard. The whole time you were flirting with me, drinking port with me, sending roses, you were investigating my father!' She let out a yelp of disgust. 'No wonder you came to my aid at the opera—it was a perfect opportunity for you and you just kept coming. I was so foolish. I kept thinking he's not as bad as everyone makes him out to be. Society has misjudged him. Beneath this rakish exterior is a romantic, an honourable man.' She rose from her chair and gave her foot a little stomp of frustration. 'I cannot believe I was so stupid.'

Caine fought the urge to go to her. She would not want to be touched, not by him. 'You're overwhelmed, Mary. Take some time, think through it and you'll see that is not true. I care for you. I took you away from Amesbury, I saw you to safety.'

Mary held up a hand. 'Stop. You are not making it better. You are no different than Amesbury, just aggressive in a different way. You both want me to make you look decent. You spirited me away to have me to yourself.'

That stung. 'Mary, you're not thinking straight. The scandal is on the other foot now. It's not me who needs *you* to become decent, it's you who needs me—the Marquess—to redeem yourself in society's eyes,' he growled—the comparison to Amesbury had hurt. He was ten times the man Amesbury was. 'Marry me for your safety, if nothing else, Mary.'

'Absolutely not. This, this whole proposal, is just Horsemen work and I will not be the next disaster the Four Horsemen avert.' She grabbed the bow and poche from their resting spots and stormed off, headed for the house as the first clap of thunder rumbled through the sky.

Chapter Twenty-One

She was furious! With Caine certainly, but with herself even more so. She'd been entirely taken in! She'd even been his champion, thinking him maligned by society, and all the while *he'd* been duping *her*.

Mary shut the door of her chamber behind her and leaned against it, her anger mixed now with sad disbelief. She was in an impossible situation. What did she do now that there was no one to turn to? No one to trust? She was beset on all sides: her family on the brink of ruin, her own freedom traded in marriage to offset familial debt and the one man she'd trusted to see her safe had done so only because he intended to marry her instead.

She couldn't go home, couldn't return to her old life. It didn't exist. Rumours and gossip had seen to that even if her parents would forgive her behaviour. Although, she thought, the need for forgiveness ran both ways. Her father needed to explain himself. She could only go forward, into a new life, with a new name.

Caine has offered you both of those things, her conscience whispered. *A new life and a new name as his Marchioness. Surely you can work through your differences, build something together if you forgave him. He can protect you. You might not like what he had to say, but it was truthful and it was not wrong.*

He was right. Amesbury would not give up, not if he thought he had access to her. If she meant to go, she had to go now before Amesbury and her father came looking for her, before Caine had a chance to persuade her into a decision she'd regret. Love had to work both ways. She could not be the only one willing to love in her marriage.

Outside, the rain began to fall, drops trickling down her windowpanes. Perhaps that would work in her favour. In the rain, no one would come after her. Maybe they would forgive her for taking a few things with her. She stripped two pillows of their cases. They would work as sacks.

She would take the nightgown, a spare dress and a few of the underclothes. She had her jewellery and she wrapped it carefully in a washcloth. She could sell it piece by piece for passage, for food, for lodging. If she was careful, it would last until she could settle somewhere and do something. That part of the plan was still unclear to her. But Sussex was on the coast. She would make for the closest port town and catch the first packet, the first ship, to anywhere: France, Portugal, even the Americas.

Thunder rumbled. She debated taking a horse. It would make travel faster, but it would also alert people to her absence. Better to walk the two miles to the village and catch a coach from there, although it would be a muddy two miles. With luck, there'd be an evening coach. With even more luck, Caine wouldn't miss her until after supper when it was too dark to do anything about it. She didn't relish the idea of Caine storming the inn and attempting to drag her back here in front of the village. Assuming he came at all. Perhaps he'd just let her go. Perhaps he'd decide she wasn't worth the trouble. At least if he came for her, it meant she mattered just a little.

Tears stung her eyes and threatened to spill as she tied a knot at the mouth of the pillowcase. She hadn't needed two after all, such was the state of her worldly goods. For now. This was just a temporary setback, she told herself. She swiped at the tears. She was *not* going to cry over Caine Parkhurst. Perhaps she was starting to understand Lady Morestad's bitterness. Perhaps that elegant lady had been taken in by him, too, thought she'd understood him only to be taught otherwise. Mary took a final look at the room, at the bed where a few hours ago she'd slept in blissful contentment beside a man she thought she'd loved.

Was it worth it?

Perhaps it still was. She'd learned a valuable lesson or two about men. She said a silent goodbye and shut the door behind her, slipping down the servants' stairs, pillowcase bag in one hand, out of the house and into the storm.

Mary was soaked through by the time she had walked the two miles to the village and more than thankful for the simple comfort of the inn's fire in the common room. It was a quiet night and there were few people about. Once she warmed up, she'd make enquiries about a coach. She kept herself busy with plans in the meantime so that her mind didn't have time to think about the enormity of what she had done and what she *was* doing. If she thought too much, she'd run out of courage and that was simply not an option. She just had to take one step at a time, focus on the present. She could do this. She had to.

Intent on warming herself, she'd sat with her back to the door and as a result, she did not hear the danger or see it until it was too late. 'Mary, what a pleasant surprise to find you here, all packed and ready to go.' The man's voice at her ear made her jump in surprise. She whipped her head around and came face to face with a smiling Amesbury. Her blood ran cold with memories of the last time they'd been together.

'What are you doing here?' She tried to keep the tremble of fear from her voice. She would not give him the satisfaction of knowing he'd succeeded in frightening her.

'Looking for you, my dear,' he said in silken tones. He captured her chin between his thumb and forefinger, turning it from side to side. 'It's a pity about your cheek, but it will heal. You'll have to be more careful in the future, dear. We can't have you running into things.'

He crooked his arm. 'My coach is outside. I dare say you'll find it a bit drier than whatever you were travelling by. You are alone, aren't you?' She knew better than to think he was really asking that question. He was using it to remind her that she was indeed alone in a strange place where no one knew her and those that did know her did not know where she was or even that she was gone. It was starting to look like a bad idea to wish no one at Sandmore discovered she'd gone until after supper. By then, she'd be long gone from here, but not in the direction or with the company she'd hoped to be.

'Perhaps I don't wish to go with you.' All she

wished at the moment was to be back at Sandmore. He would not dare go to Sandmore. He'd be outmatched there.

'It doesn't matter what you want. I thought I made that clear the other night. You are mine, bought and paid for. You shall go where I want, when I want and, right now, I want to head back to town. We don't want to be late for our own wedding. It's all been arranged. St. George's in the morning, dusky pink roses, a string quartet, and a wedding breakfast at Amesbury House before we leave for our wedding trip. I thought Brussels. Your mother has exquisite taste, by the way. She made the arrangements. Everyone is clamouring for an invitation.'

He gave another of his seemingly benign smiles and showed all of his teeth. 'We'll spend the night before the crossing to Ostend at an inn on the coast. I think you'll like it. I've reserved their bridal suite.' He took her hand and kissed it. 'My dear, your parents will be so relieved I've caught up to you. They've been beside themselves with worry. As have I, but all is well that ends well.' Fear was in her throat, but she refused to give in to it. He was trying to scare her on purpose.

Caine would never frighten her, never try to use fear to motivate her, never try to steal her sense of choice.

Even this afternoon when there was something he so clearly wanted, he'd left the choice up to her at great cost to himself. She saw that now, too late.

She pulled her hand away. 'You mean monetarily worried.' What could she do but stall him? Keep him talking in the hopes that maybe someone from Sandmore would come looking for her.

'Caine explained it all to me. The munitions factory, the arms deal that failed, the attempted sabotage on the ship so that the Prometheus Club would be forced to buy a second round of arms, this time from you.' Caine had told her all of it, had not hidden it from her like her father had, like Amesbury had. He had shared hard truths with her and she'd rewarded him poorly for it.

Amesbury made a tsking noise with his tongue. 'That is all true, your father has lost a lot of money.' He shook his head. 'But you can make it right for him and for me. I want this marriage very badly and I am not sure how your father survives his situation if you don't honour his agreement with me. I've seen men blow their brains out for less and your father seemed quite agitated when I left him. He was absolutely distraught.'

That last frightened her. She might not care for her father at present, but he *was* her father. Caine's words came to her: *'We don't know how much your father knows.'*

'Does he know what kind of a scoundrel he's doing business with?'

Amesbury grinned as if she'd made a joke. 'I think he's figuring it out. Now, let's be off.' If she fought, if she screamed, would anyone come to her aid? Besides the innkeeper, his wife and a barmaid, there were only two others in common room—two older men playing chess by the window. She'd thought there was a third, but he was gone now. Would any of them stand up to a duke for her?

'Your Grace.' The innkeeper bustled over, his eager subservience answering Mary's question. No one would stand up for her here. 'We've just received word there's been a mudslide on the London road a mile from here. You won't be getting through tonight. Shall I see to a room for you? Our best room is available and there's a private parlour where you can sup.'

'That's unfortunate. But we'll make the best of it, won't we, my dear?' Amesbury said, ushering her out of view to the private parlour, ushering her out of sight. They were alone. He might do anything to her and no one would stop it unless she stopped it.

'It certainly is unfortunate,' she replied coolly. 'If Caine Parkhurst finds you here, he will kill you.' She hoped that was true. She'd been a fool twice today. First in refusing Caine, in being more interested in her anger than his explanations, and second in running. She should not have left Sandmore. She'd been mad and she'd not thought clearly. Now, here she was in the clutches of the very man Caine had warned her against.

He sneered. 'You assume he'll come for you? Then again, he might just be done with you and happy to leave you to your fate—which isn't all that bad, Mary. There are a lot of girls who'd gladly wed me.' There was a bottle left on the sideboard and he pulled the cork, pouring two glasses. 'Wine, my dear? We can toast our future.'

'I was hoping we would be toasting the future Marquess and Marchioness of Barrow.' His grandfather pulled the cork from a bottle of French burgundy with a rueful glance his direction.

'I *did* ask her.' It was just the two of them for supper, if one didn't count the storm, which was making its presence known loudly enough to warrant its own seat at the table, but of Mary there was no sign. She'd not come down for supper and no one reported having seen her since she'd stomped back into the house and slammed her bedroom door.

'Why did she refuse?' Grandfather poured two glasses.

'She doesn't trust me. She thinks I was courting her because I was investigating her father. In other words, using her to gain access to her father. Marrying her is just "Horseman's work", not true love.'

His grandfather put his nose to the wine and inhaled before sipping. 'Angry women say angry things. She was hurting. She's been through a lot in a short period. She needs time. Perhaps she'll be more receptive if you check in on her. After all, she liked you quite a bit last night. Maybe it wouldn't hurt to remind her of that.' He took another swallow of his wine. 'And, Caine, it wouldn't hurt either of you if you said the words she needs to hear.'

The footmen came forward with the supper— they were eating simply—a single entrée of rabbit in a creamy mustard sauce with peas on the side. Caine had just taken his first bite when a messenger arrived. His grandfather tossed him a wry smile. 'Some day, these interruptions will be all yours.'

'I'm in no hurry for that.' Caine smiled back, but he watched his grandfather's face change. 'What is it?'

'Amesbury is in the village. Our man was in the inn when he arrived and he's got Mary,' he said grimly.

'How is that even possible? She's in her room...'

But even as he said the words he knew they were wrong. Caine sprinted out of the dining room and up the stairs, throwing open Mary's door. He didn't need to look about to know the truth. She was gone. The room felt empty. Sterile. Not like the room he'd slept in with her last night. Still, he threw open the wardrobe and pulled open drawers. She'd only taken a few things with her.

Downstairs, he gave the order, 'Saddle a horse for me.' Damn, but he wished Argonaut was here instead of in London, getting fat on hay. He needed a sure-footed mount in this weather.

'Take the coach instead,' his grandfather countermanded. 'You want to arrive with your powder and your thoughts dry.'

'Coach is slower.' And speed seemed to be the preference of the moment. 'If he's managed to get her into a coach and he's on the road already, it will be difficult to make up time in the rain.'

'Our man says the London road's out. No one is going anywhere tonight.' Grandfather put a firm hand on his arm. 'Make sure you're thinking with your head. Amesbury is dangerous. This is about Lady Mary's safety, but it's also about something much larger, don't forget that. I do wish Kieran was here to go with you. Take two of the footmen, they're trained for emergencies.' Caine nodded. Of course they were.

* * *

It seemed to take an eternity to cover the two miles to the inn. There was too much time for Caine to be with his thoughts. It was a nightmare come to life, the very thing he'd warned his grandfather about earlier today. To be associated with him put one in danger and now the person in danger was Mary.

At the inn, he strode inside and scanned the common room in hopes Amesbury was there, but that hope had been slim. Amesbury wasn't stupid. If he was stuck here overnight, he'd want to be out of sight in order to minimise the chances of being recognised or Mary being recognised. That meant they were upstairs. In a room. Together. Mary would be terrified, alone with a man she detested, a man who had hit her once before, a man who had bought her, who had no morals, no scruples.

Caine pulled his pistol from his greatcoat and charged up the stairs, ignoring the innkeeper's shout of outrage. Amesbury would have the best room. That one, at the top of the stairs. 'Amesbury!' he yelled, launching a kick at the door that sent it splintering as he crashed through. Inside, his eyes took in the chaos. Mary's hands were tied to the bedstead, Amesbury in a state of dishabille scrambling for the pistol on the table, but Caine got there first, pistol raised as he stepped between the table and Amesbury, his body shielding Mary should Amesbury pull a knife from a boot.

'You've resorted to tying your women up, I see.' He gestured with the pistol to the chair set before the fire. 'Sit down over there, Amesbury, nice and slow—you and I are going to have a talk about your business with Cabot Roan.'

The sight of Amesbury paling was almost worth the trouble. Caine didn't think he'd ever seen blood drain out of a man's face so quickly before. 'Why did you try to sabotage the arms cargo? And before you try to deny it, let me assure you that I know what you attempted in Wapping. I saw the munitions expert who was so desperate to escape us he jumped into the water. I do not believe for a moment it was for the reasons you used to persuade the Earl.'

Amesbury glared. 'I am not telling you anything. Do you have the balls to make me?'

Caine cocked his pistol. 'I do and the aim to go with it. I can't say the same for you. You might have one less ball when we're through.' He levelled his pistol. 'Mary, you may want to look away.' He wanted answers and he wanted them fast. He wanted to get Mary back to Sandmore, wanted to settle things between them. 'I will give you until the count of three. One, two.' The lever pulled back on the pistol.

'Wait!' Amesbury was ashen. He crossed his legs. 'The Ottomans paid us. They couldn't afford to let such largesse reach the Greeks. That would change the balance of their little war. Roan was playing both parties against each other. When we didn't get the bid for the munitions, we told the Ottomans about the shipment and the loan. Carys gave us all the information and it was easy to pass it on. Then, the Ottomans hired us to blow up the ship, which suited us fine. We'd get the next contract and in the meanwhile we were being paid by the enemy.'

Amesbury rose slowly, hands raised, and stepped towards the table. 'Now you can put that pistol down, Parkhurst. You have your answer for all the good it will do you. You'll never be able to prove it.'

'Does my father know you sold his information to the Ottomans?' Mary's voice trembled with anger behind Caine.

'No, nor does he know about the Ottoman money.' Amesbury smiled wickedly. 'He only knows I'm his friend, the one keeping him afloat, and I'll keep doing it as long as he keeps doing what I say.' Amesbury lunged then, suddenly, wildly, for Caine, thinking to knock the pistol from his grasp or to grab the other pistol from the table.

Caine didn't take time to make the distinction. His only thought was for Mary. If Amesbury got his hands on a gun, he would not hesitate to use it against him by threatening to harm Mary. Caine fired. At close range there was no margin of error. Mary screamed, Amesbury crumpled, a stunned look on his face, and then he was gone.

Caine felt the twin emotions of regret and relief. Amesbury could pose no further threat to Mary and yet it was never easy to take a life. He went to Mary and sliced through her bonds, some of that regret fading at the sight of the red marks on her wrists. Amesbury had deliberately tied the ropes far tighter than needed. She fell against him.

He swept her up in his arms and carried her downstairs to the coach. There would be loose ends to wrap up tomorrow, but for the moment all that mattered was holding Mary close, wanting to assure himself she was safe and unhurt as they made the trip back to Sandmore.

'When I heard he was here and that he had you, I nearly lost my mind with worry. I was afraid I wouldn't get here in time, that he would hurt you, that he would be gone with you.' He cupped her face with his hands, wanting her to see him when he said it. 'But most of all, Mary, I was afraid I wouldn't get to tell you what I should have told you today when you asked. I love you. There are a lot of reasons I could marry you, but that's the only one that counts.'

Tears welled up in her eyes. 'I was afraid, too.' She swallowed hard. 'That I wouldn't get the chance to apologise. Today was upsetting and I let that obscure the importance of what you were willing to do for me. Instead of being angry, I should have been honoured by your proposal. I should not have doubted you or doubted that you were telling me the truth just because I didn't like hearing it. Amesbury could have taken everything from me tonight if you'd not come. I do not want to ever feel like that again—that everything was over before I'd even begun to live.'

'Life with a Horseman is dangerous,' Caine warned.

She shook her head. 'I think life without a Horseman is even more dangerous.' She leaned towards him. 'I wouldn't want to live without you, Caine. You've brought me to life, the real me. I'm alive when I'm with you, everything is vibrant and precious and every minute matters when it's spent with you.' She curled her arm about his neck and drew him close. 'You set me free.' She pressed her lips to his and his body began to hum with want. 'So, is that proposal of yours still on the table?' she murmured against his mouth.

'Yes.' He let his tongue tease her bottom lip and she laughed.

'Yes is supposed to be my line. When do you think we can wed?'

He drew her on to his lap, her hands already working his breeches loose. 'Well, very soon would be best at this rate.' Because when a man who thought never to be able to marry decides to wed, he doesn't want to waste any time.

Epilogue

Caine stood at the front of the little chapel at Sandmore and checked his pocket watch before discreetly tucking it into his waistcoat. In five minutes, he'd be a married man and he was as nervous as hell. Kieran stood beside him. 'Counting down the last moments of bachelorhood?' His brother joked.

'No, counting the moments until I become the happiest man in England.' Once she was here, he'd relax. Then he'd know it was really happening, that the divine Lady Mary Kimber was going to be his wife—the wild, reckless rake had fallen for the *ton*'s most refined woman and she had fallen for him, against the odds. Love had settled him. Whatever the future held, they would face it together, and it promised to hold quite a bit.

They would establish their household at Longstead and begin the gradual process of running Grandfather's diplomatic network from there. In the days since the debacle with Amesbury at the inn, he and Mary had talked about that future. There would be night visitors, there would be secret messages and things he simply couldn't tell her. She could be *a part* of that world, but she'd also have to be *apart* from it as well. It would require trust and bravery. But they'd already had some practice with that.

Her family remained difficult. Embarrassed over the situation with Amesbury, the Earl had relinquished his holdings in the munitions company, and retreated from society in exchange for Grandfather's promise that his role in the events at Wapping would not be publicised. He would be able to save face. The Earl had had no knowledge of how deep Amesbury's treachery had run, but that did not erase the Earl's callous disregard for his daughter, nor did it erase the Earl's role, no matter how unintentional, in the accident that had befallen Caine's brother, both of which made for tension between the two families at present.

The Earl and his wife were not here today, which was actually a relief for both Caine and Mary. They wanted today to be about joy. His family was on hand, however. His father and mother sat in the front pew. Behind them sat Luce, whom his father had managed to drag away from his new book collec-

tion, and his sister's husband, the Duke of Creighton—ironically, a man once considered for Mary.

Caine was rather glad that hadn't worked out for
them. He felt the love of his family surround him on
this day, one of the most important days of his life.
Amid all that love, he also keenly felt the absence
of Stepan. He was reminded of Mary's words that
every moment was precious.

The door to the chapel opened and Caine's sister,
who had agreed to serve as Mary's bridesmaid despite being nearly six months gone with child, made
a graceful walk down the short, flower-festooned
aisle, stopping to kiss his cheek before taking up
her post at the bride's side of the altar.

Then it was Mary's turn. She stood framed in the
doorway for an ethereal moment, bathed in the sun's
light so that she appeared to be a dark-haired angel
gowned in white. Caine felt his breath leave him.
She was beautiful to him today, but he suspected
that as time went on she would become even more
beautiful and more precious to him as their lives
grew together.

At the back of the church, his grandfather stepped
forward to escort her down the aisle. When they
reached him, his grandfather placed her hand in his
and Caine felt that rarest of all things descend over

him: peace. As long as she was beside him, there *would* be peace. He was still getting used to that.

He would not remember much of the ceremony. But he would remember that kiss, their first as husband and wife; how she'd leaned into him, how her mouth had opened to him, how her arms had wrapped about him and his arms had enveloped her until it had seemed impossible for him to tell where one began and the other ended. He'd have liked to have gone straight to the honeymoon after that, but there was still celebrating to do.

The wedding breakfast at Sandmore was a small, tasteful affair attended by members of the Prometheus Club and a few other close friends of the family. There was plenty of champagne and plenty of kisses. They had just cut the cake when Grandfather stepped outside. Caine tried to ignore the prickle of awareness rising on the nape of his neck.

Grandfather came back inside and made his way to him. Kieran, Luce came to join them. 'There's been word of the Ottoman sympathiser,' Grandfather began in low tones. 'Kieran, I need you to take a meeting with an informant who says they know who Roan dealt with. Luce, you should go with him in case all is not what it seems. You should leave as soon as we send the bride and groom off. This may have some urgency to it, I wouldn't want to wait.'

'Perhaps I should go? We could stop on the way to Longstead,' Caine put in.

Grandfather clapped him on the shoulder. 'You've done your time. You're a married man now and soon to be the head of the network. Your field days are over, or at least temporarily suspended. You will co-ordinate from a desk, just as I have for years. Let your brothers handle it. You go enjoy your new bride and set up house.' He lowered his voice. 'And make that enjoyment obvious so the gossip columns have something to write about, distract them so that no one's watching your brothers.'

Caine nodded. If anyone *was* watching from the shadows, the wedding, the honeymoon, the opening up of Longstead would suggest that the Horsemen had been satisfied with catching Amesbury and that they believed the riddle was solved.

Mary joined them, looping an arm through his. 'Is everything all right?'

'Yes.' Caine smiled at his wife. 'I was just getting my marching orders. It's time for us to go.' Time to take the final step into his new life, a life he'd believed he couldn't have. Mary thought she'd come alive when she'd met him, but she might have that backwards. He was fairly certain she'd put the life back into him.

Epilogue Two

All the life had nearly left the body on the beach. Almost. Ellen Kingsley bent down and unwrapped a bit of polished glass from her apron pocket. She held it in front of the man's lips. Nothing. She moved it closer. Ah, there it was. A breath strong enough to fog her glass only at the closest of distances. A sign of life and also a sign of how little of that life remained.

'Is he dead?' Her sister, Anne, came to stand beside her, all curiosity. 'I hope not, he's rather handsome.'

'No, not yet. But he's close to it.' They'd come to the beach in the hopes of scavenging some wreckage. They were in desperate need of supplies. This was not the sort of wreckage she'd thought to find. What could she do for him? Would it even be worthwhile to go to the trouble of hauling him to the cottage? He'd likely die anyway. But her conscience wouldn't allow it. A life was a life no matter how much of it remained. All life was sacred to Quakers.

'Annie, run back to the house and have the boys come down, have them bring a quilt so we can carry him in it, then put the pot on, we'll need hot water.'

Alone on the beach, Ellen ran her hands over the body, searching for other injuries. She unbuttoned his shirt, feeling for broken ribs and found none. That was good. It meant there was unlikely any internal bleeding. There was a gash though, on his arm, not terribly old. It looked as if it hadn't been treated. A knife wound maybe? Such a wound spoke of violent living. She moved to study it, her fingers gently probing. Not gently enough. The man moaned, a thin, reedy sound escaping those cracked lips. 'It's all right, you're safe,' she soothed.

His eyelids opened, revealing the most beautiful pair of brown eyes she'd ever seen. They were dark, like melted chocolate she'd tasted once at Christmas. His mouth moved, trying to form words. 'You mustn't try to talk. You need water. Help is coming, my brothers will bring something to carry you home on,' she tried to explain. There was anxiousness and panic in his eyes at the mention of brothers.

'Don't worry, we'll take care of you. There will be time to talk. You're safe,' she repeated. 'You are alive and for now that is enough.'

* * * * *

MILLS & BOON®

Coming next month

THE TAMING OF THE COUNTESS
Michelle Willingham

'What did Papa want to talk with you about?'

James hesitated a moment before answering, 'He wants me to marry you.'

She blinked a moment, as if she hadn't heard him correctly. 'He what?'

'He believes I should marry you and offer the protection of my title.' He took the remainder of the brandy and finished it in one swallow. 'It would be quite difficult to arrest a countess.'

Evangeline's disbelief transformed into dismay. 'That's a terrible idea. You and I are not suited at all.' But there was a faint undertone in her voice, as if she were trying to convince herself.

'I agree.' Though he hated the idea of hurting her feelings, he couldn't let her build him up into the man she wanted him to be. 'We both know I'll never be the right man for you.'

Her eyes grew luminous with unshed tears, and she nodded. 'You made that clear enough when you sailed half a world away.'

'You could have any man you desire, Evangeline,' he murmured. 'Just choose one of them instead.' He wanted her to find her own happiness with someone who could give her the life she deserved.

The very thought made his hands curl into fists. And that was the problem. Every time he tried to do the right thing and let Evie go, he kept imagining her in someone else's arms. And the idea only provoked jealousy he had no right to feel.

Continue reading

THE TAMING OF THE COUNTESS
Michelle Willingham

Available next month
millsandboon.co.uk

COMING
SOON!

We really hope you enjoyed reading this book.
If you're looking for more romance
be sure to head to the shops when
new books are available on

Thursday 24th
April

To see which titles are coming soon, please visit
millsandboon.co.uk/nextmonth

MILLS & BOON

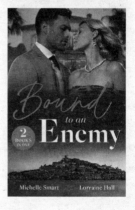

Afterglow Books is a trend-led, trope-filled list of books with diverse, authentic and relatable characters, a wide array of voices and representations, plus real world trials and tribulations. Featuring all the tropes you could possibly want (think small-town settings, fake relationships, grumpy vs sunshine, enemies to lovers) and all with a generous dose of spice in every story.

♪ @millsandboonuk
◎ @millsandboonuk
afterglowbooks.co.uk

#AfterglowBooks

For all the latest book news, exclusive content and giveaways scan the QR code below to sign up to the Afterglow newsletter:

afterglow BOOKS

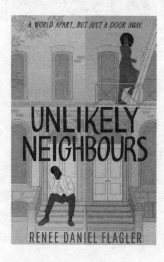

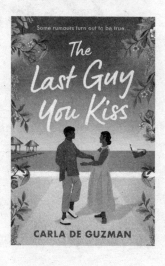

(((♥))) Forced proximity

🖤 Workplace romance

🛏 One night

✈ International

⧗ Slow burn

🌶 Spicy

LET'S TALK

Romance

For exclusive extracts, competitions
and special offers, find us online:

f MillsandBoon

X @MillsandBoon

⊙ @MillsandBoonUK

♪ @MillsandBoonUK

Get in touch on 01413 063 232